A WOMAN CALLED EVE

C. A. Mitchell

BOOKS

Also by C. A. Mitchell

Beneath the Veils
Beneath the Lies
Beneath the Conflict
Girl in the Middle
Third Child
Sixth Victim
Double Deception
Angel
Tinker Tailor Conman
Children of the Mask
A Woman Called EVE

A WOMAN
CALLED
EVE

1

'Your father is still a very handsome man, and you've got to accept women will find him attractive. I do,' said Sophia.

Sophia knew how to wind me up. She says we do it to each other all the time, although I don't know where she gets the idea from that I goad her. But it hadn't passed my eyes that when I first introduced her to Dominic, my father, her eyes alighted to his with a compelling attraction. This is not unusual. I have seen that look on many women's faces, both young and old. Every one of them melts under my father's gaze. A man who had just touched fifty-five and looks ten years younger can still turn many heads. Male or female. My father, I hate to admit, is a marvel.

I am incredibly fond of my father, as I am very interested in everything he does. I am very proud of him; his good genes mean I will look as young and handsome as him when that time arrives. Admiration. Oh, I have plenty. Never vain, never unkind, and always generous; this is my father.

And yet, we were never as close as what would be expected between a father and his only son. If you were to ask me why, I would say rivalry, but not from him—from me. Insecure, I always felt this way because I knew if he wanted, he could take any girl away from me. I suppose you could say I was lucky he didn't.

I've watched Sophia when my father is about. She likes to chat with him, her blonde hair bobbing, and her blue eyes sparkling staring into his blue crystal orbs. She cannot take her eyes off him; I've observed this phenomenon when I pretend to leave the room. It's fascinating to see what she does and how she behaves when my father is about. She becomes alive with flirtation when she is around him. I believe if he was to click his fingers, she would leave me in an instant.

Can you imagine how insecure this has made me? How paranoid. Can you imagine what it is like to be this man's son?

I call my father by his first name. So, out of curiosity, I asked him if he minded. 'Whatever you want to call me, Aiden. That's fine by me.' We have a good relationship; nothing is going to interfere with that.

I thank him for his answers, but this thought fulfilled leads to another.

I asked him what did he think of Sophia? Did he find her beautiful, or intelligent? His eyes betrayed his amusement. Was I serious? Testing him again, for I believe if he were to click his fingers, well, you know the rest.

'Your girlfriend?' his bright blue eyes, always merry, looked surprised that I should ask such a question. 'She is beautiful, Aiden and from what I know of her, intelligent and kind; I am sure she will look after you. Although life is a lottery, it really depends on how you treat her. Be kind to her and she will always stay with you. But never, never take her for granted.'

These answers, though, are never enough; he never gave me the answer I looked for or wanted to hear. A nice man like my father bothers me. And so, I had to probe further.

'Are you attracted to Sophia?' I asked.

He laughed. 'Aiden, what is this about? We are never in competition, are we?'

'But if you were to meet her, say, when I was not around; would you make a pass at her? You are a good-looking man, and you're not married. Would you make a pass at Sophia?'

'I'm going to let this conversation pass, Aiden. What you are asking me is something which would never happen, given what we know about each other. Don't be insecure, Aiden. I would do nothing like that to you, as I know you would never interfere in my relationships. Because we respect each other. You are my son; let it be enough that I am happy for you; I wish you two well. Maybe, one day, I will find someone who will make me happy too. This is what I am hoping for, hoping for both of us, to find happiness.'

And then he bowed out, smiling, and nodding, and gracefully walked away. A truly handsome man, tall and straight with a rich head of chestnut hair which had only recently been teased by grey. This change only stood to make him look more attractive and more distinguished. Fate could not have adorned him more, and that was not all. She had given him even more. He was well read, an outstanding scholar; there was not enough fate could do for him, so she had to saturate him with every August gift she could find.

I love my father; don't get me wrong. My admiration is boundless—is it possible I could admire him too much?

Perhaps I have painted myself in a poor light. I was not deprived of looks. In fact, I would say I had my fair share of them, more than most of my friends. As my father would say, while I regard my face and then my figure and now turning to the sides, delighting in my sleek flat stomach; no double chin, at least not yet—so I should not be lacking in confidence. For I am truly a good-looking man and need not busy myself looking at my father and the perfection of his face. The shape and contours of mine I know can be just as good as his. And maybe now decorated with youth, even better.

Perhaps you have caught me on a bad day.

The days of life turn autumn into winter, and spring into summer. While the pool outside glistens waiting for a ruffle of wind to disturb it. I felt seduced by the thought that life changes only when you want it to.

And then that day came when indolence kicks out for the adventure of something new. In mid-May, a friend invited my father to spend three weeks with him at his villa in Italy, and as strange as it be, he accepted. This was an interesting change of events; my father didn't know the meaning of spontaneous.

Day after day passed while the water in the pool still breathed and quivered; it didn't seem the same without my father; I do not know why. A life lived well is always worth living. I know I was waiting for my father to come home, and a quick glance at Sophia told me she was waiting for him, too. And then we received a message, a telegram of all things saying he would not be home for a while. Something had cropped up, but what?

Should I be worried? You tell me because I don't know, but one thing I know for certain is that I was not happy with this event. Not that I was worried about my father because he had always taken care of himself, and yet, something was bothering me. It was so out of character, my father always did everything by habit and routine. God, how my father liked his routines. So, what was it that made him stay longer?

When he left, he told Sophia and me he was going for three weeks. Three weeks and no more. While back home here in England, there was a fine arts exhibition he was interested in seeing. My father, you understand, is a collector of fine art. And that was another thing. My father was very rich, another quality which made him interesting to the ladies. He would never miss an exhibition at Astern, or anywhere else. Unless, of course, he could not help it. No, I would say he missed nothing that interested him. What then had caused him to stay?

'Your father is a grown man. He will let you know if there is anything wrong,' complained Sophia, irritated I was probing again. 'Don't worry.'

'I'm not worried. I am just curious. Just concerned that whatever he is doing, he is not, I hope, doing anything stupid.'

'I have never found your father to be stupid; he is the most sensible man I have met. In fact, if there is anyone to worry about, I would say it is you.'

But I knew something was going on, as I knew if there was anyone who could keep a secret, it would always be my father, for there was nothing he couldn't do.

Two weeks later, the communication came; my father, who had never sprung a surprise, and who always kept to a method of care not wanting to shock or hurt anyone, suddenly sent a telegraph telling Sophia and myself that he had met someone and married her. He had instantly fallen in love with. Her name was Eve, and she had a sensational personality. And as a wife, he felt she would bring balance into their relationship.

'I think what your father is trying to tell you is that you

don't need to fear him running off with any of your girl-friends, Aiden. You will be safe.' Remarked Sophia, at the time while applying black mascara to her eyelashes.

'I have never feared he would take any of my girlfriends.'

'Haven't you? Well, if you haven't then now's the time you should be happy for him.'

'I have always been happy for him,' and yet, as I spoke, I began wondering about the manner of this woman and what she had done to secure her claws into my father so quickly.

Hope to God it was not blackmail. She must have set him up, for my father was so blessed, the angels themselves would fall in love with him.

'You should be pleased for him,' said Sophia, irritated, setting one of the diamond earrings into her lobes. 'At last, your father will be happy because I don't believe he has been contented during the last four years since I have known him. Don't ruin it for him, Aiden, please.'

Following Sophia into the sun and out to the pool, I walked in her long footsteps, wondering why she always wore high heels in the pool area.

'I think this woman is after his money.' I stood over her, my arms crossed adamantly while my shadow fell over her stomach, making her perfect tan imperfect.

'Aiden, do you have to? Sit down, if you are going to, and be good.' she was trying to swat my shadow as it was destroying the effect.

I stood back, not exactly irritated but feeling I was not appreciated, while her only concern was getting herself positioned comfortably. I watched as she wriggled and then she looked to see how she looked and always with that queer smile. If it wasn't for me, she would not be lying around the pool enjoying the late June sunshine and trying to improve her beautiful self, if that were possible. Yes, I could see she had lovely long tanned legs. She was an expensive possession I could not afford. Not because I was living off my father's money, but because she always wanted more. And more meant something else with Sophia. One argument we often fought about was why wasn't I working. Why would I need to work?

'For self-respect, Aiden. A man who doesn't work cannot have any self-respect.'

'You don't work.'

'No, I don't. Because I am a woman and I look after you and keep you entertained, which is every man's desire.' She laid back on the sunbed and put her sunglasses back on. 'Besides, if she is ugly, which I am sure she isn't. And if she makes your father happy, we should be happy for them both.'

'Are you happy for my father?'

'It's not up to me, Aiden. Your father has already decided he will marry the one he wants. Maybe he didn't tell you because you might object.'

'It's not about objecting. I would tell him to wait; what is the use of hurrying? Take some time to get to know each other.'

'Like you and me, Aiden? When are we ever going to get married? We have been living together for nearly four years. I think it can safely be said that we know each other very well. There are going to be no nasty surprises to find out about each other. Why can't you take a leaf out of your father's book and marry me?'

I walked away; Sophia was obviously not listening to me. There was something about their affair which was not right. To me, it appeared very wrong for them to get married so quickly. My father had been impounded by this woman, and he needs rescuing. If I saw to it before too much time had passed, then I could get my father to secure an annulment. It might cost him a little money now, but it would save most of the fortune.

'Then you would make a fool of yourself,' said Sophia later when I passed my plan by her in our bedroom. 'And if you did, what do you think you would achieve?'

She walked about our room, while she changed for dinner. Her golden-tanned body was now a perfect host for the white dress she planned to wear and the white gold necklace with diamonds. She adored diamonds. Diamonds for everything: birthdays, Christmas, holidays, and any other excuse she found. This was her safety net just in case things did not work out between us. Do not be under no illusions. Sophie is a tough cookie and a realist. That's why I like her.

I watched her long legs crossing backwards and forwards, now in white high heels.

'You would not be making a fool of him, only of yourself. You know your father is far from being a simpleton. Pass me my shawl, Aiden; it's a little cooler this evening.'

'It was your idea we sit out by the pool to dine. And as to my father, even a man as handsome and as clever as him can be duped by love.'

'I am certain she must be wonderful to him. And when they first arrive home, we will do the grown-up thing and invite them for dinner. A civilised meal together where we can talk about everything other than how did they meet or what did they first say to each other? And perhaps it might inspire you to propose to me?'

She stopped and looked at her beautiful reflection in the mirror. 'Aiden, we will be happy for them, as I know they will be happy for us. I have a good feeling about this. And this, Aiden, is not a suggestion; this is a command.'

No, unfortunately, Sophia does not understand.

I endured the extra time waiting for my father and his new wife, Eve, to come home, knowing in one way Sophia was right. And yet, this was my father we were talking about, and my father was rich, and should anything happen which, of course, would not be for a long time yet, then everything should be passed to me as I was the only child. But a young woman—?

I was forced to imagine now the two of them taking a honeymoon. A honeymoon, why? Where else could be more beautiful than the place where they had first met—Camogli, Liguria? A fishing village by the sea crowded with confectionary-coloured houses hugging the shelves of the cliff. While the white regal villa they were staying at over-looked the bay. The reason I know how lovely it is, is because I had been to the villa many times. It was perfect and good enough for a honeymoon, but she obviously wanted to go somewhere else. Demands and wants and whims. This is what my father would have to put up with now he was married. A never-ending bombardment of wants and demands and probably no gratitude.

Turkey, then Greece, I understand; my father sent another telegram saying they would be home by the end of July and ready for his bride to meet his family.

'It would be nice,' began Sophia, dipping her feet in the pool, which she frequently did, 'if we could surprise your father and new stepmother—'

'Now hold it there. She is not my stepmother in any form. What makes you think that if I am calling my father by his first name, I will ever refer to this woman—as mother?'

'I didn't say you would be, Aiden; don't be so touchy. What I was trying to say to you, or rather, introduce the idea, is that it would be nice if we were to tell them we had set the date.'

I walked away from the pool, not wanting to discuss the issue any further.

'Aiden, come back; we should be able to talk about this. I am ready to marry you. The only thing I need is for you to pop the question. Are you ever going to ask me to marry you?'

'I don't like being pushed or hassled. I prefer to take my time and make up my own mind rather than having a woman shoving me.'

'Hardly just any woman, Aiden. Do you know what I am inclined to do?'

Movement in the pool and splashes of water told me that Sophia had pulled her feet from the pool. I could hear the drips falling as she padded towards me.

'Aiden, wait for me. Don't you love me anymore? When we were first together, you used to say how much you loved me. Should I have held off until I got a firm commitment? You know, Aiden, there is only so long I will wait for you. I want to get married; I want to settle down and raise a family. I don't want to wait forever until you decide to make up your mind. Aiden, wait for me. What is wrong with me, Aiden? Why won't you marry me?'

'There is nothing wrong with you, Sophia.'

I turned and faced her, admiring her figure, her perfect ample cleavage, and natural. I held out my hands for her. But she stopped where she was, not near enough for temptation, because that would involve me going to her.

'No. I am not coming to you anymore. This is an ultimatum. Do you want to marry me or don't you? And another thing, I'm not sleeping with you again until you decide what you want. No, Aiden, I am not coming to you until you ask me to marry you. I want to move on with my life.'

'I can't, Sophia. You have always known about my fears of commitment. Why can't we carry on as before?'

'Because, my darling, with every day that passes, we are getting older, and my biological clock is ticking away rapidly. Aiden, please don't walk away from me. I want children. You know you want children. I know this about you, even though you say no. You would make such a wonderful father.'

2

———

My Father and Eve's flight would arrive late in the evening, so we would need to be there to pick them up. It was Sophia's idea they should come to stay with us. She was excited about their visit because she, too, had some good news. I had proposed to her. She and I, she kept on telling me, were getting married.

One step at a time, I told myself, knowing there was no way I was marrying her. This agreement was only made to keep her a little longer. I was prepared to say anything and do anything. I don't like commitment, but abandonment is worse.

At twenty-nine, Sophia was panicking. She was trying to get me to become hysterical, too. But why should I worry when there are always other pretty fish in the sea? And the sea was a big place with opportunities everywhere, but for now, she and I would enjoy ourselves. When she is nice, she is very nice, and when she is a nuisance, then she is disposable.

'I have ordered some nice fish for your cook, Aiden. And I have planned a wonderful menu for everyone. I have spoken to your wine merchant and ordered some excellent wine. It will cost you a great deal—'

'Correction, Sophia, it will not be me who bears the cost, but my father.'

'Why do you always say that? When we are married, your father will expect you to get yourself a job to support yourself and your wife. His new wife won't approve of you living off her husband.'

'Then she will just have to get used to it because, by the time she is finished, she too will have a claim on Dominic as well.'

'I think you will be disappointed when you see how happy your father and his new wife are. And I will be glad for them,' she said, with wide eyes as she looked at me. 'I hope they will because once you see how happy they are, then perhaps you will settle down to marriage?'

'Have you finished?'

'Aiden, why are you so afraid of happiness? We could be so happy together, you and—'

'Maybe it's because I don't believe in love. Love is nothing other than an emotional straitjacket. You don't really love me. And as you know, I don't love you. What you want is an easy ride through life with someone who can take care of you and give you everything you want.'

'That's not true, Aiden, and you know it. I have always loved you; you just don't want to believe it. I would do anything you want of me—'

'If my father was to dump this woman because he realises it was always you he wanted, I know you would go to him like that.' I snapped my fingers. 'That Sophia is some- thing I am sure of.'

She shook her head and stared at me with meaning, and then walked away.

Yes, you would Sophia, I know you would. I know I am right.

On days like these when we have had a disagreement, or when Sophia does not like it when she knows I am right, she takes the car for a drive; it makes her feel better about things, although I am not sure how. But today is different. Sitting beside her on our way to the airport, she is wearing her glasses, and I know why that is. She is insecure. Sometimes I find her reading books. This interests me, but I don't ask her what she is reading, as I get the impression this is what she would like me to ask. I have in the past noticed her huffs when I don't say anything and then she crosses her long legs.

It's not that I like to see her upset, but to see every aspect of her in all her different moods because then she does not bore me.

And now she is wearing glasses while driving.

I have looked at these glasses when she has not been around and tried them on to see how they feel. I have perfect vision and do not need glasses and neither does Sophia. She likes the effect they produce. Intelligence. This is her grand illusion.

As we approached the airport; Sophia reminds me again that we were picking up my parents. I sigh. She looks and smiles.

'We have already done this argument; could we please have a new one?'

'Aiden, I am thinking of dying my hair?'

'Why would you want to do that?'

'I'm not,' she smirks. 'I just wanted to see what your reaction would be.'

She is looking at the road and grinning. Do you see what I mean about her? How can anyone marry a person like that? And then she stretched across and taps me on the knee.

'Just teasing, Aiden. Isn't that what we do to each other?'

'No,' I frowned. 'I dislike being teased, as you call it.'

It came to my mind to tell her to stop the car because I wanted to drive. But then I caught my reflection in the rearview mirror and check myself from frowning. No, the signs don't show yet, but given enough time and this undesired habit will produce the result of a very fractious man.

Over the years, I have examined my father for the effects on his skin. As he has led such a good life, all his lines are attached only to his eyes. He has what is called laughter lines. It is peculiar, for what does happiness mean to my father?

'We will say hello, good to see you, and did you have a pleasant journey?' Sophia was so full of herself. This is what driving does to her. 'Your father, I think, will do the introducing; he is very good at that, as he has perfect manners, she laughed.'

I remained silent as I looked in front of me. I was more concerned with how she was driving. Will she miss the turnoff if she doesn't look where she is going?

'I thought you should shake hands with Eve, but then again, a pleasant touch would be if you kissed her on the cheeks—both sides. Yes, I think that would be a nice touch. It would also break the ice. I see her as being nervous, probably wondering what you will be like. I was going to say your father would have described you, but probably not.'

I glanced across to her, wondering what she meant by that, and then if she was paying attention to the road.

'I think I will give her a couple of kisses. After all, we are family, so we might as well start out on a good footing. I think she will like that from me,' I said.

'What shall you call her?' this thought suddenly intrigued me.

'Eve.'

'Not mother then?'

She suddenly swerved and shot across the road while breaking heavily. Then she changed gear.

'I know what your game is, Aiden. I didn't forget the turnoff. We will meet your father and his new wife, and everyone will be happy.'

Everything was thrown into changes now at the airport, crossing over, going underneath, and looking for the directions for arrivals; Sophia was also trying to show me what an excellent driver she was. I had never any doubts about her driving skills, but it was amusing to see how hard she was trying to impress me. Even with my distractions.

In her blue slacks, white shirt and lightweight jacket, Sophia threw over her shoulder a casual bag she liked to carry. This time she was wearing light blue high heels to match her leisure clothes. At five feet eight, she was hardly tiny, and now with three-inch heels, her eyes were just below my eye level.

Slamming the car door; we walked to the arrivals area. Two slim and very attractive people were catching every-one's eye. I knew Sophia loved this, as did I. Heads were turning, arms nudging, people wondering if we were royalty. I felt that smile crawling and poking at my lips. We, the beautiful people, were being spoken about.

'I like it here,' Sophia whispered to me, doing her best to ignore the attention.

Standing in the waiting area, looking up and checking the times, the plane had arrived seven minutes early. Looking at me, Sophia nodded. Her silent language bore fruit as we walked over to where the arrivals came out from the customs checkpoint.

I shrugged okay and followed her lamely. Someone walked past me and winked at me; I winked back. Someone else smiled at me, so of course I smiled back and then Sophia turned around and frowned at me; I frowned back.

What are you doing? Her eyes were saying. Nothing darling, sweet nothing.

A crowd of people were coming out through customs. Some were jubilant, mouthing that it was good to be home, but not for everyone.

'I should imagine your parents would have a fair amount of luggage,' said Sophia after another ten minutes had passed. What was keeping them?

I shrugged; this was her outing; I had nothing to do with it. Looking at the clock overhead and then at my watch while my eyes were still on the tunnel, I kept dumb and waited.

'Okay,' said Sophia. 'What is it? You can tell me.'

'Tell you what?'

'I am tired of all the games you play, Aiden. What was the point of coming all this way here knowing they would not be here?'

'I tried to tell you they took an earlier flight, Sophia, but you were so intense about getting to the airport.' I called out as I chased after her.

'Childish—' she spat. 'Something you should have grown out of a long time ago.'

She was dashing towards the exit, her long blonde hair had slipped to her back; she was furious.

'I have done nothing wrong. If you had listened to me in the first place, we would not be here. But you wouldn't listen.'

'Liar,' she stopped to turn on me.

'How dare you call me a liar, I—'

'I call you a liar because it's true. You said nothing to me about it. And Aiden, I listen and pay attention to every word you say, mainly because you are important to me, and also because I love you. But sometimes—just sometimes—I don't understand what's wrong with you. Why do you play these jokes on me?'

'Nothing is wrong with me. Nothing,' I said, trailing behind.

With a dash, I caught up with her. I don't know how she manages to move so fast on those heels. I've tried them on myself because she has not got little feet, and I nearly fell over.

'Believe me,' I caught her shoulder. 'I told you I had another telegram from them saying they were catching an earlier flight.'

She stopped again.

'Why do you lie to me? What do you get out of it? Do you think it's funny that we came all this way for nothing? What are you trying to prove? Honestly, Aiden, sometimes I really don't understand you. We should be on each other's side and not playing tricks. Why couldn't you tell me there was no point going to the airport?'

'But I did. I can't help it if you don't believe me.'

We said nothing on the journey home. She was furious, not because of the misunderstanding at the airport, but because she was upset by what my father thought and his new hag of a wife by us not being there. Who cares, for God's sake?

'Aiden,' Sophia said when we entered the house. Standing by the door, she had the look of thunder in her eyes while her lower lip was pulled down. She was resolving to do something. 'Do you want me to leave you? Do you want me to pack my things and never come back? Is this what you want?'

'Yes,' I said, raising my chin a little. If she calls my bluff, then I will answer it.

'Very well,' she walked ahead to the stairs when out from a room Mr Mears came over to me.

Appearing incongruously in our drama, he politely ignored the scene.

'Your father and his new wife arrived about an hour and a half ago, sir.' He fluttered his eyelashes. 'They give their regrets at not be here to greet you on your return, sir.'

'Oh—'

'He said their journey had been long and tiring, so they have taken themselves to their rooms.' Mears back stepped and with a cursory nod, he said goodnight and moved off toward his rooms.

'What do you want to do?' I asked when we were alone again. I was now looking deep into her dark blue eyes and wondering if she would really leave me when something exciting like this was about to happen. 'Are you leaving now?' How can I ever keep Sophia entertained?

'Good night, Aiden. You can sleep in one of the spare bedrooms.'

Ah, so there was a reprieve, but I only had to tell her I was sorry for her to share our bed again. But I was not sorry. Besides, this was my house, and if anyone should go to a spare room, it should be her. But she would never leave me. What? Hey, leave the luxury of my life, a kept woman enjoying the benefits of the pool, house, money, and our circle of friends.

As I lay in bed listening to the noises of the house watching the reflection of the pool imaging on the ceiling, I saw the door to my bedroom open and a figure stole in. Ah, I sighed, smiling in the shadows. She has come; it's about time. A nymph crept to the bottom of the bed, her breath nearing my face as she opened the covers and slid in. I grinned, shaking my head gently. No, she would never leave me.

Sophia was gone when I opened my eyes at that quiet moment of the morning. I wondered where I was when I pinned my eyes on the drapes, smelling the perfume of lavender. I thought I heard laughter while still half asleep in that strange halfway house between waking and dreaming. Sophia and I were riding the Carousel at a funfair, and every time I went up, she went down. She kept on stretching out to me, but she would never reach me. Such a lovely dream.

And so, I was going to see my father and his hag. I stepped into the shower and cooled myself down. There was no reason for me to say anything until later and then have a quiet word with my father to find out exactly what damage he had done.

Perhaps this would bring my father and me closer to a more meaningful relationship. Yeah, well, don't hold your breath.

That was Sophia's voice coming from the outside. I could swear to it talking to another female. Padding from the bathroom across to the window while towelling myself, I pushed the curtains gently apart. What a perfect pool scene. Sophia was sitting by the pool showing how entertaining she could be, but as for the person she was talking to, she remained hidden beneath the parasol. Even so, she had an interesting voice.

If only I could get my father on his own to have that quick word with him, I would put some sense into him;

show him what he neglected and let him see she was only after his money.

Doing up my shirt buttons, I examined my physique again. My father looks good now, but in a few years from now, his figure will slip, while mine—well, mine would still look good for another twenty-plus years.

'Aiden?' Sophia knocked on the door. 'They are asking after you. Are you going to come down?'

'Yes, I'll be down in a minute.'

She was listening at the door and wondering if I was still lying in bed and being idle.

'Aiden?'

'What—?'

'Don't tell them we had an argument last night, will you? Not even in jest.'

Going to the door to open it, Sophia was gone.

3

I could see my father sitting near the pool and keeping Sophia company. Their laughter was tumbling through the house when I stepped out. His white trousers and blue shirt flattered his chestnut hair—what a shame it would be if he went bald.

The last few days of June sunshine promised more golden bodies to come. Sophie, the nymph, had straddled her sunbed and was leaning across towards my father in a very compromising position. This was how it looked to me —always provoking, but I would say nothing.

'There you are, Aiden.' Sophia had caught my entrance, her face dissolving from one expression to another, embarrassed probably that she had been caught. 'Your father and I were just talking about you.'

'And what were you saying?' I stood by my father's side, looking down at my girlfriend. We were a family; a team and she was the outsider. Interesting that I could show loyalty just from where I stood.

'Yes, Dominic, what were we saying?' grinned Sophia to my father.

He turned around with the sun in his eyes but with not so much a grin as an expression of pleasure.

'Come here, my son,' my father put out a hand to me in a gesture of not only friendship but now of love. 'Sophia has been telling me you have missed me. Is that true?'

I must admit I looked from my father to Sophia and wondered again at what she was playing.

'I told you he missed you,' said Sophia, nodding, now referring her observations to Dominic. 'Aiden is going to tell you it's not true, aren't you, Aiden?'

'Aiden.' My father took my hand, sandwiching it between his. Clearly, he was moved by what Sophia had told him. 'I have missed you as well. You have been in my thoughts a great deal; I've been talking a lot about you to Eve. Sit down, son, and let me look at you.'

Never have I known my father to be an emotional man, but now I see he has become one. Regarding him with distant affection, I see many changes in him. His hair is a little longer and at the wings, a little silvery, but he is more handsome for it. While the lines on his face were also a little deeper and yet still effective. He has forgotten to moisturise, proving that his new wife does not know how to take care of him.

To the side of us, I could see Sophia regarding us with perfect understanding. I hate how she watches me, as I hated every part of this emotional rubbish my father is trying to impart to me. She was thinking about how well we looked together. Family is what she's thinking; because this is what she wants.

He never asked my counsel whether he should marry, but went straight ahead and did it.

'Aiden is worried you might have forgotten him.' Again, Sophia was doing her best to upset me.

'Father, do you think I could have a quiet word before you introduce me to your new wife?' I indicated towards the house with my head.

'Aiden is worried that—'

'Shut up Sophia and keep out of my business.'

Keeping her mouth dutifully closed, Sophia looked to Dominic to imply they had discussed something while I was not there.

'You are nervous about meeting my new wife, Eve. I know because Sophia has been telling me all about it. But I can assure you once you see her, you will fall in love with her as I did. It will be instantaneous—'

'What will be instantaneous?' asked another voice coming to join us around the pool.

She was standing in the sunshine, dazzling herself in the rays. At first, I could not see this petite creature of some five feet two.

'Aiden, my son, allow me to introduce you to Eve, my new wife.'

When I stood, the sun fell from my eyes, yet reformed to produce a new sparkling presence. Was this possible? Ethereal or sublime? My eyes took in this shape of wonder that only music, if it were possible, could describe. Long, dark hair slid from her elegant neck down her back. Large grey eyes generated interest, while her skin was the colour of milk. Everything was detailed with perfection. I have seen no one as beautiful as her. While my heart, the most redundant of my organs, fell into a rhythm which had never been constructed. Yes, I could. My body echoed with the same desire to fall in love with her.

Did she know what I was thinking when she slipped her little hand while smiling into mine? Her cool white hand was perfect. I marvelled at her touch, perhaps with an open mouth. I was unsure whether I should squeeze this little hand, believing almost certainly I would break her fragile bones.

'It's good to meet you, Aiden. I have heard so much about you from your father that I could swear I would never meet up to your expectations. The mean and nasty step-mother; I know this is what you would have called me. And I don't blame you.' She giggled while I stood there with my mouth open wide.

'No, you must never say that.' My face drew white, while my heart asked me what had happened. To function from our blindness, we must be told what is going on. But how could I when I had never expected to meet such perfect artistry? Not even in my dreams had I expected to feast my eyes on someone so lovely who was still human. I was trying to make sense of what was happening. Though I tried to appear natural, all this fell apart when I became angry. 'You are anything but ugly.'

Again, Eve exchanged looks with my father. She never said she was ugly, but ugly she must be to me. She smiled with features that drew perfection, but her thoughts held their own reservations. Anyhow, that can be left until later.

'You must call me Eve. Everyone does. It is the shortest name my parents could find for me and a reminder that I must not think well of myself.'

'But you should think well of yourself,' I said, blasting out like an idiot again. 'You must think—I mean, Sophia has been looking forward to meeting you.'

Even Sophia, my blond-haired beauty, was enjoying my embarrassment. Leaning on her knees with her head in her hands, and eyes that were now looping up; yes, this was her Aiden. This was the man she was in love with.

'Sophia,' continued Eve, turning away, as if she did not

know the effect, she was having on me. While still standing
beside me, she held her head to one side in lively conversation, her pink mouth in a bow of a gentle smile. I could not
move. 'Said that you did not receive our last telegram. I am
afraid this was my fault. And I shall explain. Friends—don't
we all need friends? But with friendship, you need to spend
time in their company. I needed these friends when I was on
my own. They protected me until I met this wonderful man.'
Eve looked across at my father and grinned spiritedly. 'So,
what do I do?' her eyes were merry because a tease was
coming on. 'Divorce your father, so I can say hello to my
friends and therefore lose the best thing that has ever
happened to me in my life? You explain to your son,
Dominic.'

'No, my dear, you are doing very well on your own. I will
not interfere.'

How much he loved her; I could see everything of his
feelings in his upturned face; he could not conceal them.
They were there in his voice, his eyes, and how he looked at
her. Even their love was going to be perfect.

'If you wish,' she smiled, or was it merriment? Turning
her charitable face to him, she was going to let us into the
secret. 'This wonderful man suggested divorce would be too
dramatic. I did not have to leave my friends, as I did not have
to leave him. That we could do a compromise. A compromise,' she repeated in a whisper, more like a sigh. 'What a
wonderful word. It means I can do whatever I want in the
enclosure of a compromise.' Her head nodded to her new
husband. 'He suggested we should see my friends because
we all need friends. So, before we left, this marvellous man
took me to visit them.' She touched my father's shoulder
gently, and then she took his hand. This was most sympa-
thetically done. 'Which was why the telegram was late.'

Of course, the reason was ridiculous and warranted no attention. Listening to her voice—I could not believe how perfectly she spoke. Her voice was a music box of charms which I could listen to for the rest of my life.

'I want to say I am sorry you had to go all the way to the airport for nothing. It's my fault entirely. I will take the blame.'

Again, my eyes turned to Sophia for the mischief she had caused and for the embarrassment. When I get her on my own—? But I thought the better.

'Please, think nothing of it. Sophia is a wonderful driver; did I tell you?'

'Oh, I am glad everything turned out all right in the end. Sophia told us many things while you were away and also some splendid news as well,' said Eve, while my father started nodding and smiling. 'And it is congratulations to you two. I hope you will be as happy as your father and me.' She turned to him, and I watched as my father put his arm around his new wife.

It was sickening, and I hated it. I hated the way he looked and touched her. The need to shout out and tell him to take his hands off her was blocked by the residue of sense for I still held on to my reason, only just. What I was unaware of was that while I was watching my father and Eve. Sophia had got off her sunbed and walked across to me. In a gesture of ownership, she had put her arms around me. It took all my might not to shake her off being so angry with her.

'Dominic and I thought it would be nice if we took you two out for dinner. And make it a grand occasion, weren't we, Dominic?'

'Well,' Sophia said after a while, perhaps noticing how idiotic we looked together, pretending to be in love. 'I thought it would be nice if we ate here, in front of the pool. Our chef has ordered some wonderful ingredients. What do you think? We could be cosy together. Moonlight on the pool. Plenty of wine when we want it. We could be private and intimate and there will be no one listening in to our conversation.'

'Yes, a better idea as we have a lot to talk about,' said Eve, smiling as she walked across to Sophia, and placed her hands on her arm in a show of camaraderie. 'I think that will be charming.'

She looked at me and then at my father before turning her attention back to Sophia.

'Come, I am interested in what food you have for us tonight.'

As the two ladies walked off, Dominic stared after them. He looked as if he was missing Eve already.

Once out of sight, my father moved, making himself ready to talk to me.

'The two ladies appeared to have hit it off. I am glad everything is going well. There was always a worry, you know. Changes.'

The awkward silence between us was now filled with awkward thoughts. Now that status between us had changed, came the realisation we never talked.

'How have you been, Aiden?'

'What do you mean? I have been well. I have done all the things I've wanted to do and enjoyed myself.'

I don't know why it is, but everything my father says to me feels like an assault.

'Yes,' sighed my father, 'Enjoyed yourself.'

I could see he was bracing himself for something which was on his mind, mainly because he could not look at me.

'So, you have asked Sophia to marry you? It's a big step, Aiden.'

This direct hit was tackled with his eyes on me. Rooting away in the ashes of my mind, he was hoping to get an answer. What I was reading, though, was his disappointment in me. I was angry, and it showed in my eyes because I could not help launching an attack on him. None of us is above censure.

'And one which seems you can take without asking for anyone's blessings. I am your son, and you never told me. In fact, I was one of the last to find out. And why is that? Had you forgotten you are my father?'

'No, I have not forgotten, Aiden. I would have told you if I thought you would have approved.'

His smile had been vanquished twenty years ago; we were much better enemies than we were friends. Now here we were again, telling each other how much we disapproved of each other's behaviour.

'I know your feelings about marriage and any other form of commitment; I don't judge because they are yours, but not everyone thinks the same. Which is why I wonder about your decision to take this step.'

'Oh, if that's the only thing you are worrying about, don't.' I sulked.

'What do you mean?' he frowned.

'I only promised marriage to shut her up. She is always going on about wanting me to marry her. What's the difference whether we're married or not? We live together, share the same space; she is seen with me, and I with her. I don't know what the big fuss is about.'

'Love, Aiden, is about wanting. Being with someone all the time and wanting no one else. This, Aiden, is what love is about. When one makes this commitment, it's saying you will not be with another—'

'I seem to remember you used to go off when you were married to my mother. Why did you marry her when you had no intentions of keeping your promise?'

'This is different, Aiden—'

'Is it? I don't think so.'

Like a dog still tethered, I walked away but was compelled to come back knowing all the time my father's eyes were hanging on me. I still had something more to say.

'Do you think what you did had nothing to do with breaking my mother's heart? Because it did. You broke my mother's heart. I remember her sitting on her own, crying. While you—well, where were you?'

'Aiden, that's in the past now and I have changed—'

'Oh yes,' I jeered. 'You have changed, but my mother's heart didn't once you broke it.'

'Will you never forgive me?'

'It's not a case of forgiveness, father. My mother can't forgive because she is dead. Let me put this question to you; do you forgive yourself?'

'Eve forgives me.'

'Eve would forgive anyone if you were to ask her. I can see how wonderful she is. And yes, I think she is too good for you. This is one of those questions which should not be asked of another but of oneself. Do you forgive yourself?'

'No, Aiden, if that's what this is all about. I don't forgive myself, but I must carry on living. I cannot forever live in regret with you as my punisher and my conscience—you are my son, and not my judge and executioner.'

'Pretty words, but they never saved my mother.'

A pained sigh from my father, a man who was exhausted by this son and father relationship.

'Dominic, Aiden,' came the call of a sweet maiden's voice.

Her flute-like voice, mellow in tone, rang out to us just at the right time. Did she have some prophetic abilities? We both raised our heads in the direction from where it came from, relieved we had been released from this argument. Eve was walking across the lawn past the swimming pool, walking with a purpose and directly to Dominic. There was something in her manner which suggested a new idea had crept into her mind. While the worn expression which sat heavily on Dominic's brow vanished when he saw her person. At last, I read this in his eyes and mouth; she was directing her steps to him—she was his saviour, the one he had searched his entire life for.

In less than a second of Eve reaching us, she had read the situation between us. Guessing what was said and who was the haranguer, she could not help passing her eyes to me. She knew what had gone on, and then she smiled, a gentle smile, for like my father she could forgive as well. Dominic needed her, which was why she was here. This was her calling in life to be there for him.

'I have to tell you, it was Sophia's idea. She is the inspiration.' She winked at Dominic and then at me. 'That we should have a day out tomorrow and go for a picnic. What do you say to that?'

'What do I say to that?' laughed my father. 'I say that—'

What was on his lips was so thoughtfully held back? Should I guess? I didn't need to. I knew what my father was thinking I should do, for many times in the past, my father passed me the idea that I would be happier if I was working. In fact, he would prefer it if I was more occupied because I was that constant reminder of how he failed my mother.

'I say it's a wonderful idea,' picked up my father. 'And you, Aiden, what do you say?'

'Yes, why not?'

'Did you talk to him?' asked Eve significantly, her long black hair slipping over her shoulder, making a screen between them and me.

I looked from Eve to my father. What were they talking about? Already they had made plans together, excluding me.

'I have not had a chance to or the occasion.'

A deep conference was going on between them. I felt peeved to be left out. What's going on here? What were they talking about?

'Isn't it wonderful news, Aiden?'

The tall, blonde, still in her swimming costume showing off her fabulous shape, came bounding across the lawn and so dangerously near the pool that in one light breath, I could see her tumbling. Even Dominic's looks expressed those sentiments that he found her beautiful. But what I saw made me laugh, although there was no doubt she was lovely. But honestly. She looked like an Afghan hound that hadn't exercised for a long time.

Catching hold of my shoulder, she swung around to perch herself on my lap.

'Get off me, you big lump,' I said without thinking. 'I am not a doormat for you to dump yourself on.'

'Oh Aiden, don't be such a grudge. But isn't it exciting news? And so romantic.'

'What?' I looked from Sophia to my father.

'I haven't had time to tell him.' Said Dominic, apologetically while his eyes sought for Eve's kind face.

'For goodness' sake, what is going on here?' I could not help being distracted and even feeling a little paranoid.

'Don't worry, Aiden,' Eve's light touch on my shoulder was enough to calm me down. 'I shall tell you our good news because you must hear now, especially as we have to leave soon. I am so excited I find it difficult to keep quiet about it any longer. Dear Aiden, it's because I love Italy so much,' began Eve. 'Dominic has promised to get us a villa on the edge of this beautiful island, a place called Pantelleria, in Italy. Have you heard of it?'

'Never,' I smarted resentfully.

'Yes, you have, Aiden. Your mother and I took you there when you were a baby,' said Dominic.

'Well then, of course, I would have heard of it. Makes sense, doesn't it, even though I was too young to remember it?'

'He's right,' said Eve, turning her attention to me with a gesture of a caress across my face, taking any response I had. What were these messages Eve was sending me?

'We have come across a piece of land—'

'More like cliffs if you were to ask me,' said Dominic indulgently.

'Yes, but we will make it beautiful. Oh, Aiden, I am so excited about what your father is going to do for me. I have always wanted a place in Italy and always by the coast. And now I shall have it. It's my dream come true.'

Excitement had caused her to spin as if in a dance. She was much younger than I thought before.

'This is what I fell in love with,' said Dominic, touching my hand and then nodding. 'She used to be a dancer once upon a time. She could have carried on.'

We marvelled at her while she danced. Her long black hair spun outwards like ribbons of silk as she sprung in the air. I was enchanted. I wanted to know everything about her, her birthplace, her parents, because I could swear she came from royalty. While she danced, I was captivated.

'I wish I could dance like her,' complained Sophia. 'She looks so small, so light, like an angel leaving heaven to come and entertain us. What is the dance?'

'It's called the tarantella. A dance which was performed in Italy in a place called Taranto Puglia. The dance is done to rid the victim of the poison of the wolf spider, whose bite is deadly poisonous. That's the myth, but in fact, the spiders are not. But it makes for a wonderful story.'

Whirling around one more time, Eve dropped to her knees.

'Superb,' I said, clapping and then holding my hand out to raise her from the floor. 'You were wonderful.'

'It's nothing.' She took hold of my outstretched hand and allowed me to pull her up.

She was so light, as she was exquisitely lovely. Nothing was out of proportion; the mathematics was based on grace. I pulled her towards me for a moment, forgetting myself because her body balanced itself on me. A mistake perhaps, but she was worth it as she fell into my arms; it was an accident.

'When I am so happy, I forget myself,' said Eve, leaving me for Dominic.

She slid her arm around my father's shoulder and kissed him gently on the cheek. With that, I wondered about their love. Perhaps my father had lost his virility, and perhaps their love for each other might only be platonic. She needs a man, someone like me.

'Well, are you ready, Aiden?'

I nodded while still thinking of her beauty.

'We are going out there even though the house is not yet built. Dominic said it doesn't matter. We are going to lease somewhere—but Dominic said he would buy it, but I told him, no, don't be silly, why would we want two villas? Anyhow, back to what I was saying. We will leave in a couple of days, and we want you both to come with us. But only if you want to, of course. What do you say to that, Aiden? Are you excited and happy for me?'

'Say we can go with them, Aiden,' cried Sophie, excited. 'Don't be a spoilsport. Say you want to go.'

Sophia tapped me on the shoulder with energetic excitement. While Eve's eyes had left themselves at my doorstep. What was I going to say to this news?

'I am delighted for you. And yes, Sophia, we will go.'

'Now that's settled, we will make arrangements.' Eve smiled and clapped her hands.

4

We sat at the table outside with my father and Eve sitting opposite each other. My father, who liked his wine, was rationed by the effect of an observant eye. I listened to their chatter, although most of it passed over my head. Nothing important had been said but the nice sighs and twitters from the ladies. The wine bubbled into the glasses, while knives and forks scrapped against china plates. In the background, the lapping of pool water on the edge of the pool filled the air. It would have been a wonderful evening to relax, if there wasn't something already on my mind. In fact, it was touched on many times.

'How I envy you,' said Sophia, gazing at Eve. 'To have a man who wants to make you happy that he is prepared to buy you anything.'

'Yes, I know. I am very lucky. But your turn will come, I am certain of it.'

'I don't know. Sometimes, I am not so sure of what is going to happen the next day.'

Sophia's eyes looked at my deadpan face. Was I listening? She did not care. Now she was pouring herself another drink.

'What is your secret?' I heard Sophia ask Eve when my father proposed we walk around the pool. 'How do you get a man to part with his money for you?'

'We are thinking of leaving for Italy next Monday,' began my father. 'It was Eve's suggestion that you should come out for a while. She is trying very hard to make a success of this relationship.'

'This relationship?' I questioned. 'Do you mean to say that your relationship is already in trouble?'

'No, Aiden, you have me wrong. Eve is trying to patch up the relationship between us two. She is convinced that you and I could be friends.'

'Friends?' I raised my eyebrow.

'Yes, friends. I told her you and I could never be friends again, even though I have tried so hard to make a go of it. But you always blame me for everything—'

'Just mother. And yes, I blame you for mother. You pretend nothing happened to her, and then when she committed suicide from grief, the next thing you said was that she was mentally unstable and that it was inevitable she would kill herself. Do you have any idea about grief and what it can do to you?'

'Yes, Aiden. We have been through this before. Shall we let it drop?'

He looked at me in a way I had never seen before. A way that convinced me that my father wanted to part waves with me. He had taken me on this walk around the pool without the women hearing. I felt strange. It felt weird. I felt lost.

'Of course, I will always make sure you will have sufficient money; there is no need for you to worry on that part. I won't cut you off. In fact, I shall increase your allowance—

you know I have plenty of money. There is no problem with that.'

'I don't understand what you are saying?' I felt myself becoming frantic.

'Don't you, Aiden? I thought I had outlined it well enough for you. It's not been a secret that you and I don't get on. This sort of thing happens in families through nobody's fault. Now at last, I have a new life with Eve, and I can stand up on my own two feet and leave you. You have proposed to Sophia, which suggests to me you are prepared to get on with your life. There is no need for either of us to get in touch with the other. It's what you have always wanted. Isn't it? For me to get out of your hair, as they say.'

When Dominic looked over to the other side of the pool to see how the ladies were doing, I felt an unexpected change had happened to him. More relaxed than he had ever been, as if something had been resolved in his mind, meaning he would never be unhappy again. He had fought his demons and come out the victor. And she was the reward for his fight; she was that light in his life. So, what about me?

Yes, what about me? I could say nothing else. My lips were suddenly sealed and if I should say anything, he would either not hear or heed me. Breathless, he had left me breathless. He had taken the wind out of my sails as surely as he had punched me in the guts.

'Isn't this what you have always wanted?'

I could not reply; this strange feeling of loss came over me. I was being abandoned.

'Besides, it is not as if you are a child anymore, Aiden. How old are you now? Thirty-one or thirty-two?'

One of the two women laughed. Turning our heads at the same time to the distraction. Sophia had become over-excited; she was clapping her hands like a child. I looked at her; her blonde hair was a delightful contrast to Eve's black mane. These were two thoroughbreds, two wonderful beauties. My father, though, had not noticed my silence. Perhaps he had rehearsed this conversation so many times in his head that he did not need the influence of my voice.

'I don't think you could do much better than Sophia. She has a sound brain in her head. She's funny and amusing; you two will have many conversations into the night. You have not done badly with her. To be honest, I like her. My request to you is to treat her kindly. She is exquisite, which is a bonus and good to look at.'

In the dark, our voices came like the sages, prophetic determining the fate for us all. I felt so strange.

Staring at the two ladies, I could not hear what was being said or it would be more correct to say that I did not understand. But my father was accurate. They were enjoying each other's company. These two attractive women were getting on with each other. There was no disparity because they were of the same age. It seemed a shame to split them up when they had just got to know each other.

'I was thinking of leaving tonight. In fact, I was thinking of never returning ever again to this place. What have I got to come back to, Aiden? I don't have any family here.'

'What about me?'

'I told you I won't cut you off, Aiden, so there is no need for you to panic. I realise now that you won't ever get a job. It was at my advice that you made something of yourself. It's not good for your morale to hang around and do nothing. That's what happened to my younger brother, although you never knew him. It was tragic how his life ended; I couldn't help thinking at the time that it was a waste. What I am trying to advise you is to take care of your life, and I also mean the people in your life. But I guess this will fall on disinterested ears. You do nothing I suggest—'

'Was I always a disappointment to you?' I found myself saying this without being able to monitor it.

'No, no, you were a delightful child. Very clever, in fact, I would go so far as to say you could have had a future in anything you touched.' He mused, smiling to himself. 'In truth, I could see you with a future in medicine—perhaps even in research. And then you were also musical. You had everything at your feet. And one day, you closed down the lid of your piano, put your books away and you never went back to them. It was such a shame.'

He stared ahead with the eyes of destiny.

'What happened to you, Aiden? What made you want to give up on life? Is there nothing that you appreciate anymore? Does the food you put into your mouth lack the taste of hope and desire?'

We had been walking slowly around the pool, and our footsteps were becoming shorter and slower every time we turned the circle until we came to a stop.

'What happened to you, Aiden?'

'I don't know, Father.'

My father squinted. What was this he heard me say? Was it true that I had called him Father for the first time in years? Did I really call him Father? Yes, I had. So, what was wrong with me? He accepted he had no place in my life.

'Are you okay, Aiden?'

There was a degree of gentleness in his voice instead of the tone he introduced while we made our laps. With every step he was taking, he was distancing himself from me. I was his son; he reasoned with himself, but there were many men with sons who they never saw. Because life does not dictate that when you have children, you must love them.

Life only wants you to give life to them, and once they have been born and nurtured; this child belongs to everyone for the future and not yours alone.

Halfway round we had gone and now we were standing still on the other side of the pool opposite the ladies.

'I don't know, but I feel that something has happened to me—'

I felt my father's eyes spin on to me like a limpet while wondering what had happened. This was not the time to say anything, but a time to listen. We move about this earth wondering with uncertainty where to put our feet while trying to hear our next thought and what it could do for us.

'I have never felt like this before.'

Time stopped also to listen to me, the Prodigal Son. Where had I been on my journey? Why had my life gone so wrong? I was hearing every sound about me; my ears had tuned into the sounds of the stratosphere. I was lost with no destiny. Life poured on. Sounds came and went; a blackbird made its last bid for a good night in the trees some thirty yards away. And the mating frogs only rarely came to the pool daunted by the blue, perhaps or from the chlorine. Only the other day I had found one floating in there. Again, from the babble of two women's voices, someone burst out laughing. It was Sophia, of course.

'Don't you want to see me again?'

'I didn't say that, but I think in this case, there is no point in it. I want you to be happy, Aiden, but I do not know how or why I am ever going to do that. We need to move on with our lives; you do see, don't you, Aiden? I don't want to be reminded by you for the rest of my life that it was my fault your mother killed herself. I don't want to carry on feeling so bad about it. If I could relive my life right from the beginning, I would do so, and that would mean I would never hurt your mother. But it is done now, and there is no turning back. With Eve in my life, I have a chance. She has given me that chance and a reason. And I want to start again. I want to be happy. And now I find I also want to be free of you, but that does not mean I have stopped loving you, far from it. I am fifty-five now; I have a few good years ahead of me which I can enjoy—'

'But what about your art? Your paintings—what about them?'

'Paintings?' he grinned. He thought this was absurd.

'Yes, paintings.'

'Do you know why I collected paintings or a part of the reason?'

I said nothing. I just looked at him.

'So, that I could have something beautiful in my life. But I don't need paintings anymore when I have got Eve. You know, Aiden, you should try love; it really is a wonderful feeling; it completely alters your conception of life. Shall we return to the ladies?'

To stop him, I put my hand out. 'I can change, Father. I can be different.'

He looked baffled, even confused, and then he gently took my hand from him.

'You don't have to change, Aiden. This is what I am trying to tell you. You can carry on being the man you want to be. You don't need me getting on at you or showing my disapproval. Don't you understand, Aiden? You, too, can be free of me. Isn't that wonderful? We can both lead our lives and be our own man, with no one looking over our shoulders in displeasure. Wouldn't that be wonderful, to be our own selves?'

'What do you want me to do?'

'To do? To do what, Aiden?'

'Okay, so you want me to get a job—I will get a job.'

'No, Aiden.'

This time, he laid his hand on top of mine.

'I don't want you to do anything, and I mean anything. No jobs, no routine, just lie in bed if you like and be happy. Oh yes, there is only one thing, don't harm your lady.'

'I will get a job; I will be smarter; I will do everything you want me to do.'

He frowned. What on earth was I talking about? Hadn't he just given me his good wishes that I could carry on being a bum?

'Aiden, you're all right,' he now smiled, patting me on the shoulder, as if he had not heard a word of what I was saying. 'Everything will be all right. We should return to the ladies. It's getting cold now and it will be dark soon, and it will soon be time for bed. I am glad we have talked.'

'Don't Father,' I knocked his arm from me. 'Will it help if I say I am sorry?'

'Aiden,' now he was frowning, as if he found this interview very harrowing. 'There is nothing for you to apologise about. You have done nothing wrong. These are your feelings, and I must respect them, but I don't have to agree with them. Let us return to the ladies.'

'Please Father, give me a chance.' I was holding on to him, wrestling with his arm. 'Please don't make me grovel. I am thirty-two years old, but I am not past begging.'

'What is it you want?' he was completely bewildered as to know what to say or even do for me.

'I want to come with you to Italy.' My eyes were determined; I had always got what I wanted.

'Why?' this was making no sense to him.

'Why? Because I want to. Do you remember Saul on his way to Damascus?'

Squinting, he was totally perplexed at the game I was playing. But knowing me, as he did, it must have been another of my tricks.

'Or the Prodigal Son—you remember him? Well, that's me. I am Saul. I am the Prodigal Son. You can't do this to me, Father.'

'Aiden, please, what is this all about?'

'Don't cut me off. Take me with you.'

He grinned. 'This is some sort of joke, isn't it? Well, you are not very funny—'

'No.' I grabbed hold of his arm again. 'I mean it. What you said to me suddenly made sense. I don't know why that is. Perhaps it is because you are going away. But you are right. I should not punish you for what my mother did. I remember now how she used to be. She was always so possessive of you, she—'

'Aiden, stop this. Your mother loved you; I won't allow you to take this away from her. She loved you, Aiden. Please remember that.'

'But you are going to leave me, aren't you?'

Again, that frown trying to work out what this all meant. This must be some very peculiar and long-winded game I was up to because he still did not trust me. He still believed that I was playing a game.

'I am not leaving you, Aiden. I am starting a new life with a woman I am deeply in love with. Please be happy for me.'

'I am sorry, Father. You do not know how sorry I am. If you don't let me come with you; I don't know what I will do.'

'You sound just like your mother. But Aiden, don't you see? Even in Italy, we will still carry on with our old destructive relationship. I hate it you hate me, and I am tired of always being the bad guy, the one who murdered your mother—'

'I never said you did.'

'Oh yes, you did, Aiden. Yes, you did. We need to be apart from each other. I will call you from time to time—'

'No, you won't. You will be glad you won't have to see me again. Please, Father, give me this one chance, and please understand that I have changed. I want to make it up to you. And I am glad you are happy. I am glad for everything that makes you happy, and you will be happy, and because of that—but I am asking you to give me a chance. Please allow me to come with you so I can prove how much I've changed. And I will show you, father. Please.'

'Oh Aiden, I don't know. I've got to think about this—'

'I won't ruin your life with Eve if that's what you are worried about.'

He was. I could see by the concern on his brow.

'I don't know. I will have to talk about this with Eve.'

'She wants Sophia and me to come with you. Didn't you say she wanted us as one big, happy family?'

My father was staring at me with great incredulity; he had seen himself free from me and it had been a relief. And now I realised how much he distrusted me.

'Just give me a chance, Father. I will be on trial. If we have one bad word, just one bad word, then I will be on a plane on my way home. Is that good enough for you?'

The two ladies looked up when we reached the table. Sophia was attached to the wine bottle, and this was her second.

'We were guessing what you two were talking about,' said Sophia, twiddling the glass stem in her fingers. 'Eve guessed it had to do with Italy, but I thought it was something different. Now what was it then? Oh yes, the last argument you had, and who said what, you know that sort of thing? Who was right? Eve or me?'

'Neither of you.' I jumped in. 'But Eve was closer to the truth. We were talking about Italy, weren't we, Father? We were talking about the house. I asked him if I could do some labouring. It's about time I pulled myself out of my idleness—'

'I don't believe you, Aiden,' said Sophia, her hand seeking to top herself up with more wine. 'You are always about yourself. Why would you do anything for anyone?'

I put my hand over her glass to prevent her from pouring the wine.

'Why are you doing that?'

'Because you've had enough, Sophia. You know you will wake up with a hangover in the morning and regret what you've done. I am stopping you from being ill.'

From the side, Eve smiled, approving of my care. I could see her having these pleasant ideas about me.

'What is wrong with you, Aiden?' said Sophia, now on her feet. 'Don't you like me having fun?'

'It's time for us to go to bed. I wish everyone goodnight. Say goodnight, Sophia.'

'Okay, bother. Goodnight, everyone. I hope to see only one of you tomorrow. Seeing twins is making me giddy.'

'Goodnight, dears,' replied Eve, still smiling approvingly.

My arm was around Sophia as I gently steered her away; I did not look at my father, but I knew he was watching me and perhaps wondering if I was acting.

'By the way, Eve,' I stopped as the idea came to me. 'Sophia and I will take you up on the offer to come with you if that's all right with you?'

I did not look at my father; I had made this decision even if he had not been sure of it. Seeing Eve, I knew she was genuinely pleased about this arrangement. The delightful response touched her mouth and lit up her eyes. This was a success.

'Isn't this wonderful?' Eve said to my father. 'We are going to Italy now as a family. I am so happy.'

I did not look at my father; as I knew he could not look at me, but I guessed something of what he was feeling.

'You know,' said Sophia when we were alone in our room. 'I was surprised when you told Eve we were coming with them. I am pleased you changed your mind, but what happened to you to change it so suddenly?'

She had taken off her dress and was now looking at herself in front of the long mirror. She wobbled a bit—in the morning she was going to regret drinking so much.

'Well, it must have something to do with seeing you two happy together. You and Eve appeared to be getting on well.'

'Yes, isn't she nice? I wasn't sure if I liked her at first because she is so beautiful, but she's very down to earth. We chatted about so many things. You know, Aiden, I have never had a best friend before or even a sister. She said she was going to help me learn how to cook—'

'You—learn how to cook?' I could not help being sceptical. With a leery grin picking at my cheeks, I probed her face for the jest I thought it would contain, but there was none. She had lost an excellent opportunity. 'You are one of the fussiest people I have come across with food.'

'When I was a model, we always had to watch what we ate, or any unattractive bulges would mean you wouldn't be working. Anyhow, since I have been with you, my life has completely changed. I have decided what I want to do in life and that's being a good wife to you and have lots of children. Aiden, I think I will make a wonderful mother. What do you think?'

'That you need some juice and a couple of painkillers? And I am going to get them for you. Just get yourself ready for bed, and I will bring them.'

'Do you know what, Aiden? I have decided to dedicate my life to you. You will find I will be the best wife ever. I shall love, honour and respect you. I can change, Aiden. And when I do, you will wonder how you ever got on without me.'

I yawned. This was becoming very boring.

When I returned with the juice and the pills, Sophia had crashed out on the bed, with her makeup smudged around her eyes where she had been rubbing them. She looked, in her vulnerability, adorable. I should be able to love her; I should be content with her because of who she was. But now I was dissatisfied because I had seen someone more beautiful, more perfect than her.

Poor Sophia. I lifted her to sit up and blew on her face, but she refused to open her eyes.

'Take this, Sophia,' I said, holding the drink to her mouth. She was difficult, but eventually, I got her to drink and take the tablets. She was trying to push my hand away from hers because she just wanted to sleep. Why do I prefer her like that? Dependent.

At my gentlest, I wiped off the makeup around her eyes, applied some moisturiser as I had seen her do in the past, and tucked her into bed. What is it like to be a woman? Dependent on men for their identity. I had tried on one of her dresses once, well, a few times, but they never looked the same on me as they did her. Perhaps that's just as well. She would be safe tonight; I am not that desperate.

Time for bed, and Sophia and I had got into a routine just as if we were married. But tonight, I was not tired enough to sleep. Instead, I thought I would take another walk around the pool to relive the memory of our talk. As I often did, I picked over the skeleton of Dominic's and my conversation, searching for the carnage to refuel another fight.

My father had changed in a way I had never imagined. I would even say that he had become hard or even indifferent to me. We had had our arguments in the past, but they had never been like this. This confused me. I needed to think about it. When he said he still loved me, I believed him. But something much bigger had happened. I had lost my power over him.

Surprisingly enough, though, I hardly touched the alcohol tonight. You could say I had been watching Eve. She had one glass of wine, but no more. If she did not drink, so neither would I. But before going out to the pool, I went to the drinks cabinet and poured myself a long drink. Don't ask me what it was because I just threw it together, and yes, it tasted disgusting, but it gave me something to think about.

This life, I thought when I pulled out a chair. This crazy life. My father said I would fall in love with Eve. How prophetic he would be if he only realised. I had watched my father as I had regarded Eve with indelible interest. There were secrets between these two. This, I knew, would provoke my interest to find out. But not yet, perhaps, not yet in this dark, thoughtful tiredness.

Two in the morning and still the frogs were out, leaping across the lawn, attracted by the pool's light. I was watching them jump while sitting on the white chair with my legs outstretched and listening to their garbled chat. A male frog in pursuit of his ladylove. If life could be as simple as that for us mere humans, when the sound of a splash invited me to think that a frog had leapt into the pool. If I don't get it out, the frog will drown. The idea that a frog could drown was pathetic.

He should have thought of what he was doing when he leapt. I could see the frog swimming about, unhappy at being in the chemical-saturated water. He was panicking. But this male might also be a female. If she was a female, she would be worth saving, but only if I can catch her. I saw the frog race to the other side of the pool, eager to get out of there.

It was inevitable for me to save it; meant I would have to take off my shoes and strip down to my underclothes. What was I doing, for goodness' sake? I never use the pool; it's only for decoration.

Catching hold of the frog which took me at least a minute, I went to the other side to climb out. While this cold frog was wriggling from the heat of my hands.

I had not seen her because I had been concentrating on climbing out of the pool without damaging or squashing the frog. She was holding up one of the white towel robes as if she was one of my servants.

'Eve,' I cried, startled. 'I didn't see you there,' I said, raising myself out of the pool. 'What are you doing up? I thought you would be in bed and asleep hours ago. Thank you.'

The soft robe was wrapped around me as if I was a child.

'What were you doing in the water? I was worried when I saw you climb in. I thought...' and then she frowned interestedly. 'What is it you've got in your hand?'

'A frog,' I said, as if this sort of thing happened every day.

'Is it still alive? What are you going to do with it?'

'Wash it and put it on the lawn and trust that it will know its way back to its nest or wherever they live.'

'Can I have a look?'

'You will see it when I put it down.'

'I mean, I would like to have a closer look.'

I opened my hand enough so she could peek into the cup of my palm. A beaky nose pushed out, with heart throbbing.

'Oh,' she said, marvelling at its invention. 'I like frogs. When I see frogs in nature, it makes you think that all is well. Experts always tell us we are on the brink of disaster, so it is nice to be reassured by nature that we have got some things right. Is it a boy or a girl?'

'I don't know,' I said, placing it back on the grass to watch it hop away before assuring itself that all was well with its world. 'I believe they can change their sex to suit the situation.'

'Yes,' sighed Eve, 'Dominic said you were clever.'

'Did he? How strange.'

'Perhaps you didn't know it, but he is very fond of you. No, I did not get that right; he loves you.'

'Well, he has a strange way of showing it sometimes.'

'What do you mean?' her face was so close that I had this irresistible feeling I could stretch across and kiss her lips.

'You must know.'

'Know what? Oh, look, there he goes, or it could be a female. I think he knows where he is now. Aiden, I think you might have rescued a toad.'

Instantly, I laughed. She was funny. Her face, so youthful in its expressions, was staring into mine as if we understood each other, or perhaps, we were even now sharing a secret.

'You are very sweet; I envy my father. But whatever it was, a frog or a toad, at least I have saved it.'

Stretching up to avoid the closeness of my face made me realise I had overstepped the mark.

'I never thought I would save a frog or a toad.' But it was worth it, and I knew Eve was more than listening to me.

'I should go to bed,' Eve said, looking at an invisible watch.

'Why couldn't you sleep?'

My body was guiding hers over to the deckchairs and tables.

'Just couldn't. I think it's being here. It's so different from everything else where we have stayed, but fresh places always affect me like this. I just can't sleep with all the thoughts going on. Has that ever happened to you?'

'No, not really. When I can't sleep, it's usually because something has been bothering me.'

I showed her the chair I wished her to take.

'And why is that?' she sounded like she was interested.

'My father,' I sighed, before taking my chair. 'You must know things haven't been going well with us for years. You cannot pretend you didn't know?' I looked at her face, forcing her to be honest.

'You two have had your problems. I understand that.'

'Problems?' I jeered. 'Sorry, I did not mean to seem rude. My father and I have not seen eye-to-eye for years. I blame my father for my mother—you must know that?'

'Yes, I know.'

'I never realised this was having an effect on him. I should have. You see, when I get to see my father, I always behave like an irritable child. I have never grown up or become a man to him. Do you understand what I am talking about?'

'Oh yes, I understand absolutely. The last people to find out their children have become adults are our parents. I always thought it strange they can only see us as children.'

'So, I suppose this also happened to you with your parents?'

'My parents are dead. I never had that opportunity for them to comment or even find fault with me—'

'They could never find fault with you. That I am sure of.'

She smiled prettily. While I was listening to her voice, enchanted by its music, and endowed with her loveliness, I imagined so much about her.

'And so, this was what was bothering you? Your father?'

'Did you know he does not want me to come to Italy with you?'

A crossbow in her brow showed me she did not.

'So, when he said he did not want to see me again after reassuring me he still loved me, I was confused, and also strangely lost. At thirty-two, I still feel like a child. Why is that? It's very demoralising.'

'I wish I could tell you. But I don't understand; are you coming with us or are you staying here?'

'I believe this decision might have something to do with you. If you are happy to have Sophia and myself come to Italy with you, then my father would agree to it.'

'Oh dear, such a responsibility.'

'Not really. You either want us or not. I have seen already how famously you are getting on with Sophia—'

'She is lovely. Absolutely adorable.' Eve smiled. 'I'm too young to be her mother, but I could easily be her sister.'

'And what about me?'

I didn't have that ability to smile while asking this question. It was a tough question to answer. The percentage of luck on my side was going down.

'Let me put it this way,' I began. 'I have identified there are issues in my life that I need to resolve in order to move on. I am still wearing an identity I should have cast off years ago. Look,' I held up my arms. 'Can't you see it? It says dick-head, stupid, vain, arrogant and such a miserable and whiney creature that if you had a strongbox, you would lock me away forever and throw away the key.'

She was laughing, giggling a pretty tune like cups cack-ling while moving irritably together before being dropped.

'Oh, Aiden, you paint such a lovely but silly picture of yourself. I am sure you are not like that—'

'Believe me, I have been.'

Without realising, I had my hand on her hand in a grip which was firm and which said—I am here. I took my hand off hers.

'Which is why I need to be with my father and talk to him. Isn't it odd? I never saw myself for what I had become until my father and I chatted. Did you know we were going to have this chat when we walked around the pool? Did you know he would tell me he never wanted to see me again? It was such a blow. But it worked. I jumped out of that identity to stand on the lawn—just as you caught me, I saw myself as that ugly frog or toad.'

Eve stare at me with the gravity of the sphinx, her eyes blinking and closing slowly, celebrating an age of time which has never been judged.

'And I am still naked with that damn identity. Don't you think it looks stupid on me at my grand age? I need to change it to something more sophisticated and elegant. Something I can admire, and not this fool with this cap I am wearing now. And the only way I can do it is to talk to my father, you know, do all the things he wished for me, and more. Do you see what I am saying?'

Her grey eyes blinked, her thoughtful head nodded. Yes, she understood. But did she approve of it?

'I think it will be wonderful if you come with us to Italy

because I believe your father still needs and wants you. And I think it would be good for him. All the things you have been talking about, I think—' she frowned again. The stapler in her brow was pinching. 'I think he needs—yes, he needs to have your forgiveness.'

'I have given it to him. Personally, this really is all about me. I am sure my father can benefit, but I can only think for myself, and as usual,' I sighed, 'I can't get over being selfish. Why is a lovely woman like you listening to me? I know I go on and on and can be very boring. But isn't that what they say about people who are mentally ill? They can't talk about anyone else except themselves.'

She was staring at me; her thoughts were deep, unlike Sophia, who was a little like me, but this also depends on the day and the time you come across her.

'Have you any idea of what the time is?'

'I should imagine it's gone three and going on four by now. And you are right; we should try to get some sleep. By the way,' I said, standing up from the chair. 'Thank you for the gown. You are quite my guardian angel.'

5

I am I have discovered a man of senses if not reason. Sensing things which have never been written down. It had been a tough childhood, as my father had chosen to ignore the first years of my life. Being without a father remained with me while poking about in the embers of my mind.

The agreement was that my father and Eve were to stay with Sophia and me for the next week. They would stay with me instead of the other way around. The order of relationships had changed, which made it mildly interesting; I was the host, which meant that my father was obliged to follow my rules.

There would naturally be expectations of the other. But since Dominic and Eve were hardly in my company, I faced the idea that my father was doing everything he could to keep out of our way, or rather, my way. I could ask you for your opinion on what this would suggest to you, but I will not. Bubbling away in the core of my thoughts is the guess that he knew I had a significant influence on his Eve. Which was flattering; after all, I was closer to her age than he was.

This made me smile. For every time I spoke to her, he would whisk her away to some place quiet to give her his version of the story. Although I could be wrong. A bit of paranoia does no one any harm.

The day after tomorrow, my father and Eve are leaving for Italy. I think I can be disobliged that he had used my house without its company.

They were getting up early and returning late. Every day. Sightseeing, Mears told me this, for he was seeing more of my father than I was.

'When you see my father again, tell him I would appreciate his company on the last day. Sophia and I are planning another one of those delightful evenings,' which I knew was always going to be a strain on him until he did something about it.

We were to have Sunday together. Sophia wanted to have the full traditional, the solid rituals in life were having more meaning to her in her attempt for us to be a family. She was experiencing a renewal of values; an apron appeared which I have never seen before. It was amusing if not baffling.

I have never been a religious person, although when it comes to it, I am very good at using the Parables to my advantage. This was the first time that Sophia had requested she would like to go to church. I was surprised and then I was bemused. Why not? Why not do something outlandishly different?

During that long chat Sophia had with Eve; she had expressed a great pleasure at going to church. She loved the rituals and particularly the blessings; they made her feel cleansed, renewed, and able to restart her life refreshed. My first response was to laugh, being a sophisticated and cultivated man of the time. But then I held back. This was very strange. Very, very strange because I was moved to go too. By purging and cleansing myself. Would it be possible for me to get rid of whatever there was that my soul had wanted to throw out?

There is a nice little country church about three miles from here. The sort of place you need a camera. I remember that day when Sophia and I went clicking. I love taking photographs. Whatever I wanted in my world was contained in the frame. Beautiful things, I like perfection. I don't like a broken-field gate which says charm to one person but not to me. Damage does not inspire me to glean over its worth for what had been and what was not now. Sophia looked very mystic—she liked her photograph being taken as well. Of course, she did, once being a model. And such lovely poses we made, especially in the little cemetery.

My father is taller than me; I noticed this when we were standing side by side together in the church. At five feet ten, I always felt taller than my father, but standing by him in the pews with his chest full, I experienced a sensation of being overwhelmed; he was more real than I could ever be.

Inside, the church was buzzing. And the four of us were the centre of attraction; it seemed everyone was impressed by us hoping we would visit the church regularly. The reverend, a man of five foot five, was a head shorter than us. He was pleased with our new flamboyancy; we gave the congregation glamour, while his eyes kept on stretching towards us with another kind of worship. When the service was over, he was going to check us out. Unfortunately, this was going to be the first and only time we were going to be part of the congregation. Tomorrow, my father was heading off to sunny Italy. While we would leave a few days later. But before we went, we would make an impression.

Sophia's croaky voice risked its notes with enthusiasm.

Up and down, there was something about her voice which was strangely moving. If only she could hold a note. I tried not to smile, for she was earnest in her praises, and yet, overall—this had been fun and a great idea. As the basket went around, first to my father and then to me, I saw he had been feeling morally guilty because two fifty-pound notes laid in the basket which could only be from him. And then I thought, actual physical money; where had they come from, I could not imagine? Was he carrying a bank vault around with him?

'We ought to do this more often,' I said to Sophia when the service was over, nodding to faces as if we knew them.

'Oh,' she said, her blue eyes delighted with the suggestion. 'I am so glad you have seen the way. God is everywhere and we must thank him for what he has done for us. We are not always grateful.'

'Are you sickening for something? What is the matter with you? Don't tell me you have been taken in by what the priest has said. It's big business, Sophia. Get the blood and wine out of your head or else you will be unbearable to live with.'

She may well be a little disappointed for now, but it will be gone by this afternoon, I'll wager.

'You know what the father was talking to us about,' I said now that we had been released by him to walk through man's pollution.

'What is that, Aiden?'

'I feel like I have been made to feel guilty for the rest of my life. This religion thing can be top-heavy.'

'When you die, where are the rest of your family buried?' Sophia was following a specific train of thought.

'You want to be buried, do you?' I sniggered while shaking my head.

'I find it is more reassuring to know where one's remains are instead of being thrown out to sea. I always have this fear that should someone open their mouth, perhaps to yawn, it's possible to find your resting place inside of someone's stomach. Does the family have any churchyards where they can be placed and found?'

'Apparently, Mozart's resting place has never been found. A mass grave. Don't you think that's strange that one of the most famous composers' graves is lost to us now?'

Sophia pondered my strange question.

'It's symbolic,' I said, feeling more mischief coming on. 'It suggests he is everywhere. The world owns him and not one particular country.'

Eve looked up at her, a smile dimpling her cheeks delightfully. I love that she too had a sense of humour. What had she seen in my father, apart from his money?

We went for a drive and then stopped off for something to eat. I don't believe anyone from our party usually ate at that time of the day. While my father had a wet lunch, we three played at our salads while an interested bee zoomed around our table. A fine little fat furry chap, although I should remember that he too is probably female.

We chatted like conspirators about what we were going to do and see when we were in Italy. This sudden thirst to be in Italy was growing by the minute, especially when I looked across at Eve. She could have been an Italian aristocrat herself, who kept her milk-white skin away from the harsh rays of the brilliant sunshine. I could not help looking at her, delighting at her vivid expressions, which always showed me how much she enjoyed her life.

'What are you thinking about, Aiden?' Sophia asked, catching my attention.

'What do you mean?'

'You keep on looking at Eve?'

'Do I?' I was surprised and not annoyed, for this was what I was feeling. 'If I am, then please forgive me, Sophia. I was just thinking that she reminded me of someone. I was trying to think who it was.'

The two pretty ladies were on a perch watching me, intrigued by this new idea. They also wanted to see what I was seeing. Who was it Eve reminded me of?

'Would you believe it?' I countered my face with an expression of wonder. 'I know who it is, and if I was to tell you, Eve, please take it as a compliment.'

She was waiting for me to speak. Her lips quivered, ready to smile if she found it agreeable. She was absolutely delightful.

'Eve, you remind me of my mother. You must understand, she also was exquisite. She did not have the same colouring as you, as she had light brown with blue eyes—I know yours are grey, and she was taller, but in many ways, she had the same delightful expressions that you have.'

'Well, it sounds to me,' began Sophia, always being morbidly down to earth, 'that Eve doesn't look anything like your mother.'

It was wonderful to hear Eve laugh again, and especially on a Sunday. She seemed to throw off the clothes of old age in preference for youth. What was she doing with an old man like my father?

'You never really spoke about Aiden's mother,' said Eve when my father returned from the bar.

'Yes, there was no reason to. As you know, she died a long time ago. So, what is the point of bringing it up?' they moved away from the table to continue their conversation.

I was not thinking about what I had said because my attention was now focused on my father and Eve and what they were saying and doing. Was he trying to persuade Eve that he did not want me in Italy with them? I had a fancy this was more like what he was talking about.

'Aiden?' snapped Sophia, irritable and frowning. 'You don't look at me or even talk to me anymore. Why is that? We are supposed to be getting married, or is this another one of your jokes?'

What was she saying?

'You know, I have this nagging feeling that if our wedding is off, then so is the invitation to Italy. Am I that uninteresting, Aiden?'

'I am sorry Sophia; I was much reminded of my mother by Eve, that I could not help looking at her.'

'Yes, I have seen you look at her. You do it all the time. I don't know, Aiden. Have you fallen in love with her?'

'No, absolutely not. I don't know where you get that idea from.'

'You had better not let Dominic see you look at her because that trip to Italy would be off instantly.'

With the opposite intentions, Sophia had sobered me up. If she could notice my eyes on Eve, then so could my father. I made a mental note to myself that I must not look at Eve. Well, perhaps not so much. But it would be difficult doing this when we were having dinner together this evening.

EVE CAME out to the table by the lawn in green velvet, bringing with her the eyes of wow, which included Sophia, who yet again was dressed in white. She was no virgin, that was for sure.

We dined on trout; this was Sophia's menu, which was to

be followed by crepe Suzette. This time, instead of regarding Eve, I concentrated my eyes on my father. Again, he was putting down the wine. Clearly, something was upsetting him, and I had a feeling that it could be me.

'Father, you seem bothered. Is everything well with you?'

He looked up from his trout without the smiles that he had been blessed with before our conversation and my epiphany moment. I crossed my knife and fork as if I was planning for an in-depth debate. Although this should not be held at the dining table. But my father had been effectively absent after the other night. Now what was I going to suggest lay redundant in his eyes? He was waiting.

'You have been looking very unhappy just lately, and I am convinced that it's me.'

Eve's ears and eyes looked focused on our conversation, feeling it to be of great importance to her.

'Everyone knows I have turned over a new leaf. I have changed suddenly and dramatically. I can't explain why this has happened except that it has. For me, this makes sense; everything has fallen into place, but I think not for you. It's understandable that you distrust me, Father, after years of what I have put you through. I want you to be proud of me, but if it causes you unhappiness, this will make me selfish. And I can't do that to you. I have decided when you go to Italy, I will stay back here in England.'

'Oh Dominic,' hearing this, Eve was so moved by my sacrifice that she touched her husband's hand. 'That's so wonderful of you, Aiden, isn't it Dominic?'

Not smiling, I carried on looking profound and seriously contrite with the expression of accepting punishment.

'As I said before, I mean it. I don't want you being distressed, Father. Saying one is sorry should not be without penance. But I won't stop you from visiting, Sophia. You are your own person.'

'But if you are not going, then neither will I.' Sophia looked like a child whose ice cream had been swiftly removed from its hand.

'No, Sophia, I will be fine. I would hate it for you to stay with me when you would rather be somewhere else. Sincerely, I want you to have a good time. And when you return home, you can tell me all about it.'

No one else said anything more. The indirect attention was now turned to my father. He, I knew, wanted to accept my offer, but this, he guessed, would not be possible.

'What do you say to that, Dominic?' Eve touched his hand again. The little school mam was disappointed in her student.

'If Aiden wants to stay home as he suggests, then I will not tear him away screaming and complaining about coming to Italy with us.'

'No, Dominic, Aiden has told me he wants to come. What harm will he do? None. I am sure they will do a lot of sightseeing,' Eve nodded to me and then to Sophia to ensure she was correct in what she was saying. 'It would be churlish to say no to your only child when he is trying his very best to make it up to you.'

'Oh Eve,' Dominic sighed again. 'This is our life and a new beginning. I don't say he will intentionally destroy things for us.' And then he sighed again and turned his attention smoothly to me. 'Do you really want to come to Italy, Aiden?'

'I don't know what to say to you, Father. I can see you don't want me. It hurts, of course, and yet I can't blame you. Sophia is a witness; she can validate that I had been an absolute pig to you and worse. And if I should step out of line; I will put myself on a flight straight back. You only have to say that you find me unbearable.'

I knew then I had won. My father was not pleased for me to stay with them. But it could work in the end and mainly because Eve wanted it to.

'WHAT ARE YOU DOING?' Sophia still had on her table light; she was reading. It was something I was not used to seeing her do. And she was wearing those damn glasses in bed. I opened my side of the bed and bounced in, disrupting her, which was my intention.

'Do you have to?' she complained.

'What are you reading?' I tried to peep over her arm to see what it was.

'Psychology.'

'Psychology,' I mused, raising my eyebrows. 'And what brought this on?'

'You. Now let me carry on reading.'

'Me? That's interesting. Am I interesting? I must be. What have you found out that is so interesting about me?'

'Well, if you really want to know,' Sophia closed the book to fix her attention on me. 'I think you have a personality problem with narcissistic undertones.'

'Does that make me dangerous?'

'It could do.'

Sighing, I snatched her book from her hand and began paging through it.

'Aiden. Give me back my book; it's my book; it's not yours.'

'No Sophia, not yet. I am fascinated by what you are reading. You know that psychology is all hocus-pocus. If you tell somebody they are sick and that it's their mind, they will react and be like that. It is called autosuggestion. What's this?'

Sophia had been marking certain passages. *The Unsettled Mind* was one of them. *Map of an Insane Mind* was another. The reading made for disturbing thoughts.

'How long have you been reading this rubbish?'

'On and off for a few weeks. While you were drunk or sitting looking at the television. I was bored, and then I started listening to you. You know you are very intriguing, Aiden. And a big flag is that you like everything to go your way, and when it doesn't, you resort to childish behaviour. You still have this tie to your father, which is peculiar, as you should have outgrown it years ago.'

'Ah, I see. You have been studying me. Is there any hope for me?'

'No, not from what I have read. If you don't get your own way, it could end with serious consequences.'

'Tell me, Dr Sophia, are you safe with me? Will I come after you with an axe?'

'You see, you never take me seriously; I am trying to improve myself so you will find me more appealing. I feel you are going off me, Aiden. What do I have to do to make you find me more enticing?'

'Oh, Sophia,' I could not help laughing; she was extraordinarily funny and beautiful. 'How I love you.' I stretched across and took off her spectacles. 'Don't ever change.'

The morning came too quickly. My father and Eve were leaving early while we would follow in a few days, and I was glad for that. Somehow, the thought of flying terrified me. If it was possible, I would travel by sea.

'As soon as you arrive, Eve,' began Sophia, for we were not going with them to the airport. 'Send us a message to say you got there safely. And let us know how you are getting on and what the weather is like. It should be hot, shouldn't it? Oh, I wish I was going with you.'

'It won't be long before you are there.'

The next events happened quickly. A taxi collected them and took them to the airport, and then they were gone. Surprisingly, mixed feelings poured over me. I too wished I could go with them, but I wasn't ready yet.

6

Don't ask me what our journey was like because I was out of it. What I do remember, though, is a series of images. Sophia looking into my face, her head to one side, asking me if I was all right. I don't know what I said, but it was probably something uncomplimentary. The other image was of sitting in several types of chairs accompanied by many other faces, and I didn't know any of them. In that hazy passage of time came the understanding that I had arrived safely at Falcone, Borsellino airport.

'He has had a shot from the doctor,' I heard Sophia's distant voice broadcasting this information. I presumed it was for the benefit of my father and Eve. 'He will be fine once he has had a good night's sleep.'

Eve muttered something, and then my father.

'You were out of it,' said Sophia, climbing on to the bed to lie beside me. 'I could not wake you, well, I did wake you and you told me to shut up and to let you go back to sleep, so I did.'

'How long have I been asleep?'

'About forever. No, you've been asleep since this

morning for over ten hours. There is some dinner if you want it? Eve said I could find it in the kitchen. Oh, I love it here.'

She turned on to her back and stretched her legs.

'Have you seen the view from the balcony? No, of course not. The villa is overlooking the sea—it's so picturesque that you have to pinch yourself to see if it is real. Eve is so lucky to have a man who loves her so much he would do anything for her and buy her whatever she wants. Your father is so rich, Aiden. I wish you were.'

'Is that all you have come to tell me? That it's nice to know how rich and generous my father is. He is lucky. The wonder of rich parents is they give birth to children who then have everything.'

'But your father also worked for it.'

'If you call being an art dealer, work.'

'You don't do anything,' she said, now sitting up.

'I live. What else do you want me to do? And I look after you. You are my girlfriend, aren't you?'

'No. I am your fiancée if that's still on. One day, I am your girlfriend, the next your probable wife; I am always wondering what the following day will bring.'

'That's the way to do life, as there is no certainty to anything.'

'No, Aiden, in your world, nothing is for certain.'

The morning came in a flood of light, and Sophia was still sleeping when I got up to look at this new world. If I saw what she saw, it would be amazing. Morning in Palermo awoke as a jewel. The turquoise blue sea quietly awakened in the bay as an eery mist was sipped by the bright golden sun, her early morning breakfast. Don't tell me there was not a heavenly being up here who desired to please us undeserving mortals. For the first time, I felt I could breathe. I was in my father's world, and he knew how to live.

'Aiden,' Sophia had awoken and was now looking for me. 'Are you okay?' She was sitting up in bed. 'Oh, so you have now seen what I have seen.'

She scrambled out of bed; her long legs carried her quickly. Already she was leaning on my shoulders to look at the view.

'It's wonderful, isn't it? Aiden? Do you think we can have a place out here?'

'We can have all of this when my father passes on.'

'But that could be forever. I want to have a place out here now.'

'And how are we going to do that?'

'I've got my money; you've got yours.'

'Correction, I've got an allowance. My father has been generous, but with the way we live, it won't get us anything like this unless, of course, you want some shack in the outback.'

'Oh, Aiden,' Sophia was in pain. 'You could ask him to buy you a property.'

'I could do that, couldn't I? But I am not. He will tell me to get a job. And even if I get a job, I still won't be able to afford anything like this. Do we have to talk about this—?'

'Oh, it's not fair. I wish you were rich. I wish you were like your father. Sorry, Aiden.'

For I had looked up, and already, the comparisons had begun.

On the veranda below, I could hear voices. Looking down at our neighbours, Eve was serving Dominic some juice. Her thick dark hair was plaited down her back and she had on a straw hat. Nothing too pretentious. Wearing a long light-blue dress, she could easily be mistaken for an Italian peasant girl.

'It must be wonderful to rise to something like this each morning,' I muttered, trying to listen to what was being said.

Peeping over my shoulder, Sophia also saw what I was looking at; she was not so stupid as to know what I was thinking.

'We should get dressed and go down.' Sophia took her generous arms off my shoulder. 'Our host will expect us.'

Walking out on to the veranda was a spectacular event. I felt myself wanting to bow to the view; it was so perfect. Cradled by dozing arms and scooped out by the sea, the world was dazzled by the bay's perfection. My father was sitting at the table. He had been looking out and enjoying his thoughtful moments.

'Hello,' said Sophia. 'This is so beautiful.'

She went across and kissed my father on the cheek. What on earth was she doing that for?

'It must be the air,' said Sophia, full of unnatural energy, 'but I feel I could eat a five-course meal.'

'You don't want to overeat,' my father patted Sophia's knee now that she was sitting beside him.

For the first time, I realised that my father not only liked Sophia but approved of her, probably hoping she would be a stabilising influence on me.

'I always seem to make an entrance.' Eve was carrying a tray of breakfast things for the table.

'Let me,' I leapt up and caught hold of the tray and, with a smile, placed it down on the table for her. 'It's heavy.'

'Only a little.'

'Don't you have a servant, father? Eve should not be carrying something as heavy as this.'

'Aiden, would you like some fresh orange juice? I squeezed it myself this morning. It's nice and fresh.'

'Eve and I have decided to do our own lives, and that means no servants. Eve wants to do all the shopping, cooking and housework.'

'I want to be the perfect housewife.' Eve began energetically. 'I know it's not the thing to want to do these days after we have been emancipated. I know the suffragettes would disapprove of me, but I don't care; it's my life although I thank them for giving me the ability to do exactly as I want.'

'Yes,' Sophia nodded in agreement. 'That's what I want to do. I want to be the perfect self-sufficient wife. I want Aiden to appreciate and approve of me.'

'Do you, Sophia?' I said, arising with mischief lurking in my chest.

'Yes.'

'Then it might be an idea if you went to work and earned us some money?'

Both father and Eve looked startled, which instantly made me want to laugh.

'Have you seen the amount of money a model makes?'

'A top model, maybe, Aiden, but I was never at the top. Most of the models only make bread and butter money, but I got paid well considering, as you always say, Aiden, model's don't have much to do.' She lowered her head. 'I was admiring the view; you two are so lucky.'

'It's rented,' responded my father. 'But yes, a man should look after his wife.'

'I was thinking of going to the market to shop. Would anyone like to come along with me, Sophia?' asked Eve.

'I would,' squealed Sophia in delight. 'I love shopping. Perhaps we could have a walk by the bay.'

'And what about you, Aiden? Would you like to have a look around to familiarise yourself?'

'Does my father want to come?'

'Dominic will be busy. He has a meeting with one of his financiers. A few things need to be sorted out.'

It would interest me to hear what was being said between these two money-making speculators. I still did not know how wealthy my father was. It would have been nice if he would share with me now—you take the bigger half because you are younger, and I take the smaller. There was always going to be a limit to how much one could spend, no matter how much money one had.

'I am torn by two opposite forces. The need to be with my father and renew our relationship as opposed to going out with two attractive and charming females.'

'Aiden, I can promise you I won't have much time for you. Go out with the ladies and have a look around.'

Everyone was watching me, including my father.

'Very well,' I said.

Any smile I had on my face was erased by disappointment and hurt. I could see that Eve had noted it. She, the reconciler, needed everyone to be happy. Harmony, though, needed a fair deal of work before this could be achieved.

THE MORNING HAD BEEN HEATED in a whirlwind of enthusiasm, but not to its full intensity. I now found myself strolling with two lovely ladies, one on either side of me. We were heading downwards to the market, marking the streets with our footsteps. I was taken by the architecture, though very basic, yet there was a beauty to its symmetry. Everything one needs to enjoy one's life was here. I could hear

Sophia's heavy footsteps, but not Eve's. Different personalities. If you wanted to live life loud, then the choice would be Sophia. Sophia was smiling at everyone we passed, although to be honest, there were very few people to be seen; she carried the sunshine in her hair, while Eve, I felt, was happier in the shadows. But that was the romantic in me.

'It feels so different here?' Sophia waved at a child tucked away behind a corner who had been watching us. Spooked now, she disappeared out of sight. 'And I am a foreigner with lots to see and understand.' She was viewing her thoughts with her fingers cupped on her chin, caught in a Mediterranean trance. 'Even the air smells fresh. It smells of sunshine.'

'It smells of ozone.'

'Is that what it is?'

'And the other thing is dearest beloved, you are in another country, and you are most definitely the foreigner.'

From the other side of me, Eve looked up at me. Don't be unkind to her; she is also one of God's children.

It took us nearly twenty minutes to move into the main area. The buildings here were upright and straight, the same as the roads. It was as if someone had taken a ruler and mapped out a town and demanded order. If one could put a character to it, I would say from my limited experience to be unique. Many cultures had left their impression with, I woz here; great towers that outstretched everything with their ideas and dreams. Were they meant to take off and go beyond into the future? I looked at the two ladies and thought of hope.

'Your father is always busy these days,' murmured Eve, although this was not a complaint.

We had just stepped out from the shadows and into the

baking sunshine. It was exhilarating, and our footsteps echoed in the piazza. I was thinking of Eve and how a few hundred years ago, she would not be out of place. But this modern-day Eve had changed into slacks and a blouse; her hair was tied in a ribbon and then left to be free to lie on her back. I could not help marvelling at her hair and then worrying about her skin. She was so very pale. Inconsistent thoughts led me to notice the stone on these buildings and how worn they were by time; Eve's skin, though, was still radiant.

'In order for us to live well, work needs to be done. These are beautiful tomatoes, Aiden. Nowhere else in the world produces such wonderful tomatoes. Dominic is always joking with me. He says with the number of tomatoes I consume, I will turn into a one.'

I smiled and helped by holding the bag open while she collected the ripe, plump fruit.

'I can assure you with the number of tomatoes you eat, you will only get more beautiful.' The prophecy was reversed.

She looked up and blushed, uncertain about the compliment, and whether she could accept it. But I didn't mind. I had plenty more I could give her; and time and patience are the foundation of empires.

I had lost one of my doves. Sophia was doing her own shopping. Once her feet touched the market, she was gone. Her striking voice was haggling, but I am embarrassed to say that the stall owners had met his match.

'She is very beautiful.' Eve followed my eyes to where Sophia was.

'She is lovely; you are beautiful.'

'I was not saying this for a compliment. You have done well with this young lady. Your father approves and so do

I. She is everything you could want, Aiden, in a young wife.'

'She is twenty-nine—'

'She is still young,' Eve generously smiled with a shake of her head. 'Young people,' she muttered.

'Sophia is a lovely person and yet, how do you know anyone until you live with them?'

Picking up a large, dark green celery stick pungent with aroma and freshly picked, the stall owner passed the basin of his scales for weighing. Unable yet to speak Italian, Eve used her fingers for sign language to make herself understood. The stall owner smiled at Eve; he did not care what she said. Everyone loves beautiful women.

Some carrots, big fat onions, lemons, garlic and some basil, and a few apples were the fresh ingredients to set for dinner tonight. And these were pinched with light fingers by a choice of the best and the brightest. And from her purse, the notes were selected.

'You are doing very well.' I grinned, very impressed at how she was managing.

'There is a lot for me to learn, but I am determined. I want to be the best wife I can for Dominic.'

'Yes, you already said. But are you doing it out of gratitude, I wonder?'

'Aiden, you are being very personal and rude. Please do not doubt that I love your father. He is everything to me. Everything. I want our marriage to work,' and then she sighed, so out of character to what she was saying. 'I am prepared to do everything I can to be happy. Your father is a wonderful man.'

'Oh yes,' I murmured. 'He is a wonderful man.'

If she had heard, for I believe she had, she was doing a damn good job not allowing my words to affect her.

'Sophia said she wanted to see the bay.'

We found her at another stall and this time she wanted him to reduce the price of some sandals. Eve and I were standing further away, watching.

'Yes. She is always full of wants and desires. She certainly keeps me busy.'

'A lovely girl.'

'And a handful. Don't get me wrong, Sophia always wants entertaining. And she is expensive. My money never seems to be enough for her.'

'Well,' shrugged Eve, this was really none of her business.

'It can get very difficult with Sophia. With you, she is on her best behaviour.'

'A relationship always takes working at. Giving and taking.'

'Perhaps.' We directed our feet away. Sophia would be bartering for a few moments longer, so we might as well have a look at another stall.

'Sophia tells me she is determined to learn Italian,' mentioned Eve.

'Yes, I know. She told me earlier she wants Italian lessons, but I am afraid I cannot afford it.'

'Do you want me to ask Dominic for some help?'

'No, Eve, I don't. I don't want my father to know I am trying to get employment. I am committed to get a job, Eve. Do you approve?'

'You, getting a job, Aiden. But I think that's wonderful. Your father would be over the moon; it's one thing he has always wanted for you. He says—'

'Yes, I know what he says. I have been there many times. I don't want him to know about my ambition, not yet, not after I have made a success of myself. And with Sophia going on about money, I can't help feeling over-stressed. Eve,' I stopped her dead. 'If you don't know already, I have never worked. Don't look at me like that because I am ashamed of myself.'

'There is nothing to be ashamed of,' she touched me gently. 'You have not been shown how to work because it's never been required of you. And then, with all your family's tragedies, working would not be the most important thing in your life. I quite understand. It's a big step you are taking. And yes, I am impressed with you. In fact, I am very impressed with you.'

'Eve? Would you help me? You are the only one who knows about my ambition.'

'How can I help you?'

'Perhaps you can help me by finding out what I'm good at. I know I jokingly said that I would be a labourer. But look at me. I have been cosseted for a life more gentile, not labouring. I suppose I could do it after a fashion by tearing my hands to pieces and damaging my skin and my back.'

'I agree with you; you are not cut out to be a physical worker. Quite honestly, I don't know who is these days.'

She was frowning to herself; there was a long list of thoughts she was going through.

'You have given me something to think about, Aiden. I feel like I must interview you to find out what you are good at.'

'Nothing.'

This pulled a smile from her lips.

'Everyone is good at something. As I believe, everyone has a hidden talent. We've just got to find it.'

'My father would tell you something different. He would say—'

'Yes, well, your father is not always right. I feel very positive about you, Aiden, and I am in admiration of you and how you are trying to pull your life together. I was saying to your father last night that you have changed.'

'And he did not agree with you. That's okay, Eve; I have given nothing to show I am worth saving. He has done so much for me. And as for admiration, reserve it for my father. He really is the man to look up to, even though he can be very hard on me.'

Her thoughtful eyes carried on looking at me as she consulted with her thoughts about her husband and then me. They did not see the world as I saw it; hers came with so many kindnesses.

The way back was all uphill with Sophia giving us a running commentary on the bargains she almost made.

LATER THAT EVENING, my father and Sophia waited at the dinner table while I went to see if Eve wanted any help. Sophia was snacking on breadsticks and consuming my father's interest in her tour of the market. She was having fun and hoped to be returning there tomorrow. Oh, and yes, she had been on the seafront. Had he seen her? She had waved up in the villa's direction.

'Sophia has certainly monopolised my father,' I said, entering the kitchen. 'I don't think he knows what has happened to him.'

'I am glad she is keeping him entertained.'

'What is this you are making?' I picked up the wooden spoon, and like all mixtures in a pot, I began stirring.

'A sauce for the pasta. I am making spaghetti Bolognese. It's quick and easy and also delicious. I hope you like it. If not, I can always knock up a salad for you?'

'Really?' standing beside the pot, I gazed at her. 'You are too beautiful to be stuck in a hot kitchen.'

'Aiden, dear, I am enjoying myself. I have never cooked for anyone, so this is new to me.'

Picking up her arm, I showed Eve her arm.

'And is this new as well?'

A recent burn on her arm looked painful. The flesh had dried and formed a reddish scab.

'It's nothing.' She pulled her arm away. 'Anyone would think I am Cinderella.'

'You are very special, Eve. You should know this. My father is very lucky to have found you.'

'No. I would say it's the other way around. If you must know, this is not my first time—I was married before. I have told no one else except for Dominic. The first time,' she shuddered and then shook her head. 'I don't want even to think about him. It was too awful.'

'I can't believe anyone could be bad to you.' And I couldn't. Why would anybody be anything other than kind to Eve?

'Oh well, believe me, it's possible.' her face was whiter than it was before.

No, this idea was not only repugnant, as the thought of it was impossible. She looked so tiny and vulnerable, dressed in her protective apron. It could not have happened, even though she said it had. If there was a monster out there, I could easily have struck him. No, she should never be hit by another man ever again. And if my father ever raised his hand or his voice to her, then—

'You should never fear a man,' I said, feeling my chest swelling with outrage that a man could do that to someone so beautiful. 'Where is your first husband now?'

'Dead,' she murmured, shaking with a memory she had tried hard to forget.

'Good, I am glad about it. And I hope he rots in hell.'

'Aiden, do you think we could forget about it? I don't ever want to talk about him again. Suffice to say that your father cares for me. I would not be where I am now if it was not for him.'

'Yes, you are quite right. I'll go out and see how Sophia and Dominic are getting on?'

'Ok.'

'Aiden, where have you been?' Sophia still sat beside Dominic. Obviously, these two had been talking.

'I went to the bedroom to see where you were, but you weren't there. I was worried about you.'

'Well, as you can see, I am here.'

'I heard noises and wondered where they were coming from. I followed the voice and the wonderful smell of dinner and found myself in the kitchen.'

'Yes,' she leant her head to one side. 'I see.' There was a hard comment in her eyes.

'Dinner is about ready.' Eve was now on the veranda with cutlery and several bowls on a tray.

'I'll get the sauce, Eve. Please sit down.' Why was she always the one to carry? I stabbed eyes at my father. How could he treat his wife like this?

'Do you want any help, Aiden?' Sophia followed me along to the kitchen. The perfume of basil was so intoxicating that I actually felt hungry. Behind me, I could hear the gentle footsteps of Sophia wearing her new soft sandals she had brought from the market.

'I should have offered to help,' Sophia murmured, taking up the pot of spaghetti. 'I should have—'

'Don't worry. I forgot to help as well. When I looked in,

I found Eve had burnt her arm. Quite a nasty one, too. I can't believe my father doesn't want servants. I don't understand his economising when he's always had the best.'

'Perhaps she wants to please him. I think it's nice, but I would want help when we are married. Aiden, before we take this out. There is something I want to tell you.'

'What?' I did not like the way she was looking at me. The worried look in her eyes suggested I wouldn't like what she had to tell me.

'You remember I wanted lessons to learn Italian?'

'Yes.'

'You remember you said you couldn't afford it? Well, I thought it would help us all if someone from our family took lessons. So, I asked your father, and he said yes, Aiden. He is going to pay for me to have lessons. Isn't that wonderful?'

'I guess it is.'

She put the pot down and touched me.

'You're not angry with me, Aiden? I really wanted Italian lessons; it would be good for all of us. Your father, paying for them, doesn't make any difference, does it? He has all the money.'

'Yes, I know. I am not angry at you.'

But should I feel humiliated? No, I didn't know what I felt. It was as if all the fairies had collected together to promise this and give me that, and often what I didn't want.

A humble meal, and one I probably wouldn't have enjoyed if anyone else had made it. Beauty is often in the decoration, while the pasta had a history to it and the sauce was definitely in need of flavour. If life was as palatable, then everything could be achieved. I looked again, guarded by my eyelashes at Eve. Whatever she touched was wonderful, tasty, and interesting for the simple reason it had been created by her.

The red wine flowed, but not for me. I was watching Eve; she ate very little and drank even less; she listened and smiled and occasionally spoke. Now and again, she looked at Dominic to check that he was happy. Such devotion was sublime; I could not think what she reminded me of except that she adored him. If only she could look at me in that way.

Did my father really appreciate her? Now, every time he looked at Eve, I rated his expressions. A seven for his smile, two for his raised eyebrows, and a one when he shook his head at her, raising his glass and then turning to Sophia. I knew now that he was more interested in this lively, shapely body.

Yet, I was glad that Sophia wanted to chat; she was filling up the quiet moments with her interests and what she wanted to do and see. My father glanced at Eve a couple of times as they exchanged mutual opinions. There was an undercurrent of thoughts which I felt going on while Sophia talked. She drank too much, as was normal with her these days, and even Eve noticed. While I was the quieter one of the four of us, I watched and listened and speculated.

'We will do the pots,' I told Eve. 'You have cooked us a wonderful meal. It's time the cook put up her feet and let her hair down with her partner.'

Naturally, Eve protested, but for once, my father agreed with me. Not too unhappily, Sophia followed me into the kitchen carrying the dishes we had for dinner and still chatting.

'Do you know, Aiden, I could live here and be happy. I feel like I am really in my element and should have been born an Italian.'

'With your natural blonde hair?'

'Why not? Not all Italians have brown hair and eyes. And you, well, you would look good here too.'

'I don't believe I would look good anywhere.'

'Yes, you would, but I feel you would be the most comfortable here. And why do I think this?' she gave me the plate she had been washing. 'Because you look different, more relaxed. I would say you are happier here.'

No one broke any of the plates, and when it was done and everything was put away, Sophia and I said goodnight to Dominic and Eve. Sophia feeling her second evening was going well was with eager eyes looking for the next opportune.

We were getting ready for bed, and Sophia was sitting in front of the old-fashioned heavy vanity table brushing her long blonde hair. There was a flush on her face and the tops of her shoulders, preparing her skin for a tan.

'You need to look after your skin,' I warned her, coming out from the old-fashioned bathroom; my flesh still radiated the heat of the day.

I was so used to a shower; yet it was a novelty to have a bath, although it took an age for the tub to fill up.

'Is it me?' started Sophia. 'But I have noticed Eve does not look as happy as she did before.'

'Why do you think that?' this news made me feel hopeful.

'I don't know; it could be my imagination, but she looks strained. What do you think?'

'My impression, as well. I was wondering if it was some-thing to do with my father.'

'No, I don't think it's him; it's something else.'

I looked at the table beside her bed; there was that book

again. This amateur psychoanalyst had been practising her newfound knowledge.

'What do you think it is, then?'

'I don't know. She hardly touched her food—'

'You noticed?'

'Of course, I noticed. When we eat, we are taking care of ourselves. Food is a weapon. It's also a type of rebellion. There's something going on which the protester doesn't want to do but has no power to stop. I believe Eve is unhappy. That's why she restricts herself with her food.'

'Sounds good, but honestly Sophia, I think that's a load of rubbish.'

'Is it? Why do you think she is so thin? She is having to do something against her will.'

'Sounds like a load of drivel to me.' But if Eve was unhappy, then perhaps my father is the reason, and I—

'Then you watch her next time.'

'You think my father is a bully to her?'

'No. I didn't say that. But there is something playing on her mind.'

'You hardly know her and yet you are making these broad assumptions about her.'

'You wait,' said Sophia, climbing into bed. 'You'll see. I wish I had never eaten so much tonight, but it was delicious, and besides, I am happy.'

'Do you wish you were married to my father?' I crept up behind her. The cool sheets were comforting to the touch.

'When will you get it into your head that it is you I love? Now, go to sleep. I have a big day tomorrow. I am going to have my first Italian lesson.'

There was no air conditioning in this villa. We had our windows open to collect the breeze, but even with the window open, I still felt hot. Sophia had dropped asleep, laying on the edge of the bed, her long blonde hair hanging over the side. Drink had made her sleepy, as well as the second helping of spaghetti.

The first night here that I could remember was heavenly. I lay on the bed, warm and thinking. Hundreds of Italian people were sleeping tonight, dreaming their dreams, their lives with bottles of red wine and pasta. My mind suddenly free in the old Mediterranean world, was living and breathless with hope. Like Sophia, I was finding a new and welcoming self. Getting out of bed, I felt I could breathe better by standing at the window.

Such was the view from the clifftops, that the panoramic view filled me with wonder knowing that everything I ever wanted was somewhere out there. The inky darkness of the shadows against the glistening lights told a story if I listened carefully, I could hear it. Is my heart beating to the sound of time? I don't know because this feeling was too great for me that in that instance; I felt like I could be God. Is this what it's about? That I am God, and God in everything.

Beneath and on the veranda, something moved. A shadow picked itself away from the rest and showed itself to be autonomous. But it was not shadow but a person.

Leaning over the windowsill, I waited and hoped the shadow would move again. It did. Someone else was sitting there looking out at the view and keeping itself with its unshared thoughts.

It was her, Eve.

I am that thief in the night who steals downstairs. I could not believe my luck. I felt like I could clap my hands and do a jig just as I saw Sophia do. Sophia never suppressed herself, but then she never felt guilty about what she wanted.

First, though, I went to the kitchen and finding two

glasses; I filled with water from the tap. This is my wine for her.

'You couldn't sleep either,' I said, appearing on the veranda. I placed the two glasses on the table. 'I am sorry. Did I frighten you?'

She wore a coat on top of her nightdress.

'A little. I forgot myself. You know how it is when one looks at something so beautiful. I cannot believe how lovely this place is. You brought water. How kind? I am thirsty.'

'Water is the source of all life.' I said, taking my seat beside her. Closer now than I was before. 'So, why is it you can't sleep?'

'It's like this some nights.' She picked up the glass and sipped the water. 'A troubled mind, I believe. When we have done something that is unnatural to ourselves, we wonder what has happened. So, this is the best way to understand ourselves by coming to this divine beauty. You probably don't know what I am talking about.'

'Quite the opposite, actually. I do understand what you are talking about. I have my own interpretation of it.'

Her face was enchanted with my invention, as if I was the oracle that could tell everything.

'And what is your interpretation?'

'In the world out there, nothing disapproves of us— there can't be. Look at the stars and the many catastrophes going on in space, objects colliding into each other and none of these stars, comets or meteors ever apologise. In fact, I would go so far as to say that the universe and everything out there have no manners.'

And now she was giggling and putting a hand to her face to cover her mouth and enjoying the bizarre observation I offered.

'You are adorable, Aiden, but I am talking about something so profound—'

'That's just it. You have caught yourself in a mesh of inconsolable regret that I fancy if I had not been here, you might have thrown yourself over the side. Am I correct in that?'

She said nothing, nor did she look at me. The laughter which had bubbled into music had ceased. With consternation, I realised this had been a significant possibility. Whatever had happened to her in her life, I was convinced was not of her design. I also said nothing. Mimicking her thought, I tuned myself into her mind.

What had happened to her, which was too awful to live with?

Those few seconds of feeling which could not be said passed by, picked its way like the gentler embroiderer.

It was my sandal, which scuffed the ground to make her look up.

'You never said why you could not sleep?'

'Didn't I? I thought I did.'

'No.'

'Well, it was something which was bothering me, which really was not worth mentioning.' I pretended to yawn. 'My father would say I was so well pampered that I would not know what was good from bad.'

'Then your father is wrong because whatever is bothering you is something you should talk about.'

Now she looked at me. Her big grey eyes resolved to find out what disturbed me.

'Tell me.' She demanded.

'No, I can't. Really, it's too silly.'

'Which is all the more reason you should tell me. Tell me before I get angry.'

'You cannot be angry?' I said merrily.

'Yes, I can.' She gripped her lips together in resolution.

'Very well, but you will laugh at me when I tell you.'

'No, I can assure you I won't. I promise.'

'Very well, when I tell you and you laugh at me, I shall never speak to you again.'

She nodded her solemn head; this was a pledge.

'It's Sophia.'

I glanced at Eve as if I was waiting for her to explode. She nodded again for me to go on.

'Sophia knows I do not have any money of my own, and that everything I have is because of my father. It never bothered me before, but it does now.'

I waited again, as if I was expecting her disapproval. What did it matter where the money came from as long as I had it?

'When she told me she got money from my father to pay for Italian lessons, I not only felt embarrassed, but humiliated.'

'I can understand that,' Eve murmured.

'Do you? Well, I can't.'

'You are trying to get a job to make money,' continued Eve. 'This takes a great deal of courage to take responsibility for your life. You are a fledgling trying your wings, and in the beginning, it will hurt you. While your father has access to millions. If you want anything, you will always have to ask him. It must be difficult for you, Aiden. Money always is. Money means power, and to you, your father has all the power.'

'Yes,' I too murmured. 'I was so angry at Sophia and yet it made sense. She said someone should learn Italian, and as she was enthusiastic, why not her? While I thought to myself, yes, why not? It made sense, and yet, I was mad at her. She knew I was trying to make something of myself. And yet, she threw this in my face. Oh well, that's my gripe.' I smiled goofily, and then shrugged.

'Oh, Aiden,' she stretched across and took a hold of my hand. 'You are such a sweet and gentle man; I wish Dominic knew you better.'

'You mean if he could see me through your eyes?'

I was holding on to her hand and staring at her.

'Yes, I suppose I do.'

'So, why did you come out here to the veranda? What was running through your mind and stopping you from sleeping?'

'Nothing.' She shook her head. 'Nothing that can be dealt with.'

'Does my father know about it? Did you tell him?'

'Yes, he knows.'

'And what did he say?'

She shrugged. 'That it's all in the past. There is nothing anyone can do about it. It has to be endured and lived with.'

'I can't believe something can be so awful when I look at you.'

'Believe me, it can,' she said determinedly, pulling her hand out of my grasp.

'Then if nothing can be done, I will help you live with it.'

'Oh, Aiden. That's the most beautiful thing anyone has said to me. I am very touched.'

'I can help with your burden; I can carry some of it for you. A burden shared is halved. You don't have to be unhappy anymore. And besides, no matter what has happened, there is probably a reason it had to be. You know my mother committed suicide?'

'Yes, I do. She must have been so unhappy.'

'She was. I remember it well.'

Taking one of those long sighs, I looked down.

'I found it impossible to forgive my father for my mother. I blamed him, considering it his fault. But then when we were walking those laps around the pool and my father told me how it was affecting him, I guess you could say I was shocked. Because instead of my mother blaming him; it was me. And there you have it.' I shrugged. 'The beginning and the end of me. Before the swimming pool chat and afterwards. I have changed, Eve. Big time. What is it they say—to forgive is divine? And the odd thing is that once I forgave my father, I felt a hell of a lot better.' I smiled, then shrugged. 'Can you not forgive yourself or whoever else it was? You will feel better about it.'

I don't know what I said, but Eve stood out from her chair, and with her cool, perfect hands, laid them on my face and kissed the top of my head.

'You are a beautiful creature, Aiden. Don't ever change.'

Her body next to mine, the smell of her perfume, the coolness of her lips on my forehead—so much I wanted to grab hold of her and possess her. That my father had access to her anytime he wanted was driving me quietly insane.

'Goodnight, my dear,' Eve said. Nearing the door. 'You have been wonderful tonight; I believe I will sleep now. Don't stay up any later than you must.'

'Eve?'

'Yes.'

'You will help me tomorrow to find out what I am good at?'

She smiled, murmured yes and then put her hand to her lips and blew me a kiss.

7

How would I describe heaven? Everyone has their own version of what heaven would be, but I don't think you would get it more perfect than the one drawn up between Eve and me. There came an understanding that our time together was the most perfect.

I rose early in the morning, which if you knew me, would be something to remark about. Taking myself downstairs and straight to the veranda where invariably I would find Eve waiting for me. We began calling these times my lessons with Eve. She would ask me how I slept, and I would tell her I always sleep well when I knew I would awake to her. She would smile; this was our joke. And then she would pour coffee; I used to have it strong in the mornings to wake me up, but not anymore.

'It's not good for your heart to drink it so strong, Aiden. We must weaken it for you, and perhaps with a little milk to make it palatable.'

I hated the taste of milk. But under Eve's direction, I drank. Her words were like the commandments, which I gratefully followed. As she poured out the coffee, lowering her eyes always with a shy smile; she knew I was watching her; it was our secret how much I cared for her. Then we would go on to the second part of our ritual. And that was my dreams. She would say to me, and always with the same words.

'But did you sleep soundly?' her expectation was great. Her large grey eyes were always on mine with such intensity that I thought that if I did not keep my eyes on hers, she would creep through the windows into my soul. Oh, this was the best part of the morning.

'Yes, I had dreams,' I would tell her. And because of the pleasure of this part of the morning, if I had none, then I would make up some just for the pleasure of her speculating on what they could mean.

This was her way of getting to know me by disentangling my sleeping thoughts. Engrossed, I watched her, trying to figure out what was on my sleeping mind. Her dark raven hair, always plaited at this time of the morning, kept me suspended in a trance of love. One morning, I broke the ritual for one question: what was the meaning of her braids?

'Oh, Aiden, if you were to know the burden of having long hair, you would tell me to cut it.'

'Never,' I said. 'I would never ask you to do that. Your hair is part of your beauty.'

'You think I am beautiful, Aiden?'

'How can you ask that question? Of course, you are. Hasn't my father told you that?'

As soon as I asked that question, my heaven, and hers dissolved. This was a lesson to me; when we were together, I must allow no one, or anything, to enter through the gates of our world. But as to my dreams, she would press her finger on to the table and start working out my complicated and peculiar messages.

It always came down to the fact that I had been neglected as a child. And then would come the nursing time when she would come across to me and wrap her arm around my shoulder while she stood and rocked me. Of course, I would have preferred something more from it, but for once I was being patient.

After the dream telling, another of our rituals came about under the eyes of the sea and sky and the awakening world below us. I loved this part of the morning; it was the most extraordinary sharing I had ever been a part of. Throughout the day, I would smile in memory of it.

There were lots of good things that Eve found out about me. I was an excellent swimmer, but there was no money to be made in that. My poetry was good. In fact, it was above average. I showed her some of my poems, which I had written over the years. But like everything else there was about me, this other skill was nothing from which I could make a good living.

On one of those hot mornings when I stepped out on to the veranda armed with several newspapers and something to translate them with, I found my father also sitting there with my dearest heart. I wondered in that strangest of situations if I had come to the wrong veranda. Then he greeted me with a great familiarity. It was at that moment I wanted to go back inside and return to see if this was really happening.

Interloper. Thief. I clenched my newspapers and put them behind my back and nearly left these two, hoping that Eve would come after me.

'Hello, Aiden. I was hoping to see you,' my father was smiling, but it was not a smile which courted confidence. 'I believe you are the reason I don't see my wife anymore.'

'Aiden is hardly to blame, Dominic. I seek his company

as much as he looks for mine.' Eve held a pot of tea ready to pour.

'But I am not blaming you, my dear or Aiden. Understand that I miss you, and then realised what it was which was absent from my life. I apologise that because of business I have had little time for you, running out before the morning had barely started.' This was such a sweet scene, but I was not a part of it. 'But this is going to end in a day or two. All of my affairs have been sorted out. We shall move out to Pantelleria in just over a week, and there, you shall feel safe, my dear.'

It was with disbelief and sudden sickness when I saw Eve throw herself around my father as she and hugged him. I fancied if I had not been there, she would have kissed him with great passion. How was it I never knew of her fears? She had kept them so tactfully hidden from me. I felt absurdly childish that these mornings she had devoted to me had not been part of her sharing with me. Watching two people embracing, knowing that for now, I was the odd one out. And then Eve turned and looked at me and smiled. Was this an apology? Whatever it was between us, there was a rift which I hadn't noticed before.

In my hand, I gripped the newspaper and waited for it to crumble into dust while forcing myself to watch these two.

'It's okay, my dear.' My handsome father's face was flushed with pleasure. 'Didn't I always say I would take care of you? Hadn't I always sworn that you would fear nothing anymore?'

'Oh, Dominic, come, please let me kiss your lips. You are my hero, my emperor.'

'Please, my dear, we have an audience. Save your thanks for tonight.'

Turning, Eve looked at me as if she had again forgotten

me. Did she mean for me to see this? Something strange was growing inside me. The door had been left open for something dark and malignant to crawl in. Then finding a nest in my bosom and commencing to collect items of interest into its chest of ugliness. What did my father have that I didn't? Money.

'Oh yes, Aiden, I nearly forgot. Now shoo, Dominic, there are things Aiden and I have got to do.'

'Really, my dear? Oh yes,' he nodded with special knowledge. 'No, don't worry about my tea. I shall call you later; I have been neglecting you.'

Their eyes together drew upon something special that broke up inside of me with a passion. I found it difficult to handle. She loved him and not me. How could she do this to me when we had spent special time together, special to me as I thought it was the same for Eve? I could not help but feel the pangs of betrayal as an alien creature grew inside of me.

A silent conversation was going on in their looks, which I thought had only been reserved for me. Smiling with such gentleness, I watched as my father left us, and then I looked at Eve to see how she was reacting to this. Pensive, thoughtful, she was calculating coolly.

Yes, I thought so. She doesn't love him as she professes to do. Another one of her games she plays to keep herself safe. It was impossible now to trust her love or her sentiments. Long has it been my idea that women cannot love as a man because their feelings come from necessity. They need someone to protect them and give them everything required for a comfortable life. While a man, a man would lay down his life for a woman, give her everything he had, whether she was worth it or not.

'Should we look at the newspaper?' said Eve, peering at

my hands, anticipating me laying the newspaper on the table. 'And see what we can find today.'

I stopped and hesitated. The tone in her voice suggested I was another toy to fill in her idle moments.

'What is it, Aiden?' she asked gently, her voice now spoke with a tone that a mother would use. 'Have I done anything to upset you?'

'I was surprised to find my father here. I thought it would be too early for him.'

'Yes, I know,' she moved her head to look out to the view. 'If I had known—but never mind—he is completing his business and won't be back for the rest of the day. Now, where were we?'

'You and my father will soon move to your new villa?'

Her reaction to that was one of surprise.

'I have been talking to your father about you, and if you cannot manage here, he accepts you should go with us.'

'But I thought you believed in me. I thought you believed I could do anything.' My voice was indignant, and my pride was put out.

'I do believe in you, Aiden, but you need to admit we are not getting anywhere. You still don't have a job, well, a job which can satisfy your needs.'

'My father never had to work, not a proper job. Everything he had was handed to him on a plate.'

'True, but I am not sure about everything. But yes, he had a far better start in life—'

'He never had to beg, as I am doing.'

'And me,' Eve added with a smile. 'But we can use what we are given, which in your case amounts to being dealt a good hand. If nothing goes well for you, you will always have your father, while I will have no one.'

'Yes, I will always have my father right to the bitter end.'

'Aiden—don't be like that. You know I care about you.'

'It doesn't matter, Eve. I will get out of your way. I am sorry, but I feel you are being kind to me because you have nothing better to do.'

'That's not true, Aiden. Your father and I care about you.'

'If I had been anyone else—'

'Aiden, come back. I don't understand what has happened. Why are you behaving this way?'

At the door, I turned as if there was something else I wished to say, but seeing her wearing her light blue dress and looking so young, I couldn't throw my anger at her.

'It doesn't matter, Eve. I fear I've got it all wrong. I wish you and my father well and hope you will be very happy together. It's best if I returned home.'

'No, Aiden, please don't go. What have I done wrong? Please stay and explain to me what has happened.'

I could not. Like a frightened rabbit, I felt myself running for my life, but it was more like I was running for my pride. Slamming the door to the bedroom, I stared blindly into the room, not knowing what to say or do, but knowing I was furious. I had been played for a fool by Eve to fill in her time. She not only made me angry, but worse, she hurt me and betrayed my trust.

And yet, I listened for her footstep on the tread of the stairs and then outside my room, but none were forthcoming. Was she waiting for me to calm down and be more reasonable?

I am not a child, but a man. And I, like all men, have desires and passions. If I should go back now blown out with a temper, whatever she thought of me would come true. I would not give in to that.

The times we had spoken together while my father was at his business and Sophia at her classes had come from solace and understanding and covered much in the area of reason.

I told her many times about Sophia and how she doesn't fulfil me as a man. True, I agreed she is beautiful and often entertaining. Eve listened to me, her grey eyes watching my face and seeking that answer she knew was there to help me.

'But she is still young, Aiden—'

'As you are. How many years are there between you and Sophia? Five, six perhaps.'

'Yes, but I have lived a far different life from Sophia and one which I would never wish upon anyone, not even an enemy—if I had one. My husband died a dreadful death six years ago. Oh, his death was savage,' her eyes squinting with grief ravaged with time. Coming back to me, she smiled poignantly. 'You cannot make any comparisons with Sophia and me because we come from completely different worlds. If you consider her as being childlike, then I suggest you rejoice by this quality, because, my dear, you are not so different from her.'

If Eve had said that to me at any other time, I would have struck her.

Now I see that Eve's patient listening was all but a show. She was waiting for my father to return. At that thought, I felt the illness and insanity of jealousy moving loudly in my breast. How could she treat me so badly?

Then I remembered the times when we laughed and joked when out shopping together. Had this meant nothing to her? Nothing. Plunging into the wonderful happiness of madness, we behaved like a married couple decked out in our wedding clothes. On that day two weeks ago, I wore my white slacks and white linen shirt while Eve unexpectedly came wearing her plain white dress. We both drew the significance of this colour scheme and laughed. I had never been so happy.

She allowed me to love her, putting up no resistance because, look here, I have photographs to show you. Here she is with her arm around me. And look at this one and that. Do you see what I mean? Do you see the loving expression we have for each other? You cannot say there isn't anything there.

Now on the bed, I lay with my head aching with a fever knowing she cannot do this to me and come away without being scalded herself. No, I am convinced she must feel more for me than just care.

And as to her complaints about my father, and let's face it, there were some. Yes, and the twenty years between them were enough to make them a cultural generation apart.

Listening to her criticisms and her trying to be objective —my father was gentle. Financially, he gave her everything she wanted, but then he was slow, and sometimes she felt he patronise her. Yet these were her feelings and not his, so she could be wrong. But I doubted it. As she wondered sometimes if he was becoming possessive and then she laughed, if that was so, why was she nearly always on her own? But then she understood it was only going to be this way for a little longer.

At times like these, she was so strangely animated that I felt I was getting to know the real Eve. She sparkled and her merry wits sharpened, teasing me, and then she changed to become so gentle with me; I felt I could spend the rest of my days with her and still only scratch a little of the surface. Already, I was drawing a pattern of her life, most of which was telling me she was unhappy, as I was unhappy, and this was a comfort.

If I was to go, I should go now. Take my clothes and catch

a cab to the airport. This would surely upset her if she cared; it would be a test. One I was feeling reluctant to make, but I had to know.

But what about Sophia? Yes, what about her? She was getting on well with her classes; she told me so. Making friends, she said this was a different life for her. Someone asked her for a date the other day. She looked at me to see how I took it.

'Why are you telling me?' I asked, noting she was wearing light blue slacks, and a cardigan tied around her hips as if she was a regular college student—she never got a degree, preferring to go to modelling school if there is such a thing. She was also wearing her non-prescription glasses. 'What do you want me to do about it?'

'Aren't you jealous?' Sophia asked. 'Aren't you going to tell me I should stay home?'

Our voices rose—and that's something else I meant to tell Eve that Sophia was being unfaithful to me. I forgot to tell Eve. I was going to tell her today. But it's too late now. It's too late to go back to the veranda and say to her—

'By the way, Sophia is two-timing me. This is how people treat me.'

My bag was packed, but not completely. There you are. I was sitting on the bed with my head in my hands. You know, I should do something dramatic, something to show Eve how much I cared about her. I laughed and shook my head; I didn't have any tablets to take, and if I wanted to throw myself off the cliff, I would have to return to the veranda. Instead, I rolled over on to the bed and curling into the foetus position and fell asleep.

Sophia wasn't coming home until late tonight; she told me she was going to stay with a friend. We had an argument, which was why she was staying away.

'Aiden? Are you there?'

Someone was knocking on the door and trying the door handle; it cracked open. 'Aiden? Are you in here?'

Opening my eyes, I was surprised to find that it was dark, and then I realised the shutters were still closed. The dim light from the opening door came with a shock, just like my headache.

'Aiden?' her voice was sweet, timid now and cautious. 'I could not come to see how you were earlier. Dominic needed me, but I was worried about you. You aren't ill, are you? You're so quiet.'

She sat on my bed; I could smell her perfume and now she was stretching across and feeling my head.

'Aiden, you're hot. Are you ill?'

I rolled over and looked at her. 'I thought you cared about me.'

'Your shirt is wet, Aiden. You've been sweating, and you have a temperature.'

My head throbbed from the light, which was too bright for my eyes.

'No one cares for me now. I wish I was dead.'

'Oh, Aidan. I'll get you some water.'

When she stood, the little pressure she exerted on the mattress left a slight indentation of her being. But I could not think how sweet that was, for my head ached. But worse, I felt the loss of her presence. These feelings intertwined into one with the sudden fear that I might be dying. How I had longed to die, but when it was offered to me, I didn't want it.

'Here, my dear, drink the water. Oh Aiden, you are sick and have a temperature. When did this happen?'

The water was chilly in my mouth and throat, coming like a hammer blow to my body. What was happening to me? Some malignant illness attacking me. If I should die now, it would be Eve's fault. Such a beautiful death would show her how much I loved her.

'I'm calling the doctor.'

Putting on the light made me yell. I begged her to turn it off as the pain was blinding me.

'I am going to call for a doctor, Aiden. So I shan't be a long.'

She was worried I could tell this in her voice. Taking the glass from me, she put it on the side and hurried away.

Oh, how my head ached.

To die so young is always beautiful. I was thinking this when, in the distance, I heard her worried voice talking to someone.

'Yes,' she confirmed. 'No. When I saw him last, he seemed perfectly well.' And then, 'my husband's son—his only son. No, he's not a child. He's thirty-two years old. Have you any idea what it could be? I was worried about giving him a couple of painkillers, and the other thing was is, he has a temperature.'

My ears were suddenly sharp, as if I had tuned in and turned up the volume.

'You are? When? I am extremely grateful to you.'

I heard the receiver return to the cradle before Eve's sturdy legs drummed up the stairs. Why my father and Eve took on such a small villa was beyond me.

'Aiden, are you awake? I've spoken to the doctor; he wants to see you before he can do anything. You poor dear, how you must be suffering.'

She sat with me for a while, her cool soft hand touching my forehead. My enjoyment in dying was that she was suffering regret. When Eve opened the shutter to listen for the doctor, I yelled with pain and voiced that I would be sick if she kept the shutter open. Faithfully closing the shutters, she continued to sit with me in the dim light which came from the open bedroom door.

Beneath my eyelids, I watched Eve. She sat as a statue, her back straight, her face without distraction, marbled with intentions. She fascinated me. I could see her as a general waiting out the time for the next great battle. Unblinking, barely breathing, all her energies were concentrated on listening.

When a car crunched over the gravel in the courtyard; she stood and smiled, giving a quick look in my direction before hurrying downstairs. I waited too, pulling at the sheet to cover my arms.

'He is upstairs, second on the right,' Eve said while two pairs of feet mounted the stairs. 'I believe he's asleep.'

The crunch on the treads suggested a heavy man with a tough Italian accent. I've heard that tone in the market.

'Ciao, mio caro signore. I am Dr Rizzo, and I have been invited to look at you.'

Parting my eyes, I saw a man of five feet seven, wearing a brown suit, standing over me. Looking left, then right, he was making the room known to him. Instantly, knowing what the doctor needed, Eve brought a chair for him.

'I believe he is awake,' he murmured to Eve. 'Mr Bentham, I need to talk to you to find out what is ailing you. Can you please bear with me? I will be as quick as I can. First, I need to know when this started. Will you please help me?'

I murmured yes but refused to turn to him; the light was too bright for my eyes. He listened, and I fancied nodded and then coming around to me, he took my temperature. The examination did not last longer than ten minutes, I assumed, but the intrusion I felt lasted longer. He felt my pulse, checked the colour of my pallor, and then asked me to sit up. For my complaints and reluctance, he told me this was necessary.

'Have you ever experienced anything like this before, Mr Bentham?'

No, I have never felt like this before. Then, against my will, he checked my eyes after he checked my reflexes with a small tap of his reflex hammer. A most disagreeable examination because it made me feel worse.

'Well, the examination is over,' said Dr Rizzo, clicking open and shutting his case.

'What's the problem? What is the matter with Aiden?'

'We will talk outside.'

Walking down the stairs, I heard only a little of the conversation, as the arrangement of the stairs did not carry good acoustics. Hysteria, he said, I was suffering from usually a female complaint but real enough to the patient and often preceded by a shock to the system. I heard Eve gasp and then quickly apologise. After that, I could not hear anymore.

'Aiden,' Eve's voice spoke some minutes later. 'The doctor has prescribed you some tablets to help your head. I have got some water for you, my dear. As soon as you take them, you will start feeling better. Come, let me help you sit up.'

Clutching my head, I felt that any loud noise would make it crack open.

'You should feel much better after you've taken these tablets.'

'What are they?' my voice was almost extinguished as though the pain had reduced it to a mere whistle.

'Nothing, my dear. They will help you. I will give you two now and two later. There is no need for you to eat tonight, just plenty of rest. The world will be a happier place for you in the morning.'

'Eve,' I stretched up and caught her hand just as she was about to leave.

'Please don't leave me on my own. I have the feeling I might die. What has happened to me? Is it serious? Am I going to die?'

'No, you are going to be fine. You need to rest my dear, and in the resting, you will get better. Now I will pull the covers over you. Think of the beauty of Italy and those wonderful times we spent together sitting and chatting. Now close your eyes, my dear, and sleep.'

8

A s was ordered, I slept well. Never a person to take tablets and any other sort of potion, I left my trust in Eve. If she wanted me to take poison, then I would do it for her. But here I am with my eyes open and feeling so much better yet still unaccountably tired and a little shaky.

How long I slept for, I did not know. It could be weeks, but I think not. I felt so much better and almost refreshed except for this lethargy. I fancied that if I fell off to sleep again, I would not awake till the following morning. A complete sensation of peace now filled my mind. I was calm, and all anxiety had gone; nothing mattered anymore. It was wonderful.

The next mystery to me was what time it was. Creeping downstairs, an old clock on the mantlepiece had become a token ornament. Resisting the call of time, it ticked, but the hour hand refused to turn. Nothing moved in its strange old world.

My father was home. I heard his voice commanding from the veranda. Had Eve whispered to him I had been ill?

I crept into the lounge that opened on to the veranda; two glass doors opened to the massive Italian view. Unseen and unknown to them, I crept closer to listen to their conversation.

'The doctor made an extensive examination of Aiden checking his pulse and his reflexes. He said they are good, and there is nothing physically wrong with him—'

A bottle of wine was swilling. My father was helping himself to another vino. Perhaps he was listening, but he wasn't interested.

'I was worried about Aiden; you never saw him. He went down so suddenly. A fever, I thought—there was no colour in his face. I thought he had cholera.'

'Oh, nonsense my dear, Aiden is too healthy for that; he was raised on the best. You pander to him too much, and in doing so, upset yourself. This was what I was trying to tell you about Aiden. He is so like his mother.'

'Dominic, you are not listening. Aiden is suffering from mental illness. This sort of thing can lead to other things like breakdowns and severely affect his long-term health. It's a sign that we must take care of him.'

A great sigh from my father. 'I understand how afraid you must have been, my dear. But I know Aiden better than you do. It's because we are leaving for Pantelleria.'

'No, I don't think you do, Dominic. You have never really listened to him.'

'He's a grown man, and he has Sophia,' another sigh. 'He never used to be a clingy child, even after he lost his mother. It makes little sense to me. But you said the doctor gave him some medication. Shouldn't that be enough?'

'It's just like a bandage, an emergency fix, but it doesn't tackle the real problem.'

'Then what do you suggest we do? Because I am beginning to think that my grownup son will only settle down in his head if I am not married to you.'

'Would you mind, though we don't have to divorce?'

'But that's stupid. We cannot lead our lives like that. Are you saying we should consider this and sleep in separate bedrooms?'

'I don't know, Dominic—'

'I can't believe this—it's emotional blackmail—'

'But he doesn't know he is doing it. For him, this attack is real. Terrifying him; he thought he was dying. Can you imagine how he must be feeling?'

'Aren't we already doing that? Eve, you cannot seriously suggest we give up our lives at the pleasure of his?'

'It wounds me, too. When someone is ill, should we not try to help them? There must be a compromise somewhere with him, so he can lead his life as happily as we do ours. You said Aiden could come with us in the beginning. Something has happened to Aiden, and until we find out what it is, we are responsible for his illness.'

'This is preposterous, my dear.'

'Yes, I know.'

'It's becoming more bizarre by the day. You know, my son hates me—oh, and I am not fooled by his displays of filial love; he has been hating me all his life ever since his mother killed herself.'

'And what about before? Did he love you before?'

'Ironically, no. He always preferred Eleanor to me. In fact, he was almost hysterical in his possession of her.'

'You said hysterical?'

'Yes, I did, didn't I? Maybe that word being bandied around by you simply became handy?'

I peeped around the corner to look at them, amused by their conversation. My father, now standing, was looking out towards the sea with his hand gripping the wooden tail. He made a visionary pose. Remaining seated, Eve looked at him and then rose to stand by him. Two very attractive people watching the world from above.

'I can't believe there is anything wrong with him. When he was a child, he hardly suffered from any childhood illness. Eleanor and I would take him to Switzerland for the clean air. And later in life, when he was away at school, the reports suggested he was a splendid swimmer. He was loved very much by his mother, probably too much. And that was the problem.'

'Well, things have changed. He needs you in his life more than ever now. Dominic, he needs his father.'

'You should be an expert at that, given what you said about your first husband.' He sighed, and as he moved away, he shook the handrail. 'Heavens know why the owner didn't put a more secure railing up instead of this quick makeshift fence. If I were staying here longer, I would build a sturdier one and install it out of my own pocket.'

Leaning back from the wall just in case they should see me, I was fascinated to hear the things these two talked about, like peeping into another forbidden world.

'What then do you suggest we do? Give up on our plans to look after an adult child who has always looked after himself?'

'He only looks like he is caring for himself Dominic, but if you scrutinise the situation, you will see fractures in his life. For example, he has never had a job in his life, and there is a reason for it. I am seeing Aiden now for what he is, and no matter what you may think, he needs you, Dominic—'

'Which means I can never extricate myself from him.'

'I didn't say that, Dominic. What I'm saying now is to

give him some of your time. Make friends with him. Have you ever spent time in his company with no one else there?'

'Not that I can remember. But what purpose would that solve? He's always let me know he finds my company repellent.'

'No, Dominic, this is where you are wrong. He has expressed a great desire to know you and have you approve of him.'

'He may very well have expressed it whenever that was. But I fear now I don't want to know him. Eve, why should I? I just want to get on with my life. Oh yes, I pity him he has got himself into a bit of a palaver, but Eve, I am fifty-five and we have just met each other. We must get on with our lives. Do you understand?'

'I just remembered I would look in and see if Aiden is still sleeping. He hasn't eaten all day, and if he doesn't eat, that will also damage his spirit.'

Like the first dash of lightning, I rushed upstairs panting with the fear of being seen.

'Eve, before you go, can you just spare me a moment? I am feeling a bit left out here—' I heard my father say from the bottom of the stairs.

Jumping into bed, I pulled the sheet around me and made out that I was sleeping, while trying to calm down my beating breath.

Only just in time because the door was pushed open as Eve came creeping in to look over me; I could see her through the shades of my eyelashes.

'Aiden. Are you asleep? Aiden, it's me, Eve.'

Flickering my eyes open, I looked at her.

'Oh, good, Aiden,' she smiled. 'I thought you might be hungry. Would you like to come down and have something to eat?'

'Is my father home yet?'

'Yes, he is.'

She looked surprised at my question, which was what I had calculated.

'No, I shall be fine here. I have caused you enough problems as it is, and I feel slightly ashamed of myself.'

'Nonsense, Aiden. Your father is looking forward to seeing you. Come and have some dinner with us. Is Sophia coming home tonight?'

This was a chance to tell Eve what I could not tell her before. Perhaps I should elaborate a little, as there is no harm in it.

'I never imagined Sophia to be a two-timer.'

Eve was sitting on my bed and frowning, her fingers linked. 'I can't believe she would do something like that, yet I always felt she was too nice—'

'But it's not her fault, Eve. I must take the blame. I have hardly been boyfriend material.'

'Aiden, you have been wonderful. Your father has been in admiration of what you are doing.'

I smiled and raised my head; a total transformation taking place on my face, telling her I was inspired by kind words.

'Really,' I said. 'I felt he had got to the point where he despised me, and I wouldn't blame him, not one bit. I have been a monster to him, Eve. You must believe it.'

'Well, if you have, I still believe forgiveness should be the rule.'

'Oh, Eve, you make everything sound possible.'

'We love you, Aiden. Dominic and I truly love you.'

'You are kind.' I touched her hand and held on to it.

Blissful happiness because the next couple of days

produced a change of plans. My father and Eve were going to cancel their move for a few more weeks until I was well.

When Sophia returned the following evening, a great deal of discussion followed. She had returned to a house of different thoughts and feelings. I had been speaking to Eve and telling her everything about my lovely Sophia, and what her true feelings were about the rest of my family. And one thing was that Dominic had made a pass at her. Of course, this was a lie, but even lies have their roots based in reality. It could have been a possibility; except he was not interested in her. My father would never break up someone's happiness for the pleasure of himself.

At first, Eve refused to believe until my poisoned words set in. The protest began when she could not imagine that Sophia was like that. Yes, she could understand she was beautiful, but as to the manner of her morals, no. And as for Dominic, absolutely not until she remembered that much plainer women had made a pass at him. So, an absolute, became possible. Maybe? It was just too complicated. I have never heard Eve upset when understanding that Dominic could betray her.

'You think I would do that to you?' my father almost screamed. 'We haven't been married two minutes and you think I would already be looking around? Oh honey, you don't know me. I am not your first husband; please understand that.'

It was an ugly scene.

Eventually, they made up, but not after some things were said which should not have been. Finally, Eve accepted Dominic had not been unfaithful to her, but something had to be done.

'I will talk to Sophia and tell her that our relationship is off,' I told Eve the morning after Sophia had gone to college.

'You don't have to,' said Eve, looking at me heavy with sadness. 'But the trouble is, I can't have her here, not after she tried to cause mischief.'

'But you do not know for sure. It could just be me telling you this. Sophia could be completely innocent of the offence.'

'What are you saying, Aiden?' Eve's eyes were serious; this had been a hell of a journey which needed nipping in the bud.

'Oh, I don't know, Eve. I don't care about her anymore and her lies, and yet, I don't want to hurt her. Once upon a time, we were good together. I don't know what went wrong. But you are right, I must get rid of her. I am not in love with her and perhaps never was.'

~

'Is this a joke?' Sophia bobbed her head to one side as she looked at me. With her hair in a high ponytail, it made her look younger than she was.

'I don't love you anymore, Sophia.'

'But you have never loved me, Aiden. You were always telling me that, so what has that got to do with it? There is no one else in your life, so why get rid of me? I am pretty harmless, and I have a great body, which is something you already appreciate.'

I shook my head.

'But why, Aiden—it doesn't make any sense? Okay then, you are not in love with me; what does it matter? I love you, isn't that enough for the both of us? We get on well together, and you must admit we've had a lot of laughs.'

'My father has booked a flight for you tomorrow. But if you like, you can go now and stay at a hotel. It would be best for everyone. I am only thinking of you, Sophia. It really is for the best.'

Her lovely blue eyes, caught by the sunshine, opened to me with bewilderment; no amount of reason would be accepted by me. She was still wearing her absurd college clothes, white socks with a short skirt; she was supposed to look like a schoolgirl, but it only made her appear sexy. No more explanations. I had decided that our relationship was over and done with, and I would be happy if she didn't make a big thing of it.

'But Aiden, you can't mean it. We have been together now for well over three years. When did you feel like this and why didn't you warn me you were going off me?'

I shrugged. 'It's just one of those things. At least I told you now before you became any older. You will find someone rich who can look after you and do everything you wish. You will get over me quickly, you'll see.'

'But I don't want to get over you. You might say you are not in love with me, but I think somewhere in your heart, you will regret what's happened. Aiden, you might not realise it, but you are in love with me.'

And then she hurried off after bursting into tears. Weeping like a heroine, but still lovely. It was beautifully tragic.

I watched her from the upstairs window hurrying off and felt nothing, not even pity. She will get over it, I told myself while going over the last words she had imparted to me.

'I still love you, Aiden.' Her eyes were sad and weepy. 'I hate to leave you here by yourself—'

'I am hardly by myself when I have my father and Eve.'

'You may not know how much you need me because you do, Aiden. Whenever you need me, pick up the telephone and call me and I will drop everything to be there for you.'

So, that was it. Climbing into the taxi, only Eve had the heart to see her off. I watched my Amazonian Sophia hanging over Eve weeping while trying to understand why this had happened. She had supposed we were happy together. She loved Dominic as she did Eve. While Eve carried by the emotion pulled down Sophia's blonde head and kissed her cheek. I could swear this made Sophia worse.

And there she goes back to England. I watched the dust as the taxi drove off, satisfied a rift was occurring. My life has just started. I smiled while watching Eve returning to the house. It was then I knew she would soon be mine.

9

E ve had gone to the market on her own while I was still resting, insisting that I stay home. With so much time on my own, I began wondering, was she nervous of me?

Last night, Eve had given me two more of the tablets, and I slept and slept, and slept. A wonderful sleep which refused to leave the following morning. I was relaxed and still overtired.

'No, Eve, if I was to take any more of those tablets, I am afraid I will never wake again.'

'But the doctor said you should take them.'

'Yes, perhaps he did, but he is not the one to put up with the aftereffects. So, no, I will not take any more today.'

We now sat on the balcony together with oven baked fish Eve had brought from the market decorated with fresh salad. My father had poured a glass of red for everyone. I was favoured with my face to the sea instead of sitting with my back to it. The honoured guest, so it seemed which cheered my mood considerably. My father finished pouring the wine and put the bottle between us. He was smiling; something had pleased him.

Eating dinner with Eve and my father on my own was unusual, to say the least. Each of us was conscious of the one being left out, which is probably why Eve keeps on smiling at me.

Hot all day, the heat travels up the cliffs, beating its way to the villa. Unbearable even though the windows have been left open all day.

'I was talking to someone today, though there is no point in me telling you who it was because you still would not know him.' Dominic mused, enjoying the rich bouquet of the wine.

'Oh.' Eve stood, tossing her hand to her mouth. 'I've forgotten the bread. I won't be a moment. Can I bring anyone anything?'

We mutely shook our heads and waited for Eve's disappearance. I had the fancy that my father wanted to say something to me and that maybe Eve had just remembered that she should give my father a chance.

'What was it you were going to say, Father?'

'Now, isn't that strange? It's completely slipped my mind, but there was one thing I was going to ask you. How are you feeling, Aiden?'

'Feeling?' I queried.

'Well, Sophia has gone back to England. Do you miss her? That's a stupid thing for me to ask, but of course, you will miss her.' Picking up his wineglass, he tweedled the stem in his fingers. 'You'll have to help me out here. I am afraid I am treading on unknown waters. The fact is Aiden, we have never had one of those fathers, son talks; is it too late to start now?'

'Am I interrupting something?' asked Eve, returning

with the bread while looking at Dominic to see if she was safe.

'Aiden, I thought we could spend some quality time together.' He smiled, but looked uncomfortable.

Such a worn-out phrase had made a dent in his armour, but if he couldn't mean what he said, then I would make up for his inadequacy. I put out a hand and touched his.

'That would be wonderful. I would really like that. Father, I know you are doing things against your will, but I want you to know I appreciate it.'

Resigned to his lot like a dark and miserable day, Dominic would need to get used to it with a little reassurance from his wife, whose idea it was. She soon appeared and was likely listening, smiling as she returned to a happy family. In my stupidity, I might have reunited them. Because seeing us two happy together, father and son, Eve went to Dominic and put her arm around him and kissed him gently on the lips.

Yes, happy families, at least for a while.

When I was a child, yes, this was how the story went for my father. I listened to his story of when we were in Switzerland, I my father said insisted that I could eat more than I ordered. I loved the apple strudel so much so that I asked for seconds.

'You won't be able to eat all of that,' he told Eve. 'You would never believe it, Eve, but he ate the second bowl and then asked for a third. I said no. Do you remember, Aiden? I told you that you would be sick. And you were. Do you remember, Aiden? Because I do.'

'How old was I, Father?'

'You must have been eight, yes, eight.'

Perhaps he had remembered that story because it pleased him. But I remember a different story. At eight, I was at school. My mother wrote to me to let me know they could not come back to England for the holidays because my father wanted to go to another fine arts exhibition. But whoever it was my father was talking about—wasn't me.

Across the table, I saw Eve believing that Dominique and I were happy. If we are happy, then she could be happy. So, let me ask you, what is important then? And I have an answer; would you like to hear it?

As long as we are happy, the means as to how we get there is justified. Now I am happy.

10

'So, how did you get on?' asked Eve, laying the table for dinner.

'I enjoyed myself. I am not sure if my father did.'

'He would have enjoyed himself,' said Eve, laying out the cutlery and nodding because this was what she wanted to believe; she was the one who had suggested the father and son thing. 'I didn't know what to make tonight, so I made a shepherd's pie from my recipe,' she smiled, touching me lightly on the hand.

It has come to my notice that Eve enjoys touching people; I believe it's her way of reassuring herself that we are still a happy family.

'Where about did you go?' she asked, turning her head, pleased I was following her because it meant we could still carry on with the conversation.

Following her into the kitchen, I was charmed and attracted by her vivacity. What would it be like being married to her? Would it be like this?

'I don't know why my father thought we should go to the

bay.' I watched as she checked the pan where the minced beef and onions were frying.

If this was her recipe, then it smelt delicious.

'I had the impression he thought I would go running to the beach, throw off my shoes and socks and go swimming.'

Nodding and smiling, her cheeks flushing from the heat made her appear even more attractive, as if beauty could be polished further. She wanted me to continue.

'I would have obliged him, but I am almost thirty-three. Do we ever grow up in our parent's eyes?'

Quietly laughing, her eyes had narrowed into the shape of pleasure; one day, these will be the memories we shall treasure for the rest of our days.

Imagining her hair loose because she never let her hair down. Too long, she had said. She was thinking of cutting it. You must never cut it, because if you do, I will never talk to you again. That's what I said to her.

With curiosity, I asked what my father had said about her wanting to cut her hair. I imagined he would say the same. But no, for he had told her that if her hair was giving her headaches, then cut it. I guess my father was more considerate than me.

'Does my father have that effect on you?' I was smiling now because she was smiling while looking into my eyes. Happiness is infectious.

'Oh, many, many times and every time when I mention Gerard.'

Gerard, I had wanted to question. Was this the name of her first husband? But perhaps it was not the appropriate time to ask her; I might lose the fulfilment of her story. I nodded, which was enough for Eve to continue her story.

'Well, yes,' Eve bobbed her head to both sides of her shoulder. 'Not the easiest of people to live with, even at the best of times. He was always getting something in his bonnet and insisting that it was my fault.'

I carried on smiling, but felt more than thought that this would be nothing to do with happiness.

'I do not know what I did?' she threw her hands into the air, aiming for irony. 'But it was enough to lock me out of the house.'

'He locked you out of the house,' I could not help repeating.

'That's what I said. But it's not such a big thing.'

'But why? Although you said you didn't know why. What happened before that?'

'Nothing much, really. He thought I was talking about him on the telephone.'

'And were you?'

She grinned. 'Yes.' And then the grin stopped. 'If I am honest, I never loved him—oh yes, I did my very best to be the wonderful wife he expected. When we went out together, I refused everyone else's requests for dancing although I love dancing, but there you are. I was being everything he wanted me to be, but they find out, don't they —that you don't love them?'

So, what had this to do with my father? I thought. Eve had taken the basket of bread into the room and when she returned, she came back as another person.

'Men,' she said, looking at me, still with the remnants of a smile.

'Women,' I added.

'Jealousy,' she included this on the shopping list.

We both nodded; people are just people, but I stared after her thoughtfully and wondered why beauty could also inspire hate. But what was the use of wondering when there were tasks to be completed? Taking up the condiments after she had quickly hashed a tomato and cucumber salad, a last-minute extra just in case the shepherd's pie was not to her liking.

'Have you ever felt jealousy?' I asked, walking behind.

'No, I don't think so.' She looked back at me casually. 'Have you?'

'I think I might have done.'

'Continue,' she said with interest, wanting to hear more.

We stopped just inside the kitchen, although it might be more specific if I was to say that she stopped at the entrance, barring me from entering. No entry until I traded in my secret. My secret for one of hers; that was the bargain.

'You go first, Aiden. After all, you were the one who started this.'

'Oh well, should we have a glass of vino first? It's gone seven o'clock already.'

Taking two glasses, Eve got a bottle of white from the refrigerator and I uncorked it.

'I was keeping this one for later,' she said. 'In fact, it was going to be solely for me. I wasn't going to share it with anyone else. Oops.'

I frowned and then smiled.

'Pass the glasses.' I took the glasses and filled each one generously.

'You know,' began Eve, 'you won't get Dominic filling up the glass as much as this.' Her finger showing the level.

'Do you have a problem with that?'

'No, I don't,' she grinned.

'Saluti.' we both clinked our glasses and drank.

I watched her neck as she swallowed. So white and fragile, but passionate. Was it as soft as I imagined? I wanted to down my lips into the soft skin of her neck and wrap her black silky hair around me.

'You were saying.'

She licked her red lips, naturally red, but I wondered if she had done something to them. Bit them or pinched them, maybe? This sort of artifice excited me.

'I will not let you get away with anything,' she said, pouting her lips and, for me, almost suggestively. 'I love hearing stories and I want to hear everything.'

'Okay. Where was I?'

When I looked at her, the bejewelled light in her eyes masked a thousand and one stories. What a beautiful enchanter. We shared a smile.

'Yes, well then. It was about Sophia and how I felt myself to be suddenly jealous.'

'I love stories about jealousy. They are the best. Because they're about passion and fire and life.'

I smiled. I was not so sure about that.

'It was something which should not have happened, and really there was nothing much to it. In fact, it's not really a story—'

'I don't care. Carry on.'

A sudden passion was evolving within Eve, rising like a storm out of nowhere. Her body tensed. She would not be relaxed until she heard the rest of my tale, for even beautiful people are imperfect.

'We had only just arrived at this party, Sophia, and I—it was one of the first parties we went to as a couple and one of the last—'

'Oh, why was that?'

'Because of how I felt.'

'Okay, I understand. Please go on.'

'That really was that. She went into a room to get her coat, then a man went in after her. They were in there for three minutes and thirty-seven seconds. Sophia came out first, and then two seconds later, he came out as well.'

'And that's all?'

'Yes, that's all.' I opened my empty palms.

'But that's—' then she stopped, frowned, and looked at me. 'I know what this is?' she grinned. 'The power of the imagination.'

That rye look on my face was just a window to another side of a dual life. Sometimes, we let others in to remain as prisoners. I was possessed by a feeling I had yet to learn to master.

'Now it is your turn to spill the beans otherwise, it's not fair, and I will sulk, then what are you going to do with this large, indulged boy?'

Her eyes looked at mine as if she had an inkling this might be dangerous.

'Very well, but I am sure my story will not be as interesting or as deep as yours.'

'That's my problem.'

The levity which we now shared had run out of that nice, homely touch of feeling safe with each other. The door was opening into something darker. Memories had been disturbed that had been kept locked away. Biting her bottom lip, she picked up her glass and drank a little more wine.

'As I said, I never loved him when I married him. If he had never found this out, I believe he would have been happy, but some people have to probe too deeply; they want to know everything about who you are and gain entrance even to your soul. How can you help these people? I don't know. I was grateful to Gerard and prepared to dedicate my life to him.'

'Grateful?'

'Oh yes. Definitely. And I was completely grateful. My

parents were in a lot of debt—Aiden, it's something I would rather not talk about it—' She looked at the wine bottle. 'Some people have to do things which, if life had been good to them, would never have considered ever doing, if you know what I mean. And I was grateful to Gerard for getting me out of that awful situation. Aiden, how can you ever understand what I went through?'

'Then tell me, Eve. Tell me so I will understand.'

'Ah yes. If you hear my story and even if you forgive me. Will I forgive you for hearing it and knowing about that side of me I have already thrown away? No, I think not. I will see it in your eyes as I will hear it in your voice, no matter what we talk about. No, I could not live with that.'

'What about my father—does he know?'

'He knows as much as there is to know. Oh, I know what that sounds like, but that's all I am going to give you. You will use my relationship with him to prise out more of my private life.'

'Okay,' I said quickly, 'I understand your reluctance, but you made me a promise and whatever the price, I demand that you keep it.'

Tucking her lips together, gone was the affection in her eyes. What was left was an expression which I could not calculate.

'Remember, Aiden, if I tell you, then I might not forgive you.'

'I understand.' To know someone's secrets gives you power, and I would have that power at any price.

'If only Gerard didn't pry open that lid and peek inside. If only he had been contented with what he had. Whatever you give to one who has become fat and fortunate by the fates will never be satisfied. Unfortunately for him, he found out that if he pinched me hard with all his wants and desires, he will find that I was mortal. Isn't that sad? I think that's sad. Because, dear Aiden, I had believed everything people told me about not being an earthbound mortal. I was a goddess lent by the fates, and because of that, I acted as one. Oh, what a big downfall that was when I found out I was just mortal. Well, that was a big spell because it fooled me—Gerard was right. I had an affair,' Eve whispered.

'What fooled you?' asked Dominic, coming into the kitchen. 'I wondered where everyone was. Do you know what time it is, Eve? It's going on eight o'clock, and I am hungry.'

'And I shall feed you, my dear. I was just saying to Aiden that I was fooled into believing that I could cook.'

'But you can cook, my dear. Whoever told you, you couldn't? Aiden, did you say that Eve could not cook?'

AND NOW THE evening was cooling down, and in that relief came the feeling of mellowness, for the expectation flowed that this was going to be the best time of the day. We could all relax and enjoy our time together. I do not know what happened, but it happened sitting across from Eve when our eyes met. She smiled and then smiled some more. My father was talking about something, but between Eve and me, secrets had been shared, which would not be shared with anyone else. Special. In that understanding, I realised it is in the secrets we share that the best side of us is found.

This was how I loved her the most, and it was at that moment I knew there could be no one better than her. No matter where I ran or how high I climbed, she would always be the one I would come home to.

'What do you say to that, Aiden?' asked my father.

Eve laughed. She had seen my consternation and guessed where I had travelled to.

'We have agreed,' began Eve, 'that you, Aiden, would be a lot better off by not taking those tablets. He can hardly keep himself awake through the day—'

'But if the doctor prescribed the pills for Aiden, wouldn't it be better, my dear, if he continued? In the long run, he might feel better, and he might even get on with his life with no interference. Oh, and while I think about it, I have heard about the house, my dear. The men have already put the foundations down. I've had a look at the plans. You wanted a swimming pool, didn't you?'

'I believe that might have been Sophia's suggestion, but yes, a swimming pool would be nice. I'm sure all our friends would appreciate it.'

Everything Eve said, she looked at me as if there was something special in her meaning. I wanted to be nearer. I wanted to talk to her. I looked at my father and wondered what he was doing here.

Serving out only a bit of the shepherds' pie because of the heat, it was complimented with the fresh salad. After we had toyed with it, Eve went to the kitchen to fetch the fresh fruit. Picking at his bread, my father began pouring out more wine for each of us, but when it came to my glass, I put my hand over the top.

'You don't want any more wine?'

I smiled; I did not.

'Too hot to eat,' nodded Dominic. 'I've never been a sun person myself, but I am going to try because it's good for Eve to get away from everything. Her life in South America was not at all what it should have been. I needed to get her away from it all.'

Lifting my chin, I was intrigued and listened.

'If we don't like it; we can go somewhere else, but I have the feeling we will both love it. Italy is such a beautiful country, a place where you can bury your feet in the ground and grow roots. Oh yes, while I am thinking about it. I thought you should see a bit more of Palermo, Aiden, before —yes, well, I thought we would have another one of those quality times; I felt that went very well, so much so I thought we ought to do something like that again. What do you say to that?'

'Why not?' I shrugged.

'Mount Pellegrino is supposed to be something to see as a tourist. There is an interesting shrine, Santa Rosalia, to visit which, of course, would absolutely fascinate me. We could take a bus up the road, or we could hike it; what do you say to that?'

'Take the bus; we can still enjoy the views when we get there.'

'That's what I thought you would say,' Eve had returned with the dish of fruit.

It was a decadent pile of oranges, satsumas, bananas, and white grapes. Eve had brought in the rest of the white wine and set the bottle next to me.

'Isn't this a night when you make wishes?' said Eve, turning to look at the panorama. 'A time when you can throw your dreams into the night and tell the spirits out there living in the bay what is it you wish for?'

'Very romantic, my dear, and, as always, beautiful thoughts. What is it you wish for?' indulged Dominic.

'Oh, I think I have already got what I wanted.'

Did she look at me when she said this? I think she did. I felt her eyes upon me.

'But if you were granted another wish,' continued

Dominic, now intrigued to know her desires. 'Please, instruct us about your wishes.'

'Aiden might think I have been given so much already by this family. He will ask me, what more can I possibly wish for?'

'Aiden would not say that, would you, Aiden?' my father looked at me, astonished. 'He would want you to be happy because he loves you, Eve.'

I stopped breathing and nearly coughed. My father knows what ran through my head. I cleared my throat. Did my father know my feelings for Eve and was he now forgiving me for them? Was this an invitation from my father to love Eve openly?

'Don't you Aiden? You want what's best for her? This is an excellent wine, Eve. It's better than the white.'

Across the table again, our eyes met, and she was smiling at me. I was not imagining it; her eyes were saying something profoundly special.

'Aiden is kind to everyone,' began Eve. 'I've never known him to be unkind to anyone, except to himself.'

Eve meant what she said, and I was grateful.

It was too hot to go back inside, or perhaps it would be more pertinent to say that the allure of the night was calling us to stay and keep her company. The sea breeze lifting off the sea was softer now.

Clearing the table quickly, Eve hurried while I carried the table to the side so we could all sit and watch with no interruptions. The wonderful scenery stretched out in front of us, and already the stars had filled the cloudless sky on this perfect night. I placed Eve's chair next to mine so we could dream away, cuddled together. My father was okay as he brought his second bottle of red wine with him and put it on the table to his side. Nothing was going to touch him while he looked up at the constellations.

If Eve could have one affair unbeknown to her first husband, Gerard, the possibility follows that she could have another with me; this is what she was trying to tell me.

'Look,' said Dominic, pointing upward at the stars. 'We are having a rare treat here. Over there is a constellation better known as the Dolphin. We are so extraordinarily rich staying here where we are, Aiden. There is an astronomical observatory nearby. I was told by someone today, you wouldn't know him if I told you. The observatory is a must for amateur astronomers. Somewhere I would love to visit; perhaps we could do that before you go back, Aiden.'

Eve leaned forward as if she had something to say, but then changed her mind, persuaded that it might be better to keep silent. I held tight to my seat and grilled myself not to react. This was not the promise which had been made by me. I was supposed to be going with them to Pantelleria, and now my father was breaking his word to me.

'Drink, anyone?' asked my father.

'Not for me,' I muttered.

'Not the headache again?'

Sarcasm, I felt its bite. Even Eve flinched from this remark, unlike my father, whose mood increased with merriment as he poured himself out another glass. I was tempted to anger.

'Not cold at all.' He held his glass to his mouth. But something happened. His elbow knocked the edge of the bottle on the table.

I never realised how his reflexes could react so quickly because before the bottle made its way to the floor, my father's hand snatched and caught it. I noticed, as did Eve, but neither of us said anything. My father was still a healthy man and full of life.

'Can't spill good wine. Do you know what's on my mind?' continued my father, oblivious to what was happening around the orbit of his own family. 'I was just thinking this has been one of the most perfect holidays we have shared. Perhaps it didn't start so well, and perhaps we have been forced to do the things we didn't want to do. But, well done, Eve, you are a clever little schemer. We have endured each other longer than I thought we would.'

I was gripping my seat, feeling the tension rising. If I was to break this chair—then someone touched my hand. Some little light hand closed on top of mine to comfort me. Looking down at her hand, I felt Eve's hand gently reminding me that there was just her and I. And as I turned to look at her face; I saw her smiling.

11

An early start and my father had planned out his itinerary of what he wanted to do. We were to visit the church high on Mount Pellegrino, explore the mountain and stop for something to eat. I could do anything else I fancied as long as he could step into the old church.

Setting off at nine in the morning. Eve came with us to the door and kissed Dominic on the lips before kissing me on both sides of my cheeks. I watched. One day, I would make this woman mine.

Already the sun was up and threatening to beat the day with its heat. It felt fresh, although the warmth hovering around was building, ready to creep and burn through the white stones. At that time in the morning, I had no appetite. It was about as much as I could do to have a cup of coffee, but with Eve, even coffee was forbidden after my headache appeared. Since that awful attack which Dr Rizzo said was probably migraine, not one peek of pain had returned. I was grateful for that, as I was grateful for the care from my loving nurse.

Very few times in my adult life had I risen when the morning was young. It surprised me that so many people preferred this part of the day instead of the latter. People walked boldly with their eyes opened, comforted by the early chill of the morning. While knowing the sun was preparing to strike their daily routines. Oddly enough, Sophia also preferred the morning to the evening and had found it difficult to change her habit. But if she was going to be with me, the only way she would see me was when we were passing. Or perhaps I might be the one to accommodate her. Which makes me seem very arrogant, but I am not. I only want what I want.

'Anyone would think we were travelling to the ends of the earth,' said Father, carrying the bag of surprises as we stepped along, side by side.

'She is caring for us.' I do my best to be supportive of Eve's concern for us.

'She has forgotten, perhaps, there are some decent restaurants in the country.'

Ignoring my father, I felt the young sun on my face, feeling that it was good to be alive. Last night, Eve had kept her hand in mine for the rest of the night, and when her hand left mine, I felt nothing of the anxiety and unhappiness I had felt before. Whatever was to happen, I knew Eve would make sure we would be together.

After a brief wait, we caught the bus up to the mountain. Several other people joined the queue. They too were obviously tourists holding their leaflets and cameras, virgin eyes to the waiting secrets.

The bus arrived, chugging along the uneven twisting road, then it struggled to speed up when the passengers had boarded. My father always been used to first-class travel did not seem to mind the strangers packing in together. Around one tight curve to the next, the bus shook its way in the many stages to the top. And even after two minutes of screechy travelling, the views were making an appearance. Father allowed me to sit beside the window, which seemed ridiculous to treat me like a child now. I am not that little boy anymore.

Already the sun was putting in a grand appearance, stretching in through the window and laying herself down as if already exhausted. I was getting hotter; sitting by the window was not such a good idea. The bus's engine was taking a pounding, cleaning its throat to swallow some more air. I too felt the need to breathe. White heat now filled the sky and from below us while in the bag the food was sweltering, food which Eve had made was probably going to go to the wildlife.

'I thought we could go to the top first and then walk down to the church,' said Dominic. 'What do you say to that?'

I shrugged. 'It's nice just to come out with you and do the father and son bit.'

'I'm glad,' he smiled, but there was something different about his smile. 'Are you happy?' Dominic asked after a while.

'Yeah. It's great staying here with you and Eve.'

'Good, I'm pleased.'

Now, looking out of the window, I wondered what was going on with my father. He seemed different. I couldn't put my finger on it except the change of mood had happened just after we left. Obviously, some minor disturbance had awakened personal grievances, some minor occurrence which was enough to unsettle him. Usually, my father was easy-going. Nothing could ever disturb him, but time has passed, and changes alter people.

The bus rattled on the straight for the last bit, and then we were there, at the top. A few other tourists climbed out, then walked a few paces and turn around, breathed in, and then out, and then said wow as I did. As I could not help smiling either. What a view.

'This is wonderful,' I said to my father. 'I can't believe how amazing it is.'

'Yes,' he smiled and nodded, slowly turning to give his approval of the world. 'Sort of puts everything into perspective.' He carried on nodding. 'You know, you tell yourself that you have done well in life, and that you should not complain, and yet, there is still something not right. You try to tell yourself that it doesn't matter, but it keeps on bugging you to do something about it. And then you come up here.'

I did not know what he was talking about or what beef he was making about the world, but this was wonderful. What is it about being up so high and turning around three hundred and sixty degrees to make whatever you felt on the ground disappear?

The tourists we had come with had now scattered with their own tours to do. While the view was like nothing else; coming up high made you feel like a God of Olympus. A giant where you could do anything and everything.

'Let's climb to the top, Aiden, and then make our way down.'

Walking side by side, again I felt there was something on my father's mind and that even the view had not shifted it. Had he brought me up here for a talk?

'Do you have plans for the rest of your life, Aiden?'

'No, not really. As you know, I haven't been feeling too well lately. I need a little time,' I shrugged. 'But I appreciate your help and kindness and Eve's of course.'

'I have plans,' he said after a few minutes.

We reached the top, and stood looking at the view, and that was it for me. I could not recapture that sense of wonder and the glorious feeling it made on me while I wondered what was on my father's mind.

'What are your plans?' I asked as we made our way downwards while watching my feet on the loose stones and gravel.

'You know what my plans are, Aiden,' he laughed. 'Or you should know, and that's being happy. That's all I want to be. Do you think I will be happy?'

'It's not up to me; it's up to you,' I murmured.

We carried on in silence until we reached the church. I stayed outside to give my father some time on his own; I also needed time alone.

'Aren't you coming in?' he asked, stopping at the entrance. His figure, caught in the shadow and the sunshine backed by the cream stonework, gave him a godlike beauty. This man had it all—

'Churches aren't my sort of thing. If Sophia had been here—'

'Oh yes, Sophia.'

And then he went in. There was something on his mind —I could almost touch it, smell, and eat it. Where had it come from and what did it mean? It was bothering me.

He must have been inside the chapel for nearly half an hour. I wondered what he had been looking at as I wondered also what was on his mind. And then he was out, and I was doing my best to catch up with him, looking at his face and wondering why he had a grim expression. I wanted to ask but felt it was best not knowing.

'I prayed,' he said, as we took longer strides together. 'Are you not going to ask me why I prayed and what I prayed for?'

'Did you want me to ask?' I was perplexed. What's this all about?

'Why are you here, Aiden? What do you want of me?'

'For us to get to know each other, you know, catch up on what we have missed. This was what you said. For us to get to know each other—'

'Oh, I don't know, Aiden. I was watching you last night when you didn't think I was. Oh yes, Aiden, I can be as sneaky as you. You think I don't know what you are doing, but I have eyes and a mind. I maybe twenty years older, but there is nothing wrong with my faculties. Nothing.' He growled.

He went ahead, and I, who had been left on my own, was worried. What had he found out? What did he know? If he had guessed, then I would swear it was not true. Yes, Eve was beautiful, and I found her fascinating. After all, who could not love Eve? I hurried after him, deciding that it was best we got it over and done with now.

'What do you think is going on with me, father?'

'You want me to tell you?'

'Yes.'

'Okay then, I will. You can see I am happy with Eve when you have just thrown away your happiness. You are still blaming me for your mother. It's a shame.' He sighed before the final assault. 'You don't want me to have a life with someone else. You are jealous of my happiness.'

'Yes, father, you are right; I am jealous of your happiness because I would like to be happy too. But you think I would want to destroy yours?' I was angry now, and frowning. 'In the beginning perhaps, but then I got to know Eve. I couldn't do that to her. Perhaps, once I could have, but funnily enough, not anymore.'

'So, what was all this hysteria about? You have never

behaved like that before. Eve told me you have always been like that. I don't know how she would know, except, well, she wasn't there. Oh, why don't you grow up and get a life of your own, Aiden? They say a child is never free until their parent dies—that's another thing Eve said to me. A load of twaddle. You are a man, Aiden. I have given you everything you need as a man; it's about time you took responsibility for your own life.'

I touched my head, then heard my father groan.

'No, Aiden, I don't believe that. You are convincing yourself there is something wrong with you.'

'Father, I am sorry. I am not making this up. Do you believe I want to be dependent on you?'

'Here, take my hat. It could be the sun. You're like me; I'm not too keen on the sun either. Come over to the shade, it will help.'

Holding my hands to my eyes, I felt the worrying throb of blood pounding through my head. Not again, not again, I mumbled while closing my eyes. Strong hands took hold of me and walked me across to the shade. The cold body of darkness, almost physical, fell over me. It was a relief as my father pushed me to sit down.

'How are you feeling now?' Dominic asked, his body heat warming me from the side.

'Not as bad as I did a couple of minutes ago.'

'Well, just relax for a few minutes. We are in no rush.'

My head fell on to his chest. Through his cotton shirt, I could hear his heart beating and the warm feeling of his muscles and flesh. Never in my life had I been as close to him. Alarming because I had this sudden passion to put my arms around his chest and bury my nose and cry; I wanted to cry like a child.

'How are you now?'

Minutes had passed, and I had been quiet for a while. I fancied I might have fallen asleep.

'Okay.'

'Aiden, my shirt is wet. Have you been drooling?'

'No, I don't think so.'

I lifted my eyes to stare at him. Such a powerful blueness filled the sky. What was it like to be in his mind and see and know how he feels? What was it like to be him?

'How are you feeling now?'

'Better. Different. Human,' I added, as if this was the first time I had come across it.

'Yes, you are human all right, sometimes, I think too human. Shall we get up now and carry on with our tour? Or would you prefer to wait for the bus to take us back?'

'No, I'll be fine.'

We walked along in silence, ambling, listening to the sounds of the mountainside. The decision to stray off the road was mutual. Our bodies swayed to the side while our feet picked over the clumps of grass knitting through the stones. I thought my father would have preferred the well-designed and detailed road going down.

A few pebbles were kicked and crumbled for a few more measures, skipping along as if this was how they moved from one place to another. Looking at the views, I forgot the headache. My father looked freer than he had been before. I wondered again what he was thinking.

Our feet matched a pattern as if we were soldiers on the long march of life; there was a feeling of comradery between us if only in spirit.

'Look over there,' Father pointed to the bay. 'Somewhere over there is the villa where we are staying. And in there, moving about her day is Eve.'

He was thinking about Eve even now; ironically, I had forgotten her.

'I suppose we should take some pictures in case Eve doesn't believe we've been here.'

'There are over twenty years between you and her,' I said without thinking.

'Yes,' he murmured, as if constantly aware of that distance between them. 'I know.'

'Does that bother you?'

'Sometimes,' he looked to the side and then back again. 'She has had a hard life; I've done all I can to protect her, but there is nothing I can do about my age.'

'She should have married someone my age.'

'Yes,' my father looked at me. 'But men of your age have not been kind to her, and she knows it, which is why she prefers to be with me.'

'And you are sure of that, Father?'

'One can never be sure of anything, Aiden, or of anyone.'

That look I saw in his eyes before had now intensified and said warning; he was warning me not to come too close. And yet, everyone is free to do what they like and to leave when they need. We are not slaves to each other, at least we shouldn't be. And not even something like gratitude should keep us tied up with those invincible bonds.

'Aiden, we really should take photographs of each other; it's one way of remembering.'

He stopped to give me his camera and in that movement a shower of loose pebbles went running down, pleased to be released from their constraints. Running and falling pebbles always make delightful noises of escape.

Standing to the side so the bay could be seen. Head up, stomach in; he was a proud and handsome man. I took five or six pictures, all good ones though my father only takes perfect pictures.

And now it was my turn. I fey false modesty, yet this did not suit me because I am almost as handsome as my father. If there is anything wrong with me, it's that my looks have not matured.

'Where do you want to stand?' he said, holding the camera, waiting and ready.

'Where you are standing, the backdrop makes for an excellent shot.'

He said nothing, but held the camera to his eye.

'Are you ready?'

I nodded. Click, click. And then he put his camera away.

'Where do you think you will be this time next year?' he asked as we started on our way back down.

'Only the fates know.'

'Yes,' he muttered. 'The fates. But do you think they are always wise and that you have no say in the matter?'

'I believe they do not know everything. It seems to be whoever shouts the loudest gets what they want.'

I looked at my father. In the last few minutes, I thought we had been as close as we had ever been. Now there was something I wanted to ask him, as always. I was wondering what he was thinking.

'Where do you think you will be this time next year?' I asked, referring his question back to him.

'Away from you,' and then he looked at me. 'That's how it is, Aiden. I haven't done a perfect job with you, but it was good enough. And now I feel you need to go out on your own. I never thought for one minute I would be supporting you for the rest of your life. What happened to you? Why didn't you get yourself a job and a woman? Why are you hanging around me?'

'You want the truth?'

'Yes, I want the truth.'

'The truth might surprise you.'

'Go on then. Why don't you surprise me?'

'If you want to become the best painter, you study the greats. The same goes for anything else you study. You watch and learn their ways and even hope that some of their magic will rub off on you.'

'Yes, and?'

'You are the best, Father. As far as I can see, no one can compare. You have it all—rich, handsome, kind, generous and wise. Everything you do is perfect. That's why I'm here. I want to be like you.'

'You think I'll swallow that?'

'Yes, why not?'

'Because I am not that vain. But Aiden, please hear this. I want you out of my life before the end of the year. Nothing personal, I just want you gone. Do you understand?' He stopped, then squinted and looked about him. 'We are going downhill, but nothing has changed; we are still as high as when we started out.'

'No, if you look behind you, we have come down a long way,' I said, walking backwards, alluding to the distance we had travelled with a swoop of my hand. I was choked by what he had just said to me, but I could not react. And then I thought, this means war.

'Yes, I suppose you're right,' he replied, turning to see how much distance we had covered.

Looking at my father and seeing how handsome he looked was a picture which would last me a lifetime. And then something slipped as another cluster of pebbles rained down, pulling, and tugging at larger stones as they fell. My foot fell backwards, and as if to compensate, I held my hands out, but it was too late. The ground under my feet trembled and gave way.

Hearing the noise, Dominic turned to see where the noise was coming from while I felt myself slipping.

'Father,' I called, terrified at what was happening.

Without seeing where I was going, I had arrived at the crumbling cliff edge. Tempting the fates, they had taken up the offer and were reeling me in. My mind flicked to the conclusion that I was falling—falling to my death.

But life clutches onto anything and everything; I wouldn't be going down without a fight. A dry shrub, dead now, had tried also to hold on to life—this was my lifeline.

'Father,' I cried. 'Father, please help me.'

There was a peculiar expression on his face as he heeded me. What was I doing? Was I falling? He was thinking. Would he be free of me forever? Had the fates decided for him they would take me away?

'Father, please, save me. Don't let me die this way. I want to live. I am your only son. Save me. There will be no one to remember you. Father, please,' I screamed, feeling my fingers slipping while this tired weed was now loosening its bond from the dry earth. 'Father—'

Blinking, watching, he didn't react. Was this indecision? Was he thinking that now at last he would be free of me? But as his only son, why? Yet I realised Eve was young enough to give him more children if he wanted them.

'Father, I promise you that if you save me, I shall leave and never return; you shall never see me anymore. Father, I swear to you.'

He had his hand around my wrist, with his face next to mine. His eyes were focused on pulling me up. Saying nothing, he lifted me up with a strength I never knew he possessed. Higher and higher and over the threshold of the edge, and there I was sitting on the ground weeping.

'Here,' he said, taking a bottle from his bag. Opening it, he passed it to me. 'Drink.'

'I nearly died,' I sobbed.

'But you didn't.'

'I nearly did, and you were going to let me go. You were going to let me fall to my death.'

'Calm down, Aiden. You are becoming hysterical. You are safe now, so calm down.'

'But you were going to let me die. You wanted me dead.'

'I wanted no such thing. Take deep breaths, in and out, and try to calm down. You are safe now.'

'No, father, you wanted me dead. The way you looked at me, you were weighing up the consequences.'

'I never looked at you except to wonder what was happening to you. I thought you were sitting. I thought you were tired. It was only when you said you were falling, I realised what was happening to you. But you are safe now. Safe, do you understand?'

'You wanted me dead.'

Unable to believe what he was telling me. I saw that look on his face; I knew what he was thinking.

'Aiden, what happened, happened in a second. One moment you said we had covered a distance and the next moment you slipped off the edge. I couldn't get any faster to you than if I flew. So now try to calm down and take those poisonous thoughts out of your mind or you will really make yourself ill. Drink and breathe.'

He was crouched beside me; his eyes were angry while his face was deadly white.

12

There was no way that either of us was going to make the descent after what had happened. Thirty minutes later, the sound of the bus trudging along the road was halted by Dominic. He helped me into it and sat me down.

'The heat,' he said to the driver, who could speak only a limited amount of English. 'Has affected him.'

Watching my father as he took out a few notes, I stared at him. I knew I hated him and then I understood that the feeling was mutual.

At the bottom, instead of walking home, my father called a taxi and in a matter of minutes, we stopped outside the villa. Both on the bus and in the taxi, neither of us spoke to the other.

'It is not a good idea to tell Eve what happened,' Dominic said while he was helping me out of the taxi.

I said nothing to him.

'We don't want her worrying.'

'I thought you would be home later,' noted Eve rushing

to the; she was surprised to hear the door opening. Her eyes checked both of us to see what was wrong.

Not saying anything, I preferred not to look at her either, but went up to my room.

'He caught too much heat,' said my father, to Eve's concerned look.

I heard her say something to him, but I was not interested in knowing what it was.

Like a dead man, I climbed the stairs and entering my room, locked my door. Pulling the shutters shut, I kicked off my shoes and tugged off the top cover of the bed. I did not want to know the rest of the day. Nor did I have any feelings about what was happening to the other two below. My father wanted me dead, and he nearly had his way. What was it that made him decide he should save me?

I was the younger of us two, but the fates had decided that I had no more rights to live. Turning to my side, I shut my eyes tight only to see that entire awful scene again, but this time, my imagination completed the picture and had me falling.

'No,' I sat up, feeling the burn of a sweat heating inside me. 'Oh God,' he would really throw away my life. Old life for a young life; one of you must die. Old life for young. Old life for young.

'Aiden.'

Eve rapped lightly on the door. I did not answer her. As far as I could understand, she wanted me dead as well.

'Aiden, are you okay?' And then she tried the door handle. 'Aiden, I have some tablets to help your head. Aiden, will you let me in? I'm worried about you.'

She knocked again, then tried the door handle.

'Aiden, please open the door. I want to see how you are. I won't go away until you open this door. If you don't, you'll find out how stubborn I can be. I shall make a nuisance of myself.'

'Please go away, Eve. I don't want to talk to anyone.'

I heard her hands scuffling on the other side of the door as if she was trying to decide what to do, and whether she could break down the door. And then I heard her walk away, her footsteps running down the stairs as if she was exasperated with me.

What was I living for when everyone I knew wanted me dead? Had I ever enjoyed life? I should have let myself go when I had that chance, and perhaps then, my father would feel grief for me. But he had never grieved for my mother, so why should he grieve for me? My world had turned ugly.

Wrapping my head inside my arm, I wanted to discard all these awful thoughts, even though my mind willed me back to the scene. There was my father, staring at me while trying to decide if he should save me.

But if he were in danger of falling, whispered my mind, would I consider letting him go? He wasn't the only one who wanted to be free. Without him, I could also live my life with Eve to console me.

Something was scratching at the door, squeaking, chirping, and worrying away at the door lock.

'At last,' Eve said when the door popped open. 'I am going to put the light on, Aiden; I need to see how you are.'

The light was too bright for me. I hid my eyes with my forearm.

'I feared you have a headache, but it was no use trying to get this out of Dominic. He refused to say what was wrong with you. I think he might be jealous of you or if not, he feels guilty about something. He wouldn't say.'

Closing the door behind her, I heard Eve walk across to

my bed. Now interested, I was curious to know what she was going to do next.

'You're warm, but not hot, which is good, so you haven't got a fever.'

Her small, delicate hands were deliciously cool over my brow.

'Let me have a look at you, Aiden.' She tugged gently at my shoulder.

So Dominic hadn't told her he wished me dead, and that fate had given him what he wanted. His decision to save me was made at the price of others asking questions. I wager now that he rues the day his conscience got the better of him, for my death would have been an ideal demise, especially as there was no one around to witness. A tragic accident would have been recorded on my death certificate. A sad funeral, but after that, he could have been able to get on with his life.

My father's only mistake was to save me.

'So, you don't have a headache?' Eve sat on the bed, searching me with her eyes. Soberly, she tried to find out what had happened. 'And you don't feel sick, and you don't feel ill. Are you certain about that?'

'Yes, Eve, I am. But I feel different.'

'In what way do you feel different—can you say?'

'It must have been when we went to the shrine, the Holy shrine of Santa Rosalia. Father went in while I stayed outside; I thought he wanted to have some private time with the Lord.'

Her face withdrew a little, but it could have been from concern. I felt her absorption was total from the little knit in her brow. She nodded for me to carry on.

'It was quiet as there were not many tourists about; so we travelled on the bus to the top. Father was behaving strange, Eve. I think the place has a mysterious effect on travellers. Father was in the church for over thirty minutes. I never knew my father was religious because he never went to church, but it seemed to give him something because he was different when he came out.'

'I enjoy going to church,' Eve said. 'You feel as if you have been forgiven.'

'While I waited, I took a walk around the church; it's very beautiful. On the outside, it looks small, but inside it's huge as the church travels back into a cave. It's fascinating because the church is attached to the rocks, half church, half mountain. All this had an influence on us; I found myself thinking about my father, and how troubled he had been. And he has been troubled, Eve. It's me who has been burdening him. I understand now why he wants to see the back of me—'

'No, Aiden, you think wrong. Dominic was only telling me the other evening how much he cares about you and what he could do for you—'

'Really?' I eyed her, not impressed with what she had said.

'He cares about you, Aiden, even if he doesn't say it. I know he cares.'

'No, the truth is, you care for me, not he. But anyhow, it doesn't matter. While I was walking around the church, my head ached, which caused me to worry. Please God, I was saying, don't allow my head to ache now.'

Watching her facial expressions, I could see Eve's thoughts were uncomfortable.

'It was odd, Eve. I don't know how to explain, but I found myself praying for my father, and as I prayed, I saw a light.' I sighed. 'Now I must be hallucinating, but no, I swore there was a light. I watched the light move. Hovering outside, coming towards the church, and then passing through the wall and into the shrine.'

Hastily, and from the side of my eyes, I saw Eve make the sign of the cross.

'What was happening to me? I thought it must be the sun, but when my father appeared, I was surprised when he told me he also had been praying. I never mentioned I had. What do you think happened to me?'

'What happened to you was wonderful.' Eve's eye focused on me as if I was a saint.

My despondent mood lifted.

'You have been blessed to have witnessed something very special and I envy you. I wish the angels would come to me. Oh, how I need their grace.'

'You need forgiveness, but you are one of the sweetness people I have come across.'

'No, if you were to look into my soul, you would think differently.'

'I shall never think differently about you, Eve, ever.' I placed my hand on top of hers. 'But there is something else I must tell you, Eve. Is it possible that I have been healed?'

'How do you mean?'

'You talk about the battle you've had with yourself. You are not the only one; I too have been battling with myself, and it started when Sophia walked out on me.'

'Sophia?'

'Yes, Sophia.'

'I knew you cared for her; I did not realise how much— and I am glad for you.'

'Thank you. But she doesn't want me.'

'Are you certain of that?'

'Then why did she make a pass at my father?'

'Dominic said that never happened, and if it did, it only happened in her mind.'

'Yes, I wonder. I wonder what the actual truth was. You know, I've been thinking that perhaps it wasn't all Sophia's fault, it was my father.'

'No, Aiden, you are wrong about that. Dominic told me —he crossed his heart and swore on the Holy Bible that he never made any overtures to Sophia, and I believe him.'

'Then it's true, I believe him because you believe him; I am so grateful for that.'

So beautiful in her fears, her dark raven hair lying down her back, plaited; she looked like a wandering nereid asking everyone that passed for the right way home.

'Will you come down in a little while to have something to eat? I found the bag that Dominic took with him. And neither of you has eaten anything.'

'Yes, whatever you ask of me, I would gladly do as long as I don't get in my father's way.'

'Why do you say that?'

'I like to say my father loved me once, but I know since he has found you, this family you keep talking about is about you two. As it rightly should be. Eve, please believe me, I am in your way, and I won't be coming with you to Pantelleria. My father told me I would not be welcome. There, I shouldn't have told you, but I have. Though I don't want you thinking badly of him.'

'But why?'

'You two are newlywed and in love while I am thirty-two,' I grinned. 'Just allow me a few days to get myself together, then I will be on the next flight home. Please, don't be upset.' I leaned up and pulled her face towards me, only intending to kiss her on the forehead, but her lips were too near, and I kissed them, gently, softly, and then plunged in.

A kiss pleasurable to us both. When we parted, she looked at me not with hate or anger or anything of that nature, but with surprise. I knew then that if she had not met my father first, it would have been me sipping her love.

Saying nothing else, Eve left my room and went downstairs.

We were to have our dinner on the veranda again. At this time of the year, it was always alfresco. My father was already sitting at the table, his face to the view. In his hand, he held a bottle of red wine. Over half of it was already gone.

We acknowledged each other with a nod as I took my seat next to him. Sitting together for a few minutes was very uncomfortable. I kept my mind on the view.

'I am uncertain what Eve is cooking for dinner,' said my father, pouring himself another glass. 'She said something about fish. Would you like some?' he offered his bottle.

I shook my head.

'Aiden, about this afternoon—'

'I will leave as soon as I can; I trust you will be patient with me, as I've got to get in touch with Sophia to ask her to stock my kitchen with a few things.'

'What happened was just an accident—'

'I made a promise to you which I intend to keep.'

'Do we have to part this way?'

'It's for the best, Father.'

'Because it's hot, I thought we should just have fish and some salad, unless, of course, you want something else,' said Eve, bringing a tray of plates and cutlery.

'Fish will be great,' I said enthusiastically. 'And I am grateful for everything you have done for me—'

'Aiden, please, there is no need to be like that.'

'Aiden believes you don't want him around.' Eve laid

down the tray on the table without looking at her husband. 'I know because I asked. When the two of you arrive back early, I could tell there was something wrong the moment I saw your faces. I had hoped we could be friends. For goodness' sake, Dominic, there are only the two of us. We can't do our lives together with just us two. What will we talk about?'

Hurt by her words, he frowned at Eve as if he had difficulty focusing on her while anger dashed his face. She was irritable, knowing she might have said something out of place and even cruel.

'Of course, I don't mean what I've just said, but there's no reason to send your son away.' Eve fiddled with the dishes.

'Eve, my dear, I am not sending him away, not if he doesn't want to go, but there comes a time for everything—'

'Exactly, a time, the right time, you've heard him say he needs us—'

'I am sorry to interrupt. It's best that I go now. I was being childish and spoilt; please don't argue over me.'

'Aiden, please don't leave now,' said Eve. 'You need to eat. Please don't make me worry about you. Dominic, tell him—'

'Yes, Aiden, come back and have something to eat. There have been a few misunderstandings. We can sort them out before they go any further. It's just a bit of drama. Let us put whatever we feel out of the way. What do you say to that, Aiden?'

Watching and waiting, Eve was seeing how I was taking this.

'Yes, you're right. I have been over-sensitive just lately. I think it has something to do with Sophia—'

'Oh Aiden,' Eve jumped in. 'While I remember, Sophia rang while you were out. She said she would call later, at around ten. She wanted to talk to you urgently.'

Tensions raised, and as the relaxed atmosphere left, we were trying too hard to get on with one another. The conversations now consisting of nothing other than the mundane. Opening a second bottle, my father's conversation rambled on about the conservatory and that perhaps he might visit it one day.

If you knew my father, you would wonder at me, for I was furnishing him with natures he did not possess. And by knowing him, you would think that I was making everything up.

At five to ten, Eve and my father took themselves into the kitchen to give me some privacy. This was a pleasant villa, but it was hardly private.

She rang right on the dot of ten, and I was eager to talk to her to find out why she was calling me. I lifted the receiver straight away.

'Aiden?'

I responded, and then I listened for the reason for her call.

'How are you?'

'Interested as to know why you are calling.'

'Eve, let you know I was going to call?'

'Which is the reason I picked up the telephone. Are you still in my house, Sophia?'

'Yes, of course, I have nowhere else to go. The reason I am calling you is that I want to know how you are.'

'Okay. I might be coming home myself soon.'

'I thought so.'

'And why is that? Even though we were together two years—'

'Nearly four years, Aiden.'

'Okay, four years, I cannot believe that I am that predictable.'

'I've been reading. Do you remember that book on psychology? Well, I finished it. At the back, there are suggestions on what else one should read.'

'Okay, and.'

'I'm thinking of taking up psychology as a profession. I'm interested in it, and it's about time I moved on and did something with my life. I can't do modelling for the rest of my days, it's not natural. Aiden, I want to know how you are, and how things are going for you?'

'Sophia, is this the real reason you've called to analyse me?'

'Aiden, you know I still love you, and what we had was nothing more than a lover's tiff; I'm not upset anymore by the way you behaved because I understand.'

'Yes, you understand because of what you've been reading in the book.'

'Aiden, I should be worried about you. I think there is something deeply disturbing about you. If you were at home, I would suggest you had therapy.'

'Not everything can be treated or cured by analysis. Sometimes people are just who they are. They live, they feel, they think, and when it comes down to it, they react. And that's what I am doing. Situations get thrown at me, and I react in the correct and instinctive way with how I feel.'

'Okay, so can you tell me what is happening?'

'Sophia, what are you doing? There is no interpretation as to life—you just live it. Why don't you find someone who is good to you?'

'Do you want me to?'

It was not a question I was expecting Sophia to ask.

'Aiden, I am worried about you. I just want you to know that you have a friend in me. If there is anything you want to talk about, I won't judge you. This is what friends do. Do you understand that?'

'I understand you are either a saint or a lunatic, whatever, but I thank you all the same.'

'Aiden, I am sincere about this.'

She listened for me to say something more; I didn't.

'I've changed Aiden; I'm not that dumb blonde you chatted to while waiting for a train. I am getting myself together, and I am also envisaging a proper career, and I love this subject. Look, I will ring you tomorrow night, because Aiden, I figured that you of all people need a friend.'

This conversation had a strange effect on me. I guess I had been feeling disconnected from everyone, and completely messed up by my father.

The only problem with Sophia was that I never met her at a train station because I never take trains. So now I must not stop thinking about whom she had met at the station that day.

When the call was over, Eve came out with our evening drinks. We became very homely by habit, although after what had happened, we should not have done. We had got into a familiar habit of drinking bedtime drinks. Father's bedtime drink was added with brandy. Eve looked at me to find out how the call went and then smiled when she saw me smiling.

'Are you back together again?' asked my father, removing the wrapper from a cigar.

'Are you going to smoke that?' Eve looked surprised.

'Do you mind? I won't if you do. Aiden?' he looked at me.

No, I didn't mind; I shook my head quickly.

'I fancied a cigar the other evening; it's a nice way to end a day. I've got things to talk about.'

My father brought out the plans for their new house at

Pantelleria to show Eve. I can see he would have liked to view them on his own with her, but Eve also wanted me to be there. While I watched these two scrutinising the plans, I turned my attention out to the bay. Yes, I had thought about the death of my father because who hasn't? There is nothing unnatural or unusual about that. But what I hadn't speculated on was the idea that he would like to get rid of me. Now, I don't find that natural?

A death had almost happened today with the taking of a life if only symbolically, yet it had happened. I had died in my father's eyes when I saw how he could get on without me. As long as I did not become personal about it, I could see it for what it was—

Looking up. Eve had examined the plans and was now wondering where her garden was going to be; he promised her a garden. How did my father think he was going to keep a beauty like her away from everyone else? I narrowed my eyes. How did he believe he could keep her away from me?

My father was on his way down, still handsome now as some men are, maturing into their looks, which had always been too ruddy before. At that moment, Eve looked at Dominic as he lowered his head. She smiled at him in a way I had never seen before, gentle, kind, but hardly a look of one who was deeply in love. And then her eyes turned to me. That quick bright light lit her eyes, like a flame for me and not my father. Without a doubt, I was the light of attraction. She lowered her lashes and then took them back up to gaze at me once more; it happened so quickly.

I know what that look was saying. Please take me away from him; I am waiting for you.

What was I going to do? I felt the fates asking me now. They had given my father his chance, and he had used it.

There could only be one man in Eve's life, and that was me; I looked now at my father.

He had no grievance in putting his arm about Eve and kissing her on the cheek, happy with what his intentions were for me. Relaxed and happy and pulling her closer to him, he had no conscience about what he had wanted to do to me. If Sophia was concerned about there being something wrong with me, she ought to look at my father.

Eve glanced at me and whispered something in Dominic's ear. He released her.

'I'm going to bed now,' said my father, looking at Eve.

'I've just got to finish up in the kitchen,' said Eve without looking at Dominic collecting the cups together. 'I shall follow you up in less than five minutes.'

'Goodnight, Aiden,' he nodded to me. 'Don't make it too late either for bed.'

Neither Eve nor I said anything. Our thoughts were charged as we waited for my father to leave. Hearing his foot on the stairs, I sighed. She sighed and then we looked at each other and giggled in relief. We were children and our father had gone to bed. Well, that's how it felt. This was our time to talk.

When she asked how I was feeling now, I knew what she was really asking.

'Better,' I said. 'I am not so stressed as I was.'

'Good,' she smiled as if pleased with herself. 'I was looking at the plans with Dominic, and there's plenty of space. I am hoping there will be enough for you.'

Frowning was a cause for an explanation.

'You will come and live with us and have your own living quarters. A bedroom, perhaps even two bedrooms in case you have visitors, your own kitchen and, if you want, your own staff.'

'You have thought of everything.' A smile covered my lips with limited generosity. I had been factored in as if I was a part of a problem. 'You must see that it's never going to work?'

Her brow buckled; she did not understand quite what I meant; her plans were nicely arranged as if she had been laying the table for dinner. What do I say to her to make her understand I am a living creature and not a toy?

'I am thirty-two, as you remember. I cannot come and live with you, as my father so rightly pointed out; it would be like two dogs with a bitch. Please excuse the analogy. I appreciate your consideration. It will be better if I returned to Sophia. Besides, you are happy here with my father, and I am glad for you. Anyhow, it's time I went to bed.'

This had been one hell of a day, with every rule being broken. I was still figuring out who I was. But there was one thing that I knew—Eve must know that I was going to have her.

13

Before arising, I lay in bed listening to the commotion downstairs. My father had made a snap decision to take Eve with him to choose some furnishings. Eve came hurriedly to my room and told me what was happening and if I would be okay. Her concern amused me because now I didn't know what to make of it. She was going to leave me something in the refrigerator and told me I must eat. Of course, I would obey such pretty commands, especially with her concerns for me. Then the phone rang.

'Aiden, is that you? I thought I would call you earlier.'

Another female was using their time to be thoughtful about me, but is their concern a problem? I was trying to work this one out.

'Okay, so what's the matter this time?'

'I believe you're going through some sort of crisis. Aiden, you need to talk to someone. Your headache has hysterical roots.'

'How did you know about my headache? I never told you.'

'I know, Eve told me. She is also worried about you.' Was Sophia wearing her spectacles?

'Why is everyone worried about me? There is nothing wrong with me.'

I wasn't angry; I was more surprised, but I listened to Sophia and trusted her because of our history. In the end, everyone needs someone to talk to, and a kind ear can make all the difference. The promise I made to my father about what happened on the mountainside was about to be broken because I needed someone to talk to. I need to tell Sophia the whole truth.

'So, what do you think?' I asked when I'd finished. 'Do you believe my father weighed up the consequences of my death, preferring me more dead than alive? Do you think he knows I have an interest in Eve?'

'I think you should come home straightaway, Aiden. I can't say for sure what his intentions were on the mountainside, but jealousy is one of those primaeval instincts where people react without considering the consequences. If you had died on the mountain, he would tell his masculine instincts that it was one of those tragic accidents because, frankly, it would suit him. I believe he would sacrifice you to save his manhood. I call it the "Cronus syndrome." Which is a pathological fear of being replaced. Cronus ate all his children, except Zeus, who managed to escape.'

'I understand, but I have not yet been eaten by my father. If you had listened, you would know he saved me.'

'Yes, he did this time, but there will be a next time and with each time, his resolve to kill you will become stronger. I believe your father would justify himself with your death and never face up to the fact that he wanted you dead. He would deny any part in it except that your death was a tragic accident. You must come home, Aiden; you could be in great danger.'

'Thank you for your concerns. I will return home but not yet. I don't quite agree with you your interesting theory. You have certainly been thinking about me. But I am not finished with him yet. I need to spend some time with my father. I need to find out—'

'Okay,' Sophia sighed. 'I will call you again tomorrow night. I will try earlier, but if I can't get you—'

'Yes, I get the picture.'

My day, while I waited for Eve and my father, was one of leisure. I ate the meal on the veranda in my lap, idly gazing at the view while lazily picking at the hasty meal that Eve had put together. She found a tin of something and opened it; I guess. While I, in my investigations, tried to figure out what it was. Some sort of ham or it could have been beef; I had tasted nothing like it before.

The sun was heating up nicely on my stretched-out legs, which were turning a delicate shade of brown. Balancing my feet on the wooden railing, I mused to myself about the pleasures of setting up home here. The climate was wonderful, the people non-interfering and the houses quaint, but I could only do this with Eve. She decorated my life so prettily. How lucky my father was to have a willing spirit such as herself. I was thinking this while enjoying the view when I looked up from my plate to wonder what that noise was and where it was coming from. And do you know, it was my feet rattling the rails. Kicking again, I heard a repeat of the sound. Sitting up, I pushed the railing again. A wooden fracture was most noticeably threatening to break.

When Eve and my father returned home, there was a difference in their moods. The nervousness that Eve had displayed only hours ago was discarded by recklessness.

'Your father spent a fortune on me.' She took me by the hand and led me to their bedroom. 'Look, look,' she pointed to the box where lay the red stones. Big, beautiful red rubies.

'I prefer to see them on the owner.'

My father and his money, I realised, were always going to be the winner, but my day will come.

'You must wait here then while I try them on. I can't possibly wear them in this yellow dress, the colour would do nothing for them. I shall change into something else. I know which colour to wear, one of my black dresses. No peeping now.'

They used a side room as a dressing room. Their bedroom was the best room in the house because not only was it large, but it also looked out and on to the bay. Very nice. I nodded approval to Eve. While she escaped into the dressing room and shut the door, I thought of my father's money.

The view was even more spectacular from here. Now I understand why my father chose to rent this house. I turned a corner around the bed. So, she decided she was in love with my father again. How fickle women are.

'I won't be too long, Aiden,' Eve called out. 'I need to get the dress right to do justice to them. You will wait for me?'

'I will wait,' I smiled, lending an interested eye to the room and its contents.

Looking around someone's room is always fascinating, as it is surprising. I had known my father as being aloof, but here I was finding something else about him. He had allowed a female to take over his world because tumbling here and hanging over there was an impressive display of femininity. While my father, not a completely humble man, had only one side of the room with his sombre possessions. A jacket on a coat hanger waiting to be put away, and two pairs of shoes that were not needed because they were town style. While on the other side and displayed were several vivacious dresses, free and wild as they were exotic, had been laid on the furniture with meaning. Obviously, none of these dresses suited her, so what was the dress she had picked?

A dressing table and a stall behind it, waiting for their mistress to sit. I could almost picture her in front of the mirror looking at the reflection, knowing it would never disappoint. Did my father brush her long raven dark locks? No, that would be something I would do.

Hanging from a glass container was a structure to hold certain items, mainly junk jewellery, earring, and rings; I recognise these items; these were the type of jewellery Sophia liked to wear. I would soon make her get rid of them. Perhaps this was what my father was trying to do. Women are notoriously fond of their junk.

'I'm nearly ready,' Eve cried from her closet.

'Okay,' I returned, not unduly worried because I was fascinating myself on her personal effects.

Sophia's possessions were peculiarly tacky, nor was she a tidy person; stacked up in any corner was always a pile of glossy magazines. Once I found one stuffed underneath our pillow, I was acutely angry with her and banned her from reading ever again in our bedroom. We had a strange argument after that about the sacredness of the bedroom.

Tipping my eyes over her wardrobe and her other paraphernalia without touching it was rather gratifying. Don't touch came that little voice inside my head warning me that this was a ladies' chamber. I smiled and went back to her bureau and noticed that one of her drawers was ajar. What did she keep in here? Underwear perhaps? Curiously no, stationery and letters. What letters would she be receiving?

There would be none of my fathers. From what I understood, Eve and my father had met at a party. Love at first sight, and then instant marriage. Hardly the sort of thing my father would normally jump into, but Eve was no normal person.

'I won't be a moment. I thought I would put some shoes on first,' Eve called out. 'Rubies don't go with bare feet.' And then she giggled.

'That's fine with me,' I mused, peeping into her draw, for a name caught my eye.

Gerard. I saw the name Gerard. The name of her first husband. Too much temptation to resist. I slid open the drawer and saw the paper I glimpsed was the death certificate of Gerard D Sheppard.

How did he die?

Taking up the paper, aware that at any moment, Eve would come out to show me how the rubies suited her. My curiosity was greater than my fears of what I was doing.

Death certificates are not as impressive as they sound; the entirety of one's life is added with one flourish and as for Gerard. D. Sheppard, his death had come from a knife wound and had been referred to as one of those dreadful accidents.

'Oh dear,' called out Eve. 'I don't do the rubies justice, but never mind, I am coming out, so be prepared.'

The door opened to reveal Eve looking beyond compare in a low-cut black sequin gown. And then I saw why she was so pleased and merry. Rubies, my father, had bought her a necklace and bracelet with matching earrings. Even the colour of the stones coordinated perfectly, enhancing Eve's beauty severalfold.

'What do you think?' she smiled, feeling pleased with herself. Her innocence was overpowering. 'I tried to put my hair up to make myself look grand, but it really is too heavy to do that. Are you okay? You look very pale. Do you have a headache, or do you want to lie down?'

'No Eve,' I grinned. 'Don't you understand what you have done?'

A frown galloped across her brow as she worried at what displeased me.

'You have managed to look more beautiful than the rubies. How is that possible?'

'It is possible because you are a wonderful man. You see beauty in the ugliest.'

'We are not going to argue. You are astonishingly lovely; there is no argument about that.'

Dancing in front of her mirror, pleased at the decorations, this was another side to Eve that I approved of and found interesting.

Leaving the bedroom, she ran downstairs. I followed.

'What do you think?' Eve stood in front of Dominic for his opinion.

'As I knew it would be before you put on the jewels, perfect, my dear.'

Of course, it was the husband's right to kiss his wife, and yet, I could not bear his lips on hers where mine should have been. How was I going to get her from him when I didn't possess the fortune he inherited? Not wanting to see this affection, I left the room and returned to my bedroom. I was torn between staying and leaving. But if I was to leave Italy, it would be with Eve on my arm.

If I had hoped that Eve would pander to me again by coming to my room to find out if I was okay, then I was cruelly disappointed. Quite simply, she did not indulge this big child anymore. Lying on my bed plotting and planning my schemes that would never work because of the lack of money, I waited for Eve's light touch. Waiting forever before realising that it was me who must go down to them. One day—

Outside on the veranda, I saw the two of them by the trellis staring at the horizon. In those several seconds, I wondered at their future together and how long it was going to last. He could not satisfy this woman forever.

It's preposterous for a man like my father, as handsome as he is to marry a woman over twenty years younger than himself. Oh, I know people have married others where age has shown the same sort of discrepancy and more, and yet for my father to have taken a woman so beautiful as Eve was a mortal sin.

'Aiden,' at last, Eve turned for what other reason than instinct. She caught my ugly eyes watching. 'I didn't know you were standing there; you should have said.'

I should have forewarned her. The hurt in her voice seemed to suggest I might have seen something I wasn't meant to.

'Eve,' snapped my father, in a warning. 'Take your hand off that rail. It's not safe.'

Moving away quickly as if she had been burnt, her child-like eyes were grateful to Dominic. 'Aiden's here. Look how patiently he's been waiting; the perfect gentleman.'

'I raised my son to be a gentleman; I should expect no less from him.'

She smiled and stretched up to touch his lips. 'I had better get us some dinner.'

Before leaving, Eve pulled Dominic down low enough to kiss his forehead, so different from the kiss I had witnessed earlier, and the way she looked at my father was different, too. I knew she didn't love him. She might feel gratitude, but that never replaces love, not real love. Leaving the room, her eyes glanced quickly to mine, but returned to Dominic. What was this she was trying to show me? Another glance at me before she disappeared into the villa. And I could see Dominic all puffed up and proud. Some words had been said between them, which I could only guess at. Promises had been made. I thought of Eve and looked at my father; they both lied.

My father had been waiting for Eve to leave before presenting me with the next bit of information.

'I have decided to take Eve on another honeymoon.' From his jacket pocket, my father produced a cigar.

'A honeymoon? Why another one?' he was doing this deliberately, separating us. He knew.

'Nevertheless, I am taking her away again because we need a break. A man and his young wife need to be together.'

This was it. I squared myself up to my father; he was trying to save her from me. But I would fight for her. I knew who she preferred.

'Would you like a cigar?' He offered, challengingly.

There was nothing I could do about it; Eve was his wife, not mine.

'I am sorry, Father, but I don't want you to go. In fact, I forbid it.'

Picking up the lighter, he regarded me. At that moment, I was that annoying insect as he puffed at his cigar until it caught.

'Yes, I thought you would say that. When I first married Eve, I suspected you would have a problem with my new wife.'

'She is too good for you.'

'No, we are perfectly matched,' he looked at me with his head cocked to one side with something like speculation.

'She is over twenty years younger than you.'

'While I have twenty years more wisdom than Eve.'

'Let me put it this way. When you gather complaints as an old man does, she will not like pushing you around in a wheelchair. And when you forget who she is, she will never forgive you.'

'I have something already you will never have or not for many years; I have money, and it's money Eve loves more in life because it makes her feel safe. That's something you can't give her with your youth.'

'What makes you think she is not attracted to my youth instead of your money? Do you want to put it to the test?'

'No, Aiden, I know you will always win in the end, but I love her. And I know how to take care of her. I have loved no one as much as I love Eve. While you think you love her, and it probably feels like you love her, you can't take care of her as I can. And Eve needs to be taken care of. Don't you understand, Aiden?'

Now he was imploring me, holding his hands out, trying to get me to understand.

I stood back from his poisonous hands, hands that had only in the last moment decided to save me. These were my father's hands.

'If you loved Eve, which I am sure you believe you do?' Dominic said dispassionately, yet carefully detaching himself from me began again after exhaling a rush of blue smoke. 'Let her go to someone who understands her, and who can take care of her.'

'And you know how to take care of her?'

'Yes.' He was emphatic. 'I love Eve, Aiden. I am not talking to you as your father, but as man to man. One day when you find that special person, you will know what I am talking about. You will feel it here,' he punched his heart.

I shook my head. I didn't want to hear what he had to say, and suddenly it felt like I could not breathe. Air was what I needed. I needed to go further outside and on to the wooden platform of the veranda. It was out there in the dark night where I felt I could get enough oxygen to breathe. Almost in passionate tears, I looked at the skies and prayed to be free.

'Aiden, I know you love her; I am not so cold as to not understand that. You love her as it's possible for you to love her because she is beautiful. While I want to grow old with her; I don't care if she becomes ugly.'

Everything my father said was repellent. He wanted to put his old hands on her, to touch and possess her.

'Time will heal you; I promise. We will go away, and you will forget her. You will think of Sophia and remember how happy you once were with her.'

'Never,' I said, feeling the temper rising and burning my soul. 'Never.'

'Days will pass, time will ease your passions. Aiden, please. Please let her go.'

'Never,' I shouted. How could he ever think that I would forget her? I felt the flames of passion injuring me. He believed he had the right to take whatever he wanted from me; well, I would not let him. I pushed out to him to make him go away, to shut him up for good. 'Just shut up,' I shouted.

How was it possible that he was caught off balance by my push? My father fell back while he looked at me. Spinning and stumbling. The cigar in his hand flew up as a wand and then went crashing back down again as his hands, his beautiful hands stretched out to me.

'Aiden? What have you done—'

Yes, what had I done? I looked at his hands. I saw my

hands held out to him and then I saw how he had looked at me and the freedom he would have had if he had let me go. He had decided then, and now it was my turn to decide. And I decided.

He could not stop himself and he was right—the banister was unsafe. It snapped. I saw him stretch out to grab the remaining banister, which creaked. His feet slipped off the veranda and in desperation, he clung onto the rail, hanging with one arm while looking up at me. He was afraid. The post cracked as it came away from the planks.

'Help me, Aiden—remember how I saved you?'

I froze and watched him hanging there. I could not move. I watched as he yelled for help and waited as the rest of the rail broke from the posts. He fell, still clutching the rail.

The black night swallowed him up, disposing of him for me. The night and I had made a pact in that what I did not want, it would take care of.

Not able to figure out what had happened to him, he was here one moment and then he was gone. But a man like that never disappears. The law of logic says he can't while the law of physics says it's impossible. I was confused.

He would be back in a moment. I would not trouble myself with too much care, climbing up the cliffs and ranting at me, saying I had made his clothes dirty. Yes, he would be back.

No, Aiden, this time you have done it. This time, there is a mess that even your father can never clear up for you.

I looked at the veranda which had held so many parties, which gave safe dimensions to our world and then, in one swift temper, took our security away. The fence was broken, leaving a shaggy mouth of waiting promises.

My father never screamed, peering over the edge. My

father never made a sound, but went to his inevitable death. As in a mist of doubt and truth, I couldn't understand why he was not coming back up. I know what this is. I nodded, moving even closer to the edge; this is my father getting back at me, his way of frightening me, and I was scared. He had won—this big man in life always wins.

But don't you understand Aiden what this means? Without your father, you will be free to do what you want; you will be your own man and take over where he left off. Eve can now be yours.

Should I smile and clap my hands? The temptation to know where he had gone found me on the edge and looking over into the deep darkness of the sea. Was he down there staring back up at me? I could see nothing.

'What would you two like for dinner?'

Eve stood. I turned to explain when dear old gravity checked me out for resistance; my ankle went, and my foot slipped. I stretched out and screamed as my body pulled me down.

'Aiden,' Eve screamed. So quick to happen, so far to fall, I who wanted to hold on to life had struck out catching the edge of the balcony. A swinging piece of wood was holding on to me. A hundred and twenty feet of jutting cliffs and I was left hanging.

'But, Eve, I deserve to die?'

14

'Aiden, quickly, pass me your hand.'

This was the one hand that promised to save me and here I was, giving it to someone else.

'You've got to help me, Aiden. I need you to help me pull you up. I am not as strong as you, but we can do it together.'

Was she going to take hold of my hand to throw me off? I couldn't see hope anywhere except the desire to live.

Oh, my father, I had killed my father.

'Well done, Aiden; we are lifting you up together. Just one more little pull and you will be there; you will be okay.'

I grabbed the deck as if a panacea for a man's cries, and like a hunger, I would eat at anything to live. Sitting on the deck now, I stared at the balcony of the world. Too afraid to stand, I crawled into the house.

'Oh Aiden, you are safe now. Nothing is going to hurt you again.'

I pulled myself up to sit on a chair and there I shook.

With dark grey eyes, Eve considered me. Hurrying to the kitchen, and then back again, bringing me a glass and a bottle of brandy. I heard the spirit pouring into the glass and then she held the glass to my lips.

'Drink,' Eve commanded. 'You need to drink.'

My teeth chattered on the glass; my head bobbed around on the rim as I tried to obey her command.

'Everything is okay now. You are safe, Aiden. Do you understand?'

She felt my hands and then my head, and then she disappeared again to bring me a blanket, wrapping it around my shoulders. In shock, my body had thrown out the heat of my core; would I ever be warm again?

In between that blanket, she came and sat on my lap, putting her arms around my neck to hug me.

'Oh Aiden, please come out of the shock,' she whispered in my ears. 'Don't forget to live.'

I don't know how much brandy I drank, but nothing of that heady mess of thoughts did anything for me. And then I heard the telephone being dialled.

'Polizia per favore. C'è stato un incidente.' After giving the address, Eve returned the handset to its cradle.

'What did you do that for?'

She had betrayed me.

'Because we have to.' She said, returning to me. 'It was an accident, Aiden.'

'I killed my father.'

'No, you didn't kill your father. Your father was involved in an accident, tragic, but it still was an accident. These sorts of things happen when one least expects it.'

'I could not save him.'

'Yes, I know. It was never your fault. There was nothing you could do. He fell, Aiden, the fence broke when he leaned on it.'

And in my head were the words that I had pushed him. My father never leaned on the railing; it was me who pushed him to send him to his death. But why was Eve so cold? No tears and no regrets to say she had lost her husband.

'He was explaining to me the fence was dangerous.' Eve was talking to the police. The police officer could, fortunately, speak some English. 'His son, Aiden, tried to save Dominic,' she looked to me. 'I saw what happened when I was coming out. Both father and son were very close to each other. In fact, Aiden was coming to live with us when we moved. We were going to Pantelleria; it is supposed to be very beautiful there,' she smiled.

Someone called for the doctor, as I was not responding as I should. The shock had got to me. How I had got upstairs, quite honestly, I have no idea.

'Will he be, okay?' I heard Eve say from somewhere across the room.

And then the world went silent as the cold pierce of a needle allowed me to find the bottom of my fall.

'How are you feeling now?' Eve brought a tray into my bedroom.

Opening my eyes, I felt so much relief the nightmare was over.

'I had this awful dream. I thought my father was dead.'

She put the tray down and came to look at me.

'Aiden, you will have to face up to reality. Your father fell off the balcony last night, and there was nothing you could do.'

'It was real?'

'Yes, it was real?' her serious head nodded. 'Your father is dead; he died on impact. You've got to accept this.'

'Then, it's my fault.'

'No, it's not your fault. It was a tragic accident, but at least he died quickly. He didn't know any pain.'

'I can't believe he's not coming back.' I dragged my eyes across her face to look through the windows. The shutters were open. Something I was grateful for. And then I returned to her face, aware that as a wife, she had just been widowed. 'How are you?'

'Me?' she smiled, pleased to hear that I was returning to the living. 'I don't know. I think I am finding it difficult to believe as well. When I left you, Dominic smiled at me. I never knew this was going to be the last time I would see him.'

'It must have been a shock.'

'Yes, it was a shock, but when I saw you hanging on for dear life, I realised I could have lost you as well. I don't know what we are going to do without Dominic, but I have a feeling we will manage. The police could not get to this body last night, so they came to collect him this morning.'

'Did you see him?'

'The police said it was not wise, but I saw him when I looked out of our bedroom window before they came to pick him up. He looked nothing like himself. I was surprised, yet I don't know what I expected to see.' She paused and looked at me. 'Well, your father,' she explained, 'was someone special. I have never come across anyone quite like him—he was—extraordinary. Try to eat something,' she went to the table and place it on my lap. 'It will help you make better sense of the world.'

'Have you eaten?'

'Oh yes,' she smiled. 'One has to eat; one owes it to oneself to take back the reins because if you don't, someone else will. I should know.'

She tapped at my plate where a couple of slices of toasted bread lay.

'Eat up, the police will be here soon.'

'Why the police?' I was startled and worried.

'Someone has died in a sudden and violent manner, and they need to have answers to his death. It's just a formality; I have been through this many times; it's routine. Just tell them what happened, and you will be all right. That's all we can do. And then,' she scratched her head. 'Then we can get on with our lives.'

'I can't believe my father has gone.'

'No, neither can I. The next thing we have to do is to give him a burial. I am not sure if this is my responsibility or yours.'

I looked aghast. The obligation to my father for the disposal of his remains, when I was unprepared to accept, he was gone, was a thought I rejected with no consultation. Eve noticed this.

'We will do this together.' Her eyes softened with a smile. 'Doing everything together now will give us strength.'

Her smiling face belied her grief, as was the rest of her temperament. She had shown no feelings to reveal her loss or that her life would be incomplete without her husband. I was almost tempted to ask if she was pleased he was gone.

The interview with the police was difficult. Eating my dinner, on the following day, I spoke to Eve about it.

'But you should look at it like the police are doing a thorough job. You would not like it if they went through the procedure with no feeling. Oh, by the way, Sophia telephoned you earlier this morning when you were asleep. I hope you don't mind, but I told her about Dominic. She was shocked, of course, and then she asked how I was. Which I thought was kind. Perhaps she could come for the funeral; we really don't have any friends, so it will be lonely.'

'Funeral? Where? In this country?'

'Why? Did you want to take him back to England? It would be very expensive.'

'It may well be, but my father had plenty of money. He has always had the best in life, so why should it change now?'

Looking at me with those beautiful clear grey eyes, candid now in her expression as if what she was going to say was already well rehearsed.

'Aiden, Dominic expressed to me once that he would like to be buried here in Italy. He said there were too many unwelcome reminders for him back home. So, I think we should honour his last wish. The ceremony will be beautiful and quite simple. Oh, there goes the telephone.' she looked at the telephone on the other side of the room. 'It will be for you, of course. It's strange. I keep on imagining that Dominic is going to come out from the other room, complain about the phone and then answer it. So difficult to get used to life without him.'

Grateful to leaving the table, and away from the funeral feeling that was lying everywhere, I answered the phone.

'I'm so sorry, Aiden about Dominic. When Eve told me about the accident, I was shocked. How are you? How are you managing? I can't believe he is gone. He was larger than life, and a great man. He will be missed by me as well.'

'Thank you, Sophia. It's hard to say how I am feeling. Sometimes, I want to get a knife and cut myself to see if this is real. I have never come across a pain quite like this before. I keep on saying to myself that he is gone and then I question, is he really gone? And then I see my father sitting at the table eating dinner with Eve. He is not there, yet his image is still transmitted. Do you think I am going mad?'

'No, Aiden, absolutely not. You are in grief. You don't want to accept what has happened, hence the struggle, and then you are given the facts. What exactly happened? Eve never told me, and I didn't want to ask.'

'He fell off the balcony.'

'What—he fell off the balcony, how?' she went on as if she was questioning the truth about it. 'How did he manage to do that?'

'The railing was rotten. When he stepped backwards, he fell on to the wooded balustrade which gave way. I was just talking to him. It happened so quickly, too quickly for me to react.'

'Oh my God, that sounds awful. And you watched him fall?'

'Yes. There was nothing I could do. It happened so quickly. I just cannot believe he has gone.'

'A big man like that to go so quickly. I see what you mean. It doesn't make any sense.'

Sophia was thinking. Her speculating mind was patrolled with critical thoughts, for Sophia was not the type of person to let things go at their first introduction. Sophia wanted to know more of what the people were thinking about at the scene of the incident.

'Funny, isn't it,' although in this case, I think Sophia meant it ironically? 'Only a few days ago, your father was also trying to decide whether to save you. What was that Aiden?'

For I had cried like a girl. A high-pitched scream was sucked in with my breath as I held on to my mouth, trying not to break down and cry.

'Aiden? Was that you? Aiden, are you all right? Aiden, tell me the truth about what happened that night.'

I stood there sobbing and gargling, trying to keep my voice down so Eve could not hear. Trying to make sense of what had happened. My father was smoking his cigar. We were talking about the future. While that future was about to end for him, Sophia was listening without comment. Then I was looking for him over the side.

'He was gone, Sophia. I didn't even have the chance to say goodbye to him. And I didn't have the chance to tell him I had always loved him. I pushed him. Sophia, I pushed him too hard that he hit the railing and could not stop himself. I didn't mean to, but he made me angry. It was me who killed him. I am a murderer. And then when he was hanging there desperate asking me for help, I was thinking about whether to help him. I killed him, Sophia. It was me.'

And then when the tears were drenched as the appetite filled, I stopped.

'That's it, Sophia. Tell me what you think I should do. Go to the police and confessed to them? Let them put me in prison and lock me away forever.' I waited.

'It was an accident, Aiden, just one of those accidents. You didn't mean it. Dominic provoked you; it could have been the other way around. What would happen if he pushed you? It would have been you that fell over the side to your death. I am sorry, Aiden, that this should have happened to you. You must put it behind you like you do everything else and catalogue it under tragic accidents,' and then she stopped to think. For thinking was what Sophia was good at. 'Are you certain that Eve knows nothing about the accident?'

'No, why?'

'Because I don't trust her. She was Dominic's wife and no

matter what she says to you about being on your side. Her loyalty will still be with Dominic. You don't know if she is angry at you for killing her husband. You have taken everything away from her. Her status, company, a way of life and now a future with no money. Think about it. Please be wise and cautious. I don't trust her because everyone is subject to change.'

'I trust her.'

'Just wait until these things get sorted out with the police and the funeral is over. Do you know if your father made a will out?'

'As far as I know, everything has still been left to me. And I mean, everything.'

'Which means he hasn't had time to get around to making the will in Eve's favour. Aiden, do you think she knows you are going to get everything?'

'What are you saying?'

'I don't trust her. Yes, I like her, but I still don't trust her. It's better to be cautious when there is a great deal of money involved.'

'Do you believe I intentionally tried to kill my father, Sophia? I couldn't move, I couldn't think.'

She was silent, as if she did not want to commit herself.

'Tell me, Sophia, what do you think? I want to know what you think. It's important.'

'I believe you wanted your father dead. I think in that moment when he was about to fall, you thought to yourself, at last, you were free of him. But you did not kill him, Aiden. The problem was that you had no time to consider whether you should save him. It was all down to reflexes. If anything killed him; it was reflexes.'

'That sounds like some sort of witch's spell.'

'Yes,' she said. 'What it all boils down to is, do you

believe you killed him? It is up to you to decide. If you believe you killed him, you will punish yourself, and punish yourself without mercy.'

'I don't believe I killed him.'

'Then you are acquitted.'

Putting down the receiver came with a resolve. For now, it depended on what I thought and felt. Sophia was right. If I wanted to punish myself for my convinced guilt, then I would open that door to a life of torment. But to live my life without guilt, was that possible? Did I want to go through my life feeling nothing about my father? But his life was done and dusted, giving me the chance to have a life. But how would I live my life without this man who I had always wanted to be? For most of my life had been in a relief to my father. If he did this, then I would do that. This is how I determined my identity. Now I would have to identify myself on my own with no help from the old man. Was he already now looking down on me, and saying, it's difficult, isn't Aiden when you have always been trying to be me?

'How did it go with Sophia?' asked Eve when I returned to the dinner table. Her eyes were like butterflies fluttering all over my face.

'I told Sophia what happened. You probably heard me crying from the other room.'

'No,' she smiled lightly. 'That was your private business.'

'Thank you, Eve.' I was very glad she was kind to me.

Taking my seat again at the table, I was certain that her plate would be cleared. I had been away long enough, but she had eaten nothing. A lack of appetite was to be expected, and yet, she had eaten her breakfast. What Sophia had said to me came into focus. Don't trust Eve.

'I will be glad when this is all over. I've been here before,' Eve said, picking up her fork and poking her food. 'It always happens like this at the end of a life.' Turning her head, she looked out to the balcony. 'Do you believe in ghosts, Aiden?'

'No,' I shook my head because now I was severely spooked.

'When everything is finished here, we must go on holiday together and forget about this awful business.'

Regarding Eve's beautiful face, with her long dark raven hair plaited on her back. I realised again that she had shown no signs of grieving. Yet another thought puzzled me. Why did she still want to go on holiday with me? It should have been with Dominic, but she was happy enough to go with me. My demons had already started to fight with me.

She had not cried once she remained completely steadfast. Surely it must be natural to have some feelings of loss. But she showed none. Why was that? Had she ever said that she loved my father? I didn't remember anything of her displays of love for Dominic except gratitude. While my father, you only had to look into his eyes to see how much he loved her. But did it matter now? Did it matter what her feelings were for my father when I was in love with her? I don't know.

The police had put up a temporary support to block our exit to the veranda so there wouldn't be another accident. The following day, a car pulled up in front of the villa and a man climbed out. Intimidating in his hard black suit and steely blue waistcoat, a black Fedora, with a matching steel blue band around it. He looked very slim in his dark clothes, with a black cape hung on his shoulders. Looking up at the villa, he had an ominous look in his eyes. Coming to the front door, he knocked with his walking stick and poked something with his black pointed shoes.

'I'd better answer the door,' said Eve hurriedly.

A stranger visiting made me shudder. I stayed back and

hoped that Eve would tell him to leave. Five minutes later, she came back furious.

'Who does he think he is?' her brow was a mass of sharp lines as she pulled out her chair without looking at me to sit down. 'Making me believe it was my fault.'

'What was all that about?' I picked up the glass; I had been drinking water from.

'Stupid to come here, idiotic.' Eve's face twitched with enraged expressions, her eyes blazing, while her lips were drawn together in a scowl.

'He was the owner of this property. He has come to me when I am in grief, thinking that is the best time to threaten me. I can't believe the cheek he has. He wants me to know that it was not his fault because as far as he knew the railings were made of steel and completely safe and then he asked what I had done to these railings. He's threatening to take me to court over this. Then do so, I told him. I shall meet you also in court for cheap and unsafe housing electrical equipment. This place is a death trap. Then we will see who wins from that?'

'This man is taking you to court for the death of your husband?'

'Yes, this is when the rats come out.' Eve turned to me, her eyes flashing with defiance. 'I shall not be beaten into submission ever again, Aiden. Do you understand me? Men think me weak, but I am not. I shall fight like a lioness. And I shall get myself the best lawyer.' Then she stood and left, slamming the door behind her.

After she went, I sat thinking silently in my chair, turning over the pages in my mind and wondering about the consequences. It was something which Sophia said that bothered me. For some peculiar reason only known to herself, Sophia wanted to know the state of the wooden rails when I told her about the rails breaking. What troubled her was what I said had happened, was to her a work of fiction. Had Eve led Dominic to the fence, knowing that it was only a matter of time before there would be an accident? Because I had told Sophia about that time when my father said he was worried about the fence and how he wanted to replace it. Perhaps Sophia had unintentionally whispered damaging suspicions into my mind as I transferred the thoughtful scene as a possibility.

'Leave it for now, Aiden,' Eve stepped back in to the room. 'Why should I take responsibility for someone else's problems?' argued Eve, her hands on her hips and looking like fury.

'It might be easier for the moment—'

'And that is precisely what he wants us to do—cave in. I will not do that anymore. I've had enough of being passive, and I have had enough of being walked over.'

'I hear what you are saying, but we are in a foreign country. Please let us drop it; it was an accident, just an awful accident. If I could change everything, I would have my father back.' I put my hand over my eyes. I had had enough.

'Oh, Aiden, I forgot.'

A pair of arms wrapped around me. I felt her heat, her perfume stung my nose while her small, yet powerful strength covered me.

'My poor Aiden, I forgot how much your father meant to you. I will drop the court action if this robber promises to do the same.'

Her face, her lips, were so close to mine that if I had stretched up, I could have pulled her into another one of those kisses. But my father had passed just over thirty hours ago and here I was, threatening to take his young wife to bed.

'We have got to be strong, Aiden,' she took hold of my hand and squeezed. 'You see how it is when you are in another country, you are vulnerable, and this is their opportunity to take advantage of you. No, I shall threaten him; it is the only way to be. Please, Aiden,' she turned to face me with all the charms of an angel. 'We have to stay together; we must not fight between ourselves because we shall lose everything. Do you understand, Aiden?'

That night, as I lay in bed trying to find relief in sleep, in my mind, I saw the picture of the wooden railing. Earlier, when I examined it briefly, curious and covering myself with fault, I noticed a deeper breakage which I swore hadn't been there before, as if someone had put some tool to it to force the railing to fracture. A little tear sharpened by a knife. There was an artful purpose to this deft workmanship. My God, I gasped, for deep in my heart, I suspected foul play.

No, I shook my head, seeing the beautiful face of the obvious person. This was impossible. And then I remembered her first husband's death certificate. He died from a knife wound, and this too had been an accident. But how had this happened? Had he seen a knife and had run into it? An impossible task, for there must be an easier way of dying without causing too much pain.

'Aiden? Are you awake?'

Coming quickly to attention, Eve was tapping lightly on my door.

'Yes, I am awake. What do you want?' I sat up.

'To talk to you,' her voice was like that of a child.

'Then, please come in.'

The door opened as a figure in white gently closed the door to make her way to willing ears. She looked across in my direction. I could see her face by the light of the moon from the uneven shutters.

'I'm over here,' I called gently. I was smiling. She looked exquisite, her eyes two wide plates of innocence.

'I can't see you, Aiden. I'm sorry if I awoke you.'

'No, you didn't wake me. I was thinking.'

'Oh?' she said, patting for the area where she could sit. 'And what were you thinking about?'

'I'll give you a guess.'

'Oh yes, the same here.'

Waiting for her to continue came the realisation that she needed a prompt.

'And what were you thinking about?'

'You are going to think me an opportunist, but I have found out that I don't have any money. The banks have taken this opportunity to freeze all accounts. And I have nothing, absolutely nothing, even though I was Dominic's wife.' Her laughter was ironic. 'Like you, I depended completely on Dominic. Aiden, would you mind if I got into bed beside you? I feel cold.'

Well, what do you think I said? Sophia's side of the bed hardly moved to say that another had joined me. Should I touch her and pull her towards me? No, somehow, I didn't think so.

'Didn't you have any money of your own?'

'Let me say that once upon a time, I had sufficient, but I had to spend it.'

'Okay.'

It felt strange as I lay in bed with my father's wife. Things didn't feel right; the flaming passion which drew life when I saw her had reduced me to a candle, telling me this was not the time to be the man, but to treat Eve with respect. We had become children in the same bed together.

Should I press any further with my investigations? Perhaps the time had ceased when we should remain vague to each other. Now was the time to throw away the old rule sheets and start afresh.

Pulling myself up, I was tempted to put the side light on to assess the situation. The time during the night when the harshness of the day is wiped away, and in the gentle darkness, secrets are readily disposed to be shared. And yet, there is such a thing as being too dark.

From the other side of the bed, I slipped out and went across to the shutters to let more of the moonlight into the room. Her whiteness and vulnerabilities were picked out straight away, as did her startled eyes and worried countenance.

'That's better,' I said, creeping back into bed. 'Now we shall know whom we are talking to.'

'I think I preferred it the other way?' her little voice became young.

'Now Eve, we have skirted long enough around the bush. I think there are more secrets that you won't speak about than what I know of you.'

'I don't understand what you mean.'

'Is it possible for you to be as honest with me as I am honest with you?'

'Oh, what does it mean, to be honest?' She looked away, exasperated. 'Honest means different things to different people. My honest feelings are that I care about everyone. What is it you want to know?'

I was excited. Was she really going to be honest with me? This needed to be tested. 'Did you really love my father?' My eyes were grossly intent on every expression that her conscious mind made. I wanted to catch every one of them. How was it possible to love my father when he was twenty years older than her? My hope was she was going to tell me she loved him as a friend.

She looked down as if she was communing with her feelings, then her eyes flicked back up to my face. How much was this going to cost her? I found her expressions most exciting.

'Have you ever been in love, Aiden? Before I tell you, I would like you to answer this first. I want to measure your knowledge and if you are qualified to understand.'

I laughed and greeted the idea with my arms outstretched, for this was fun. 'Let me think?' I touched my mouth in deep deliberation. 'Have I ever been in love? Does this mean that I can be jealous? Well, you know the answer to that. I am jealous and I am possessive.' I looked at her, leaning my head to one side. 'But being jealous and possessive is not the same thing, is it, because you mean something completely different, don't you?'

Her face, empty of any emotion, waited.

'Quite frankly, no, because—' I nodded convulsively. 'I don't understand the rules of love and what is wanted.' But when I look at you, my heart whispers in my ears—you are beautiful. That's when I know I am in love.

'I have been in love just once; it was a feeling which took me by surprise and came as madness and stormed through my mind until it burnt out. I never want to experience it again because it stole my mind. We were young teenagers, Gerard, and me. I was fourteen, he was fifteen, too young to get married, but never too young to understand what love was all about.'

I devoured every word, every expression, everything about her while trying to predict. I wanted to know if she had suffered and what way had she been hurt. With my mouth partly opened, I felt as if all her struggles and endurances were coming from my mouth and that it was me who had borne her persecutions and not her. But I wanted to know more.

'Was he your first husband?'

'Yes, and he killed himself.'

Now I watched her struggling with herself and with the demon she had summoned. Her mouth grimaced into a smile, but it was one of pain. It was right she suffered because if we ask for everything, then we must expect to pay.

'I am so sorry. I should not have pushed you to relive those memories, but I felt it would help you.'

'No, you asked because you were curious. Although you would call it—knowing the truth.' Eve said, turning around, now fired by anger. 'Gerard was special, a talented poet. And I was very lucky when he made me his wife.' And then she stopped as if to look for someone who was not there, but he did not come to her. 'We delighted in the same things, for love makes you see the world differently; everything is special when you are in love. But, for us, it didn't last long; he fell out of love before I did. I don't know how or why it went wrong—it just did. Gerard should never have married me; we should have had our fun and then parted quickly; it would have hurt at first, but we were still young. Our love, I understand now, was that first wonderful flush of romance which is only given to youth, just like the first blossom in spring. And then,' she sighed. 'He should have married the girl his parents chose for him, for I was never going to be enduring.'

There was a fractious, almost haunted look about her eyes, as if she had been searching, turning everything over as to why their love had died. Why had he fallen out of love with her? When I saw how her first love still possessed her, I was jealous; I never thought how much this had cost me either, because I was arrogantly sure Eve could only love once, and it had to be me.

'Oh, it was a bad, bad time. It was a fever that neither of us understood, and I am glad now that I am over it.'

'You have stopped loving Gerard, then?'

'Oh yes, that sickness has long passed. I am not ill anymore, and I hope never to be again.'

'But you still have not answered my question whether you loved my father?'

'Yes, your father,' she said this as if she had almost forgotten. 'Yes, I loved your father. He was good to me, but it was a different type of love. I needed someone different from Gerard; Dominic cared for me. Is this what you wanted to know? Does it make you any happier or safer? You see, Aiden, there are many kinds of love. But compared to Gerard, now that was special. But you don't want me to go on about my love for other men? If only Gerard hadn't been so weak or young.'

She was right. I did not want to hear of her love for other men. Even if he were dead, would they still become my rival?

Spinning around, she sat up and pinned her eyes to mine to claim my attention.

'Money,' she said, getting up. 'If anything is going to destroy love, then it's money. Preposterous, isn't it?'

She flounced across the room to sit again on my bed.

'But it's true. Human beings love money. It's that which makes life so much easier and love more perfect. And that was what Gerard and I didn't have.'

'But you managed, didn't you because you married him?'

'Defiance made us manage. We both said we would not give in to their power. You see, Gerard's parents were excessively rich, and I mean rich. Whatever Gerard wanted; he could have. The only thing he needed to do was to conform to his parents' wishes and, in this case, marry the girl his parents chose. Sometimes, I wished I had never come along because I was poison to his senses. If anyone destroyed Gerard, it was me.'

'No, I don't agree with you there.'

'But of course, you don't,' she pinched my cheek like a child. 'Well, that is about it, Aiden.' She shrugged.

'No, I insist, there must be more to it. Tell me what happened when you married.'

'Not a pretty story at all,' she began with a smile of irony. 'But you don't want pretty stories, do you? People always like to know when love goes wrong. So, I will tell you. I didn't mind so much, but Gerard did. I promised I would do anything for him. I told him he didn't need to work, as I would do all that sort of thing. I didn't mind because I thought I loved him. But there was something else which was troubling. Oh, this happened, that happened. We had our first argument and then all the rest, which came when trouble was shared. Our love for each other was not looking good.'

Was I glad their love had turned sour? Yes, I was.

'It was by accident, I think, I hope, although thinking about it now, I am not so sure. While I went to work, Gerard stayed in our small modest home, rented, of course, and wrote poems. We were convinced this was where the big money lay. We were so innocent,' she sighed. 'So, innocent.'

Wanting to know everything, obsessed with everything about her, I went with her mind as an unwanted passenger. Had she gone back to that time and walked the streets, picked up the shopping, and looked for his face when she walked back? Had she seen him staring down at her, but not with love this time, but hatred?

'It was the beginning of the bad time,' Eve said with the bitter smile of regret tucked uncomfortably between her lips. 'I caught him, you see, talking to another woman. That in itself was quite harmless until I realised as I crossed from the other side of the road. She was the girl he had been betrothed to. I never thought I could be so angry. I never thought I could scream or shout that loud. I never thought. But that's what love does to you when it turns sour. I was also finding out that I could be mad with fury enough to embarrass myself. Oh, Aiden, do you really want me to go on? Do you really value honesty so much that you don't mind where it takes us?' she shook her head. 'This honesty has a price too expensive.'

Yes, I wanted to know. I wanted to know everything about Eve, so I didn't say anything except to wait for her to carry on.

Shaking her head with pain, her eyes disappearing into the folds of anger, she then took herself off again to the place where her despair had drawn red from her passion.

'We stood in the street as if we were gunfighters. Oh yes, I can look back on it now and see the absurdity of it, but it was painful, so very painful. The rawness of emotions is never beautiful and even harder to bear. In my madness, because I had gone mad, I threatened to kill Veronica if she did not leave my husband alone. At the time, I thought I was protecting him. But that was not how he saw it. He took me aside and told me to leave her alone. I didn't understand what was going on. He was threatening me, I was his wife, and she, who was she? She was not his wife. He took hold of her hand, and as I watched, they walked away. He left me in the street to carry all the shopping. Oh Aiden, when I think about it now, I go mad. I thought this memory had gone for me, but it hasn't. It's always waiting for me.'

'But he is dead now, and he can't hurt you anymore.'

She smiled in a way I would never comprehend, yet I was beginning to understand her, little by little; she was more complex than I at first realised. Perhaps I was beginning to recognise there's a limit to everything, and that I had exhausted her for now. Returning to the source of our discussion, I was beginning to appreciate that, for Eve, it was always going to be about not having any money. We were like an old married couple sitting up in bed to work out our problems.

'I am afraid I don't have much; it was my father who had all the money. Like yourself, I too am a pauper.'

'But it will be yours once the will is read.'

'I guess so, and I would imagine my father would have left you some money, too. There's no reason he wouldn't'.

'Fate took over and killed him before he had the chance to write out his will. Ironic, isn't it? If only Dominic could have waited another month, then I would never have to worry.'

Now she was looking at me with interest, leaning her face up to mine.

'This is how you have always wanted to be, Aiden. Rich, isn't it? And you will be rich very soon. I hope the money will answer your prayers to give you that happiness. And now I am going to wish you a goodnight. It is late, and I am tired.'

'But what about the money?' I held out my hand to her, trying to prevent her from walking away.

'The money can wait.'

At the door now, she turned to stare at me with another look I couldn't fathom.

'Go to sleep now, Aiden. Let no bad thoughts tear your mind with distress.'

15

Of course, I was going to make certain that Eve didn't go without money, but how much money did she want and need? If I gave her what she wanted straight away, I feared she would have no time for me. And I wanted her more than before. But before that, we had to get my father's funeral over and done with. For this was the next part of the story.

True to her word, we began doing everything together. I went with her shopping at the market and then helped her with the cooking. She kept me occupied and entertained, and I found myself laughing when I should not have been. I was carefree and hopeful about the future and not waiting for it to happen. I would be rich, and she would love me.

We were in that happy circle of giving. I would carry the shopping basket and she would select the food we needed for dinner, and then she would wait as I took my turn to pay whoever it was. She made it delightfully easy to be with her, and our needs were very simple.

'Aiden, my dear, I need you to buy me a dress.'

I was sitting at the table and breaking bread into my

soup; Eve liked to make soup for us both. We were trying many combinations and today; it was potato and leek.

'You shall have a dress,' I told her, holding a crust in my hand as I looked at her. I was teasing her as I thought she was teasing me.

'No, not just a dress. I want a special dress.'

'Very well, I shall see what I can afford. You know I am not a rich man yet.'

'I know you are not a rich man because only rich men know how to spend money. I don't want to beg for everything, Aiden.'

'Very well, you will have your dress; I shall see what I can find for you.'

'But you have not asked me what the dress is for?'

'Very well. What is the dress for?'

'Oh, Aiden, can you not guess?' she shook her head prettily, and then sighed. 'It's for your father. He will be buried in a couple of days. I received confirmation this morning that there is a plot in the cemetery for him.'

Was she angry at me, or was she teasing? Sometimes, when I am with her, I feel like an oaf and that I am boring her.

'How much do you want?'

She considered me for a couple of seconds before coming further into the room, with her head high and her chin up while passing backwards and forwards for me to delight in her figure.

'I want a great deal of money because I want to wear the best. This is nothing to do with me, Aiden. It is everything to do with Dominic. He deserves the best when we lay him to rest. After all, he has given everything to you. It's about time you did him justice.'

From out of my wallet, I took out everything I got from

the bank only yesterday evening. To me, this was a fortune because it would leave me with nothing. It was what was left of my monthly allowance. Yet, some of it had been deposited in my back in England to look after my affairs there, so I was not so badly off as I allowed Eve to believe.

'When are going to shop for this dress?' I asked, believing I would go with her.

'Now,' she said, walking to the hallway where we kept our coats.

I followed her with frowns and questions.

'Should I come with you?' I watched as she took out her dark lightweight jacket.

'No, I shall be gone for a while; I can't tell you how long because I don't know. And I don't want you coming with me, Aiden, because, well, because I don't want you to come. You will be fine here; I am sure of it. There is some food in the fridge and some other things in the larder, so you won't starve.'

'You don't want me to come.'

'Aiden, please, I just want a break from you. Even married people need a break from each other, and we have been more married to each other than wedded couples. I shall be back.'

Holding the door open, I watched her slipping from my hands with the realisation that she was eager to get away from me.

'You will be back, Eve, won't you?' for I felt suddenly very desperate. She had all the money she needed for a jaunt and an escape from me. Her happiness to get away from me was purely unexpected. The smile in her eyes and the recklessness of her feet showed she could not walk fast enough from me. 'Eve,' I called after her again. 'You will come back.'

She turned to wave to me, her raven hair twisted in a plait behind her, as she walked with jaunty steps. *Oh yes, Aiden, you have no fear that I will be back. I shall be back because you have all the money, and money is something I want.*

Her hips swinging, while her feet were light, I was certain there was a space between her feet and the ground. Watching her walk away came as a loss. If she had called out to me to come along, I wouldn't have gone back for anything but ran to her as I was. It felt strange when I closed the door to the world and turned around to myself. For the last four years, I had never been on my own.

She was gone, I told myself, but only temporarily. A few hours and she would be home. What on earth was I going to do with my life?

When Eve was here in her wonderful spirit, I could keep that savage emptiness away. But as soon as she stepped out of the door, my heart despaired. If my father had played a grand part in my life, perhaps I wouldn't have been insecure.

Now my father was gone I could live my life not needing to ask him for anything, because whatever he had was now going to be mine.

How quiet it was without her, and yet, when I thought about it, we lived our lives together in silence. There were no angry voices or screaming music; how can I explain it that when she was here, she was in every room, and in every room no matter where she was, I could hear her—I could hear her living.

'Don't be a fool,' I muttered, returning to the dining room.

She had left the clutter of the dinner still on the dining table, which was something she never did. For a few moments, I stood there looking at the dirty dishes. I suppose

I should clear the table; this is probably what she expected me to do. I felt uncomfortable thinking she could leave me behind. By the side of my eyes, I saw someone sitting there, someone kindly and familiar. But when I looked, the figure was gone. You thought it would be so different.

'Is that you, father?' I exclaimed, my ears wondering, waiting for a reply.

Nothing.

'Oh father, I'm sorry. But it wasn't my fault.' I looked and waited. There was nothing.

One day and soon, I will ask Eve to marry me. We will be so happy, and now I am coming into my father's fortune, I will lavish it on her. And she will love me all the more. At least this is one thing I can be certain of—her love for money.

Everywhere I looked, Eve filled the space with her own type of sunshine. How did this happen that I should completely depend on her? When she walked into the room, it was with grace. I would look at her, she would look at me. It was a game we played. Then she would turn away, knowing I was still looking at her with that sly smile. Then I would wait for her to return my look.

She had been gone too long. I looked to the kitchen door, convinced she had turned around and sneaked back to say this had been a joke. She had been teasing me, for this was the sort of thing she liked to play. But the door remained shut, and the only sound was the dripping tap.

I will be her third husband, I thought, rinsing the last bowl to put on to the draining board. She has not been lucky with her husbands. At only thirty-four she had outlived two of them and both were accidents. What were the statistics for that?

That last night before he died, I heard my father and

Eve arguing. This pleased me at the time, believing that his life with Eve was not exactly a honeymoon. I was glad of this, so I never thought about listening at their bedroom door to hear exactly what they were arguing about. It was only now my curiosity was pricked as to wonder why. What was their argument? It mattered to me to recall this splintered conversation. I wanted to know so to avoid upset my darling.

Checking about the kitchen to make certain there was nothing left untidy, not that Eve would check on me to see if I had completed the task to her liking. I turned off the light and left the starved little kitchen of sunlight.

It came to me, in between the kitchen and the hallway, that ever-present word—money.

'You know I need money, Dominic. Why are you keeping it from me?'

At least, I am sure the conversation went like that. Standing for that moment, I felt the sweep of time passing over me. Yes, this is what was said, I was sure of it. Climbing the stairs to go to my bedroom, on the hottest part of the day, I would have a siesta. But I stopped outside their bedroom listening and feeling for voices.

When Dominic fell off the veranda and was lying dead some hundred feet below, I had expected Eve to want to sleep somewhere else. But when we said goodnight that night, she went her way, and I went mine. I asked, why don't you sleep in the other bedrooms?

'Oh Aiden, that's very sweet of you, but I am used to sleeping in my own bed. Besides, Dominic won't harm me. I will be fine, I assure you.'

I looked at the door handle and began wondering what was she keeping safe in her room. What was it she didn't want me to see? I turned the doorhandle; she hadn't locked it and went in. It was strange to be in this room without these two people.

Yes, I remember this room well from the other day—not so long ago, but in many ways, a lifetime.

Her perfume filled the room with the aromatic scent of flowers. My eyes went to her vanity table to look for the perfume. There was a bottle of perfume unmistakable in its shape. Did she have only one bottle of perfume? Surely, my father would have decked her with hundreds. Well, that will soon be remedied by me.

I sat at her table and looked at myself in the mirror, modelling my face as she would do. Pouting at her reflection, coyly looking at herself. If she could see me now, would she be angry as I pouted mine? No, I don't think so. She might even laugh. I was missing Eve.

That drawer, the one with the death certificate of her first husband. Why would she hold on to that? Once she had told me that history was important. Really, I said, remembering the history of my family and knowing my father never wanted to talk about my mother.

'Yes, one day, Aiden you will be history, wouldn't you like people to remember you?' it was always her eyes, the most fascinating part about her which caught my attention.

'Not really, it won't matter one iota when I am dead.'

Pulling at the handle to the drawer, it opened. The certificate was gone, which pleased me. Morbid to hang on to something like that. But perhaps it was pushed further back into the drawer. There was a pile of letters at the back demanding I read them.

Rifling through the correspondence, who are these people Eve writes to? Names I have never come across and will never come across. From what Eve had told me, she knew no one. There would be no one coming to my father's funeral because they had no friends. I flicked the letters past my eyes, and then I stopped. There was a name which inter-ested me greatly—Veronica. The name of the young woman that Gerard was supposed to have married was on the back of an envelope. Why on earth would this young woman be writing to Eve?

These letters were private, and I had no right to invade Eve's privacy. And yet, if I am to marry Eve, this was some-thing that I should know. Taking out the envelope from the pile, I pulled out the letter. Handwritten with a script to admire, a feminine hand with loops and flourishes and in a clear yet clean, legible style. This was a person who was sure and certain of herself, who was used to being listened to and confident, not loud, or vulgar, but well-mannered and styl-ish. I could almost picture her standing beside me and watching over me as I was about to read.

I thank you so much for letting me know how Gerard is. His family has missed him greatly, but as long as Gerard is happy, that's all that matters to me. I found the poems Gerard wrote, and you are correct. Without a doubt, he is getting better, but I fear he still has a long way to go. You have been very good to him, and I am pleased he is happy with you. Thank you, Eve. And thank you for your bank details. No, I won't mention anything to anyone about what we are doing between us. He has always had a sensitive soul, so I am glad you are looking after him. You mentioned you needed to double the money for next month. I hate to tell you this, but I don't know if I can afford it. You are having everything I have. Please understand this. I am not withholding anything back from you, for it is the truth.

Gerard's mother has not been well. She refuses to see a doctor; we are all worried about her. I thought I should tell you this because, well, because if anything should happen to Gerard's mother... if you could tell Gerard... his mother would love to see him just one more time.

There was another letter tucked inside with this letter.

Dear Eve, thank you again for your letter. I appreciate everything you send me, and I shall confirm that I have told no one that you are writing to me. You have no worries about that, no worries at all. Did you ask Gerard if he wanted to see his mother? I know she would be grateful, and as I said before, she misses him. This I know, although she says nothing. The good news is that I have asked for a bigger allowance which has been granted. I shall transfer everything I have into your account, but please, I need more information about Gerard. What happened to his last poems? Did they go to a publisher? Did Gerard get the clothes you were talking about and the shoes? I hate to think he has holes in his shoes. I look forward to your next letter and don't forget, in an emergency, please telephone my number. Day or night, I shall always answer it. Yours in all sincerity, Veronica J Madison.

I looked at the telephone number added at the bottom of her letter. This letter, judging by the date, was written over ten years ago. So much had happened in that time that this person calling herself Veronica could probably be married with a family or even dead.

What do I do? I looked at my watch; Eve had been gone for an hour. She mentioned staying away until the evening, which would give me at least five hours to play with.

I dialled the number and heard the ringtone, but even this didn't mean anything; the number could now be allocated to someone else. With my ear to the receiver, I waited. Perhaps no one was there.

'Hello, this is 782. Who am I speaking to? Hello.'

A woman's voice answered at what age it was difficult to say, although I guessed she was not in her twenties.

'Hello, my name is Aiden. I took a chance of ringing this number because of a letter I was reading.'

'Yes,' Veronica said thoughtfully. 'Can I ask if this is a joke?'

'This is not a joke. If you will be patient with me, I will explain who I am. It's not simple, I am afraid. I just wanted to know if you existed. Am I talking to Veronica Madison?'

'Yes, you are. You said your name is Aiden?'

'Yes, Aiden Bentham. I wondered if I could talk to you.'

'I know the name, but the person I know of was called Dominic.'

'Yes, Dominic was my father. Unfortunately, my father passed away just over a week ago.'

'I am sorry for your loss.'

'Thank you.'

'What is it you want to talk to me about?'

'I wanted to know if you knew Eve Bentham, previously known as Eve Sheppard?'

I heard her quick intake of breath from hearing Eve's name.

'You knew her, didn't you?'

'Oh yes,' Veronica's voice was softer. 'I have been following her, but only from afar; I did not wish her any harm. I take it she is dead, too?'

'No, she is coming to terms with my father's death.'

'Yes, I expect she is. So, she is well? Why did you telephone me?'

'There are some things I want to know about Eve—'

'Then why don't you ask her?'

'Because I am not sure if she will tell me the truth?'

'What is the truth, Mr Bentham? The truth is gleaned from everyone who has a theory on it.'

She sounded so much like Eve in that instance, as if Eve had modelled herself on her.

'I am in love with Eve, and I was thinking about asking her to marry me, only I'm uncertain.'

'Then if you don't trust her, there must be an excellent reason for it. What is it you are uncertain about? You can talk to me. Perhaps I can help.'

'Less than four months ago, I heard my father had married this woman. She was a widow who he wanted to take care of. Less than four months, he is dead. I am worried that she may have killed him.'

'Was he rich?'

'Yes, he was rich. In fact, he was very rich. He was an art collector who, before he met Eve, lived modestly.'

'I see. Perhaps you don't know it, but the man I was supposed to marry was the same man Eve ran off with. Gerard Sheppard and I were betrothed when we were babies.' Her laughter was polite. 'Those were the days when you did what your parents wanted. I always fancied when I was young that I was in love with Gerard, but it was just one of those whims. Now what I believe will differ from what his parents believe. I never thought Eve killed her husband, but his father did. Unfortunately, Gerard's mother died a few years after the two of them ran off together.'

'You don't think Eve killed Gerard?'

'No, I don't. I don't know if that's enough to satisfy your curiosity. If you were to ask me, I would say it's best that this entire tragedy was forgotten. Let the dead grieve for themselves. But as for Gerard's father. Stanton Everard Sheppard, if he knew where she was, he would have her sent to prison for the rest of her life.'

Perhaps in my enthusiasm for an answer to this mystery, I already condemned Eve with guilt.

'I really appreciate you speaking with me.'

'It was my pleasure.'

'Are you married?' now it was my turn to be curious.

'No, I am not married?'

'Can I ask you why you are not married?'

She laughed as if she thought this was funny.

'Yes, you can ask,' she laughed to herself again, discreetly. 'If Gerard had not met Eve, then I would have been married. Everything had been planned for me, the wedding, the reception. The house where we were to live; we were to have three children, two boys and one girl. This was what I was told when I was growing up. I was to have no career because my life was to be centred on my husband and our children. I could swear that I lived my entire life and marriage before I was seventeen.' She laughed again, as if this was a big joke. 'In my mind, I had done everything I was supposed to. I had been a good wife and mother, hosted the best parties, and ran the best charities. Everything was set out for me. So, if Eve had not married Gerard, that was what my life would have been. And do I regret marrying him? Yes, and no. I am happy now, not ecstatic. It would never do to be that emotional. I read, I have friends and occasionally, I have a small party. Sometimes, it is just a question of getting through life.'

I was talking to a woman who was in every way satisfied, but to my mind, was already dead.

'Before I go, can you tell me what happened to Gerard and how he died?' I asked, wondering about the lady at the other end of the telephone.

'Yes, it is no secret. It was an accident. Eve and Gerard had been arguing yet again. She had a knife in her hand. I think she was trying to protect herself; Gerard was threatening her. Eve said that she put the knife down, but suddenly, Gerard felt she was laughing at him. He ran towards her, tripped, and fell on the knife. He died before they could get him to the hospital. And that is about it.'

I could almost see her smiling.

'You have been very helpful; I am sorry to have interrupted your day.'

'I would like to ask you to say hello to Eve from me, but that would not be wise. Is she still very beautiful?'

'Yes, she is. I don't think her beauty will ever fade.'

'Perhaps not. Are you still going to marry her after everything I have told you?'

'I think I have a chance at happiness with Eve, so yes. I know this may sound insensitive, but perhaps the two deaths were meant to prepare her for me.'

'Perhaps. Sometimes, you have to kill the one you love to move forward.' Veronica replied in her lazy, tranquil voice, predicting for another now she was safe from the threat of marriage.

'What is that supposed to mean?'

'Anything you want it to mean?'

16

It was getting late, and I expected Eve's return. I had made us a simple salad with cured ham. A bottle of red was waiting on the table and in the cooler was a bottle of white. I had even looked at my wardrobe, trying to decide what to wear. Taking out my shirts, blue, red, white, and even yellow; it was the blue shirt I chose together with my blue jeans, a sure winner because they made me look sexy.

A couple of hours later, I was sitting at the table in the dark, brooding. In a temper, I began contemplating what she was doing. When we are married, I would cut her wings. There would be no going off without her telling me where she was going. In fact, I would stop her from going anywhere because it was not safe being on her own.

As there was nothing else sounding in the house, I heard the front door opening and shutting. No mistaking that she was home. I stood while that chain of broken promises fell to the floor, grateful that she had come home. Everything I had thought had vanished because Eve was home. Now, there would be lots to talk about, and as for her apologies, why, I didn't want to hear about them because she had returned.

It was a scramble to get to her with my greetings. The front door slammed just as I came out of the dining room, but before I was there, she was running up the stairs.

'Eve?' I called after her, seeing the back of her legs as I looked up the stairwell. 'Where have you been? I've been waiting for you. Eve?'

Either she was refusing to answer, or she didn't hear me. Whatever it was, I needed answers, so I followed her upstairs. But my relief did not outmatch my temper, which had taken a turn for the worse that she could do this to me. She had to know that I had been torn into tatters worrying about her.

'Eve,' I carried on calling after her. 'Why are you back so late? Did you get the dress you were looking for?'

The light was on in her bedroom. I could see her shadow as she moved about the room, puzzled, what she was doing.

'Eve, I asked you where you were and whether you got the dress you went shopping for?'

Walking into her bedroom, I found her open suitcase on the bed. Already there were clothes piled in from her chest of drawers. What was the meaning of this?

'What are you doing, Eve?'

'What does it look like?' she called from her closet.

'It looks to me like you are packing.'

Frowning, I wondered if she was in one of her funny moods as she threw out clothes from her closet.

'Are you getting rid of your clothes? I don't understand what you are doing. What is going on with you, Eve?'

'I am leaving.'

She came out of the closet with one of her favourite

dresses, the white one. I watched as she folded this gown to place it to the side. The other clothes were going in first without thinking if she could get everything in.

'What do you mean by you are leaving?'

'That I have had enough and so, I am leaving. It is as simple as that, Aiden.' Eve glanced up.

'But you can't. You can't walk out on me. After everything we have been through together, you can't just walk out on me.'

'Watch me.'

Her eyes were defiant, beautiful, and dark. They were almost black, like jet. I was enchanted by the vivacity of her eyes, believing still she could not mean it, but I loved her drama and saw our lives together full of excitement. And then I smiled again. She could not mean this. But this animated automaton walked backwards and forwards, clearly showing her intention.

'I've made some dinner—Eve, stop this. Look at me. I don't know what your game is, but I want you to stop it. Why are you leaving?'

'You want to know why?'

'Yes, I do.'

'I've got a job and a chance to earn my own money. You know I am not afraid of working.'

'I never said you were. But there is no need for you to work. You will be married to me, and we will be happy. So, stop what you are doing and come back down and have something to eat. Let us be happy together, and we will get through everything.'

Shaking her head and grinning, loading herself with sarcasm that she would not have to endure this any longer, and still she was packing her case.

'Eve, stop this, I forbid it.'

'You forbid it. Who do you think you are? You are not my husband or my master; you are my husband's son. At least when I was married to Dominic, I didn't go short of money.'

'Short of money, I was prepared to share everything with you when we are married. What about my father's funeral? Aren't you going to stay for it? You can't leave. You were his wife.'

'Not anymore. I'm free, don't you remember?'

'Eve,' for now I was becoming afraid as well as angry. 'Stop what you are doing! I forbid you to leave.'

'You can't stop me, Aiden. I'm a free woman, and I can do as I like. You go to your father's funeral because, after all, you are going to inherit everything.'

'You think I'll keep everything—is that what it's all about?'

'Yes,' she looked up, her black eyes gleaming with perverse mischief.

'Well, I am not. Eve, stop this,' I put my hand on her case. 'I will look after you. I will take care of you like my father did. You will not want for anything. Eve,' I pleaded. 'Don't go. Please stay.'

'Yes, I know. This is how you will look after me by buying all the trinkets I want.'

'Is that not enough? To be taken care of. I need you, Eve. Please, I'm begging you not to go.'

'You just don't understand, do you?' she raised herself to her full height, standing in all her magnificence. 'I am tired of playing this game being the dutiful wife, always pacifying a man's big ego, and always grateful for what they do for me. Do you know how tiring this is, Aiden? You don't, do you? You take all of this for granted just because I'm the woman.'

'But I love you. And I know you love me. We can be so happy together, Eve. Please, listen to me.'

'No Aiden, I want you to listen to me for a change.'

There was a great deal of confidence in how she held herself. The first anger in her eyes had disappeared to be replaced with something like frustration. Or maybe it was tiredness?

'I have got to get away from here. I need to get back to normality to see and understand myself as I should be seen. Whatever you imagined for us won't work, Aiden, because for one, I don't love you. Yes, I have cared for you because you are a vulnerable man who's spent most of his life depending on his father. And two, you've got Sophia, she's more your age, and she knows how to take care of you—'

'No, stop that. I don't want her, it's you I want. How can you think I would go back to her after I have known you?'

'Well, you will have to get used to being without me,' she started folding up her clothes again. 'Oh, I am so glad I've made this decision. You should try it, Aiden. By the way, I have made certain that the rent is paid for the next two months. That's where your money has gone, and not on a dress. I am not what some people think of me. I hate being made to be the villain.'

When she walked to the closet, I stood in front of her, fighting my own shame.

'You are not going, Eve.'

'Oh yes, I am. Please stand out of my way.'

'If you leave me, I will kill myself.'

This caused her to shut up and look at me with some respect. Or was it shock?

'Aiden, in actuality, it's the reverse. If I stay with you, my fear is that you will kill me. Now please, get out of my way or else I will walk around you.'

The emptiness and the struggle to survive to overcome the black yawn of desolation became my despair.

'Please Eve,' I grabbed hold of her in desperation. 'You've got to help me here. I don't have anyone; my father has just died—you are not being fair to me; don't you understand? You can't leave me like this, as if I am a toy that you have finished playing with. You owe me Eve. At least stay with me here until I get the funeral over with. I will pay you to stay.'

'Please take your hands off me.'

Instantly, I obeyed, but had I made her stop, I don't know. Maybe she was reconsidering what she was doing because she had stopped folding her clothes and looked at me critically. If this did not prevent her from leaving, I don't know what would?

'Do you know what it is to be a man? To be a man is a myth; it's a combination of hopes and dreams learnt from others. You try to do your best to fulfil what everyone wants of you. To put yourself last when others are needing, to remind yourself that you are strong when everyone else is weak. But I get weak, I feel helpless; I feel everything you feel and more. Have some compassion for me.'

I sat on her bed and looked at Eve, hoping she was listening to me.

'If I have done something wrong, then you must tell me, I cannot do and be everything when there is so much strength in you.'

Now lowering her eyes, she too took her rest on the bed with her case wedged between us.

'Very well, I shall stay until the funeral is over, Aiden, but then, I must go. You must let me go, and you must promise me now?'

This promise came hard to my lips, but if I didn't, I knew she would walk out on me. And so, I made that promise to her. Eve had emasculated me. And yet, I could not let her go,

'I promise you, Eve, that after the funeral, you are free to go; I will not impede you in any way, Eve.'

How did she become so hard? Where was that person I once knew, the one I had seen with Dominic? She could not always have been like this, hiding herself behind smiles and her long raven hair, the veil to her real thoughts. I needed to protect myself from her famished anger.

'Then we shall make the most of our time together, and I am starving. What is it you have made for us?' she had brightened, changed. It was dramatic, but she had got her own way. Everything I felt had been dismissed. I didn't know what to make of this except that I was grateful.

Pulling the case off her bed, it crashed on to the floor, then she pushed it out of the way. She was so different now from what she was seconds ago. Who was this woman called Eve?

Smiling, she took her time walking down the stairs, merrily talking about the shops she had been in and the people she had met. I could not get it out of my head that only minutes before she had threatened to leave. Suspicion was filling my mind.

'Oh no,' she said when she saw what I had created. 'I can't eat this; I want something more substantial. By the looks of it, you do too! You've lost weight, Aiden. It doesn't suit you. You must eat.' She was pouring rice into a pan, taking out spices and herbs from the little tray above the cupboards. 'Going without food will weaken you.'

We were sitting once more at the dining table while Eve poured out the red wine. I watched her eat with an appetite. She was relaxed, as if what had happened in her room had not happened at all. I did not understand this new Eve. I did not understand her at all. And I did not trust her.

Had she really meant what she said about leaving me?

Could it be a test or was it just another one of her elaborate teases? I had a hope it was and yet, if this was true, I did not like the cruel game she was playing.

'You know,' Eve said when she had found the second bottle of wine in the cooler. 'I miss the balcony. I loved it when we all sat out there and Dominic was telling us about all the stars. That was one thing I loved about him, his vast knowledge.'

Although I tried, I could barely enter any of the discussions she started. Perhaps she knew this because, for most of the time, the conversations she had were made on her own. But every now and again, she looked at me to check to see how I was; her eyes flicking quickly over me.

How I hurt, how my insides were torn out and stretched with pain. I did not know what I was going to do with myself. Everything looked dark. Everything I heard was evil. The world had turned dark on me, and everything I saw was a knife in my mind. I tried to eat as I tried to drink, but everything was pointless and tasted of nothing.

'Do you want to go for a walk?' Eve suggested.

Perhaps she was taking pity on me and trying to quicken my spirit. I agreed straight away. I was going to accept everything she offered, for I was humbled. My passion had humiliated me. I agreed to walk down to the bay to look at the sea, but ten minutes into the stroll, I felt tired.

'Would you mind if we returned?' I stopped just as we entered another road. 'I would like to return. It has been a busy day—' and then I stopped because she would not like me reminding her of the argument.

She looked surprised and answered me with silence. Perhaps she was wondering what my next trick would be. As we neared the house, it was time for Eve to confess again that she did not buy a dress to wear for the funeral.

'It doesn't matter,' I smiled, waving away any disappointment. 'Nothing matters. Let us just get through the next two days.'

I did not want Sophia to come to the funeral; I did not want her concerned and practical voice worrying over me and telling me what to do. She cared for me and was my friend. That was enough.

'You should have let Sophia come,' said Eve, sorting some refreshments out just in case neighbours came along. These were the things that people did for a funeral, providing friendship and sustenance at a lonely time like this. Kind of them to bring offerings of food. Neighbours, they said in their bits and pieces of English, they knew what it was like to grieve. We had become popular visitors, the beautiful English people.

'Sophia would have been good for you—I like Sophia. She's a nice girl.'

'She, who would try to order me about, and I can't stand that. She thinks she owns me.'

'Do you not feel anything for her?' Eve looked at me, a pinch in her brow as she searched my face for an answer.

'No,' I smiled. 'I just wanted to get the day over and done with.'

'And then what will you do?'

'If you are worried that I will stop you from going, I won't because I promised you. You are free to go as soon as this is over. I won't stop you, Eve.'

'Then what is it you are going to do?'

'Have that holiday I was supposed to have. But whatever I do, there's no need for you to worry about me. I just need a long rest.' Eve had hurt me more than she would ever know.

❧

I CAN'T REMEMBER MUCH about the funeral except that I was looking at my father's coffin and thinking how strange my father was in that box. Too quickly, everything was over with shaking hands of people I didn't know.

When the last of them went and the door was closed, I saw Eve's suitcase had been placed by the door; she was going and keeping to her word. I took it all in and accepted it as it was. There was no use fighting something when the decision had been made.

'Thank you for being there for my father and me, Eve. You were great; you looked beautiful, and I was pleased and proud of you.'

'Would you like me to make you some tea or would you sooner have a something stronger?'

'No, go. I will be fine.' I waved her, I hope, cheerfully away.

'What are you going to do now?' she frowned.

'It's been a long day. I thought I would go to bed.'

I had a bit of a headache, but that was none of her business now; she probably would think it was stress, and that I was using this to forestall her.

'But it is not even three in the afternoon.'

'Then I shall have a siesta. You can go now. I won't stop you anymore.'

I remember climbing the stairs and thinking about my bed, and that was all I remembered.

17

E ve had sat by my bed like an angel, dabbing my head and wetting my lips, but fortunately, I don't remember. As I don't remember that my headache was hurting me, and my neck was stiff. I fell into a coma, but this, of course, I don't remember. All the while, Eve was there. I should have gone to the hospital; the doctor said, but Eve refused. She told the doctor that she could take care of me. And if anything happened to me, she would take responsibility. But this would not happen, she told the doctor when she dismissed him.

The lumbar puncture was performed in the house instead of the hospital; Eve was so insistent to save my life, the doctor and a nurse did the procedure on me between them. It was a risky time, but I survived to awake one afternoon ten days later into a world of sunshine. Eve was sitting in the chair beside me, embroidering.

As she continued sewing, I looked about the room. I had awoken and now I was trying to understand what had occurred. Undressed and in my pyjamas, I looked down to the bottom of the bed and my feet to unravel the mystery.

'Oh, you are awake?'

Eve looked at me, delighted I could do something as easy as that. Just to awaken seemed such a miracle. To this funny question, I could do nothing other than smile.

'How do you feel?' her eyes were pressing me to answer.

'Tired and puzzled why I am here in bed and why are you sitting next to me? My head aches.'

'Still?' She stood, put her needlework down and straightened out the bedclothes. 'We have been worried about you.'

'You and my father. Where is he?'

She had been tucking the blanket in at the bottom of the bed, and then she stopped. Concealed behind her eyes were plenty of thoughts going on. But it didn't matter because I was finding anew the world around me. The shutters were open wide; I knew this had to be Eve's doing. I was already guessing how much she liked the light.

'What happened to me?' because something had clearly happened for me to be in bed at this time of the day.

'You have not been well.' Eve said with her back to me. Did she not want to look at me anymore? Was I hideous?

'Have I been involved in a car accident?'

'Oh, no, nothing like that.' This time, she looked at me, her eyes still bright and radiant.

'I just thought because,' I touched my face. 'I have a beard.'

'No, not quite a beard.' She laughed as if this was one of the funniest things she had heard. 'No, not quite like that. You've been ill, but now you are well—'

'And I suppose you have been doing all the nursing and that my father has left you to it.'

'Yes,' she whispered. 'I suppose you could say that.'

'So, where is my father?' I asked, my voice becoming stronger. 'Was he really worried about me? I should imagine he was out trying to buy up all the magic potions and things to get me well.'

'Yes, that's the sort of thing your father would have done. Would you like some water? I am sure your throat must be dry. I'll fetch you a glass.'

'To be honest, I would soon have something stronger, some wine or even a glass of my father's brandy. I feel like I have been pulled through a hedge backwards.'

Eve looked at me as if she was trying to work me out. I had experienced the entire galaxy of her expressions seen since I have known her, but even these were always different. What was it like to be inside her head?

'What are you doing?'

'I am going to get up, as I've been in bed long enough. I want to get dressed and go downstairs and greet the world. My body aches: I need to stretch.'

'Well, you can't, Aiden. You've not been well. And if I were you, I would thank my lucky stars I was still alive.'

'Alive?'

'Yes, alive, Aiden. You had meningitis. We were anxious about you. So, please, for now, until the doctor sees you again, you must stay in bed. Getting up too soon could be serious.'

'So, what do I do? I can't lie here all day doing nothing. And I can't expect you to do either.'

'Patience, Aiden. Give it a day or two. You were in a coma, Aiden, and you can't expect to be doing what you did when you were well. You need to rest, and then when you are well, we can complete what was neglected.'

'Eve, you can't expect me to just lie here all day. I'll go out of my mind. Do you think I could have something for this headache?'

Dr Rizzo was very pleased I had awoken, and then I had

cognisance. He started asking me lots of ridiculous questions like what my name was, when I was born, and every other stupid enquiry. I was not dumb. I had been ill, but memory loss, I understood later, was one of the side effects.

'There doesn't appear to be anything wrong with me now,' I bragged. 'I've got off Scot free because I am healthy.'

But outside the door, I could see from the mirror that Eve and the doctor were whispering. Tomorrow, I was told by the doctor I could sit downstairs for a while, and the day after that, I could progress to sitting outside in the small side garden. Everything was to be done in stages a little at a time. This was not quick enough for me.

'Eve,' I called to her. She was sitting by my side, working intensely on her needlework. Attentive, she was eager to please me. 'I couldn't help noticing that something had happened to the veranda. Was there an accident?'

'Oh yes,' her eyes were gay. 'The landlord wanted to do some alterations so it will be out of use for a while.'

'Couldn't he have done it before you took up residence? Some people are very inconsiderate.'

I waited for Eve to agree with me, but she said nothing and went back to her needlework. One moment Eve looked merry and happy, the next, I couldn't put my finger on it. Was she concerned about something?

Nearly a week passed before I was ready to enter the outside world, for even dressing was a great effort. Everything was an endeavour, and to do even the simplest of tasks made me reliant on Eve. I might have complained, and showed my temper, but Eve remained strong while listening to all my impatience. Everything I did attracted Eve's eyes, touching me with her glances and checking me to see if I was okay. But I felt she was waiting for something, waiting for her reward.

I was thinking this when she changed the colour of her silks, snipping the skein with cosy satisfaction. Her enjoyable small conversations with herself were most interesting; she told herself off more than the materials she worked with. I loved listening to her private world.

'Eve, if I have not already told you, I must tell you now that I would not have made it this far without your care; you have been wonderful to me. And I really appreciate it. I have not come across anyone as kind or as gentle as you. I want you to know this.' I was waiting for Eve to say something. 'Eve,' I spoke her name again.

And this time when she looked up, it grieved me to see two tears bejewelled tear in her beautiful grey eyes.

'Eve, have I upset you?' Seeing her tears hurt me as much as I thought it hurt her.

'No, you haven't. It is the first real kind word anyone has ever said to me.'

'Oh, I can't believe that. You are too beautiful for anyone to be cruel to you. I am sure my father has said many kind things to you.'

She stood and went to the window; we were in the back sitting room because of the broken balustrade.

'Dear Eve, the entire world should be kind to you.'

It surprises me now how little we think about anything. When someone you trust tells you something, you accept their account as being true because why else would they tell you? Something had been on my mind for the last two days. And it was this. I kept on thinking about the veranda; I seemed to remember the three of us were sitting out enjoying the evening together and watching the views; there had been no problem on that occasion except that one post was fragile. Oh well, I thought, what does it matter when it is going to be fixed? No harm was done—

No harm had been done, I kept on repeating to myself, no harm.

'Where is my father?' I had been listening out for him and trying to predict what he would say. Would he be worried? No, if he had been worried, he would leave whatever he was doing to be with me. But it was more than likely that he would be exasperated with me for being ill, perceiving it as my fault.

Eve had returned from her room, looking for a skein of the same colour. She stopped herself from physically entering the room, and I can remember clearly how she looked. Dressed in a light lemon shirt and lightweight lavender-coloured slacks while her hair was plaited down her back. She had not dressed to adorn herself but purely for comfort; we had become easy with each other. My question had caught her by surprise, leaving her mouth slightly open, but it was her snow-white skin that warned me something was wrong.

'You are well enough to know,' she turned from me. In her hand was the skein of silk that she had gone searching for.

I watched her thoughtfully walk to her chair, taking the task of sitting down as a study in algorithms as something meaningful pressed hard on her lips. Feeling extraordinarily weak and vulnerable supposing there was going to be a confrontation, I could not afford to take part. If it came to my father, really, I didn't want to know about him.

'It is your right to know.'

'Eve—' I butted in, but she did not seem to hear me.

'Dominic and I were talking about going on another honeymoon, a proper one this time. He was going to take me to all the places I had longed to see.' There was a smile of remembrance on her lips. 'One day I will see these places, but for the moment, I am not worried about them. I went out to the kitchen to get us some dinner. I left you with Dominic; he told me there was something he wanted to say to you.'

My memory had been erased and so, therefore, it meant nothing to me, but her distress was not only puzzling but worrying.

'I don't know what happened on the veranda while I was away; I can only suppose. Too late to ask you what your father and you were talking about, and besides, what does it matter in the end? A decision had already been made by both of you, except your father had no say in his fate. That is in the past now as long as you keep to your promise.'

'Eve, I don't know what you are talking about.' A dormant fear which I had suppressed was ceasing strength by becoming corporeal.

'Yes,' she said thoughtfully, carefully. 'When I returned, there was no Dominic. You were the only person there.'

'Where was my father, then?'

'Oh, Aiden, do you not remember anything?'

Eve stared at me, willing me to remember, but I couldn't, or I preferred not to.

'What do you want me to say?' I almost whispered.

'So, the murderer got off with no punishment because he couldn't remember.'

'Murderer?' I breathed. 'Me, a murderer? Why do you say that?'

'Dominic was gone. When I came back, you were pretending to have fallen off the balcony. I saved you, or perhaps you allowed me to save you.'

'And then,' I whispered, not wanting to hear anymore and yet still compelled to ask.

'Your father had fallen off the balcony to his death. My poor dear Dominic.'

'My father is dead?' It was as if this was the first time I heard this. 'I don't believe you.'

I ran to the veranda to disprove Eve's ugly allegations, and yet, I was weak. My legs found it difficult to carry me, but I managed to reach the closed glass doors which separated me from this world to the other.

'Aiden, stop, what are you doing?' Eve ran after me.

'You tell me I have killed my father; I am telling you I don't believe you.'

'Aiden, your father is dead. Please leave it at that. I don't want you to take your own life for some sort of strange satisfaction. Besides, you made me a promise.'

She was clinging on to me while I stupidly held on to the door handle, which refused to open.

'Let me go, Eve. How on earth do you open this door?' Shaking it as if I was trying to make it come off its hinges.

'I'm sorry, Aiden. I didn't mean to tell you like this that your father is dead.'

'No.'

The heated passion of those last few seconds weakened me. My father is dead? It was a sin even to think about it, and Eve had accused me.

She had helped me back to the other room, her arm supporting my larger frame even though I had diminished. With a glass of brandy, and this time, Eve also had one. We swaddled together, finding comfort in each other's company.

'I could not believe what happened that evening,' Eve said, raising her glass to her mouth. 'When I left the balcony, the biggest problem on my mind was what could I make for our evening meal. Of all things, I was thinking of poaching a piece of fish in white wine. I didn't know if this

was going to take too long. I knew you would be upset;
Dominic and I had spoken about it. When I came from the
kitchen, I found you were hanging off the veranda and
Dominic gone.'

'I can't remember. Eve, I wish to God I could. Then I
could tell you why, because not knowing is destroying me. I
loved my father.'

'It was hard for me to accept what happened. My first
thought was that you were playing the clown once again.
And then I feared you and Dominic had shared suicide. I
was mad with these thoughts, but you were hanging on; I
knew I had to do something,' Eve replayed the tragedy. And
then she laughed. 'One moment I was married, the next a
widow. It was so ludicrous—'

'What happened next?' I asked to Eve's suspicious eyes.

To her, I must know. Surely, I knew, the sudden death of
my father could not be scrubbed out.

'I called the police; it was the only sensible thing to do. I
told them that what had happened was an accident. But it
wasn't.'

'What happened next?'

'The police came, and you told them everything.'

'What did they do?'

'It was dark and late. I told them a lie.'

'A lie. What did you tell them?'

'Yes, I lied because you made me a promise. You wanted
him dead, Aiden. You got your wish. I didn't tell the police
the truth. I was afraid of you. You are a violent and evil man.
God forgive you. When you saw me standing there as a
witness to Dominic's death, you came for me as a man
possessed.'

'I don't believe you. I wouldn't kill my father. Never.

Never. Oh yes, I have said how much I wanted him dead. But I would never do that. Never.'

'If that's what you choose to believe.' Her still grey eyes were fixed on me. 'Then so be it, but you made a promise to me, and I expect you to keep it.'

I stared at Eve as if I had never seen her before, fearful of her now, but still haunted by her beautiful face as her steel-grey eyes stared hard at me.

'Have no doubt I was angry at you. You have stolen my future, every hope I had, and everything I had planned between Dominic and myself is gone in one strike of aggression. I have always striven to be the best, Aiden. It's not been easy. I have suffered many injustices in my life, but you are Dominic's son. Despite how I feel, I cannot send Dominic's son to prison.'

'But you should have. If I am guilty, you should have sent me to prison.'

'Dominic would not have wanted it, and it was his death which decided it.'

'I can't believe I killed my father,' I muttered, staring now at my glass of brandy. 'I swear to God I didn't do it, couldn't do it. How could I kill my father?'

'This was not what I wanted to speak of, but you forced me to tell you.'

'How do I live with myself?' I moaned.

'You will live and so will I.'

'Eve, I'm sorry. If I did what you say, it must have been in madness. Please forgive me, Eve.'

Weakness made me cry. I was sitting in the armchair feeling the tears coursing down my face; I am not a man to cry, and yet, the horror of it was livid in my mind. How do I live my life knowing I was responsible for my father's death?

Eve had made something hot, but I could not eat. The

energy I had regained in health, the triumph of overcoming illness and the rush of energy which came with it were lost in the attack of guilt. Eve watched me all the time, a witness to my torture. Eat up, she kept on nodding to me. The only thing we have in this world is our lives, she added. Whatever happens, you have to go on. My thoughts to that were bitter.

And to sleep, how was I going to go to sleep with these thoughts running through my head? But I did, and I hate to say that as soon as my head hit my pillows, I went into a deep slumber and awoken afresh to the bright light of another sunny day until I remembered Eve had called me a murderer. How does anyone live with that? Some do, I am sure, tell themselves lies and coax themselves to believe this other truth.

The following morning on leaving my room, I found a pillow on the floor and wondered about its reason. Later I understood Eve had taken to sleeping outside my room just to be there for me in case I needed her.

It was not the same between us anymore, a tension woven by uncertainty, wondering what Eve would do. I must tread carefully with her now. Who wants to go to prison when there is life to still enjoy? I had become a very rich man now with everything to live for. If I was guilty of murdering my father, then I was going to do good work to pay for my soul. The only worry now was Eve and whether I could trust her to keep her silence. That's if she was telling the truth. For I was remembering a different truth.

I should marry her to keep her silence, not such a bad proposition for she was still attractive, but as for love—how could I love her now when she has so much power over me?

Walking into the dayroom, I saw her unfinished letter left on the table like an invitation. Her writing was always a pleasure to read and admire.

Running my eyes over her words, the letter's contents unfolded to me with a shock. She was answering an ad placed in a newspaper. They were looking for someone to take care of their children.

I could not allow her to do that, to work when I had so much money. It would be an insult to how I had taken care of my father's widow. I had to do something about her situation and help her, and the only way was to give her some of my money.

'Eve,' I said when she came into the room. 'I see what you've been doing, getting a job when there is no need.'

'You have been reading my letter?'

'Yes. You need money. Why didn't you come to me first?'

'Because of pride.'

'Well, there is no need for pride. I have money enough for both of us.'

'Perhaps I did not want to be beholden to you. I've every intention of working to keep myself. The money for the position is very reasonable. If you didn't know it already, I'm a very proud person and have no wish to live off you.'

'You don't need to worry about money again, but should you want to take that job, I won't forbid you.'

'Thank you—' I could see she was offended by my offer. 'Oh, by the way, I meant to tell you. Sophia called late yesterday. I told her about what happened to you, so naturally, she's worried. You must talk to her to let her know you are doing well. I'll wait for you in here while you have a word with her.'

'I would sooner not.'

Taking no notice of my wants, she ushered me to the telephone.

'Aiden,' it was Sophia, 'What's happened to you? Eve told me you were ill. I have been so worried about you. She only told me yesterday. I wondered why you never came to the phone. So, you had meningitis? That can be serious.'

'I am feeling much better, thanks to Eve; she has been a godsend, and the worse of it is over now.'

'When are you coming home? You can't stay out there forever now your father has gone. You must be practical, Aiden.'

'Well, first I need to recover, Sophia, and it might take a while. I hope to bring Eve home with me this time.'

'Oh, I thought she would have told you—'

'Told me what?'

I was going as carefully as I did not want to upset Sophia, but she was forcing my hand.

'Joyous news, at least for Eve. She told me she was hoping to marry soon. So soon after dear Dominic, well, it's none of my business.'

'To whom?' I would like to think Sophia was either joking or lying, but these were the two things Sophia wasn't capable of.

'She didn't say. I'm sure she would have told you if she was. Do you think she's making it up? Which wouldn't surprise me; she's been telling us a lot of lies. The dancer she told Dominic about was a lie. I ran her name past one of my friends, also a dancer; he couldn't locate her at all.'

'Perhaps she danced under another name. What other things has she been making up?'

'Don't think I have been checking her out to find the worse on her. I was just curious. She is clever,' began Sophia. 'When I told Eve that I was studying psychology and found the subject interesting, she told me she had studied psychology, too. Where? I asked her. Oxford, she said.' then Sophia sighed. 'I found out that she hadn't studied at Oxford or Cambridge. People who lie often have psychological problems; they are afraid of being found out and need to protect what they are concealing. Oh Aiden,' another sigh. 'I am not a nice person. I am full of nasty, unkind things. Please forget what I just told you.'

'And what are your nasty things?' I asked indulgently; it was good to hear from Sophia. She was refreshingly honest. Another thing which came as a surprise was, I had missed her. Compared to Eve, Sophia was pleasantly straightforward and unimaginative.

'I can be very jealous.'

'You jealous? Oh, I don't think so.'

'Yes, I am. I pretend to be friends with Eve because you like her, but I never liked her. I never trusted her. She said she would teach me how to cook, but when it came to it, she found it difficult to cook an omelette. Even I can cook that.'

It was so good to listen to Sophia that the stress locked up inside of me burst into laughter.

'I was so jealous that I got in touch with Oxford and spoke to someone I knew because in modelling, you get to meet many people from all walks of life. I asked if he could look up Eve Madelaine Alarie and if she had an MA in psychology. He found no one of that name on the register either. Wasn't that mean of me? But that's not the only thing she lied about. She lied about everything, including her age; she's not as young as you think. Oh, I am sorry, Aiden; it's wicked what I have done, but I cannot help it.'

'Is this the reason for your phone call, to pick Eve to pieces? What does it matter if she's lied?'

'I knew you would hate me telling you, but I don't trust Eve, and I am telling you this not because I am jealous, but because she's up to something. And there is something else I am going to tell you which you won't be happy about either.'

'And what's that?'

'I have a ticket booked for tomorrow. I'm flying out to see you, and I am due to arrive at one o'clock in the afternoon, your time.'

I wasn't as angry with Sophia as she predicted. Concerns had been passing also through my mind about Eve, one of them being how quickly she got over my father. As for my father's money, I intended to give her a third of it.

'What are you doing?' I asked, coming up behind Eve. She shook as if I had really taken her unaware.

'I was just running water. I meant to get myself a glass of water, and then I forgot.' She was watching the water run.

'Eve, I have decided that I shall give you a lump sum of money, so you don't have to work or worry.'

'You don't need to worry about me anymore.'

'But I do worry about you, Eve. You have been more than a good friend, especially just lately.'

Since my illness, my passion for Eve had evaporated. I can't say why that was, but now I was wondering if I was ever deeply in love with her. After losing my father, the passion I believed I had for her was dissolving, which seemed so odd because I had been desperately jealous. When I confessed I cared for Eve, it was true, but not as true as I thought.

But what the hell, I felt wonderful. I still cared about Eve, but not in the way that denied me my sanity. I found myself being more grateful to her than adoring her. While poor Eve began to note the changes as well, by understanding I was not her slave anymore. She had lost not just one person but two, while I was all the lighter for it.

'Something has happened to you,' she said, squinting her eyes.

'I am getting better.'

'No, there is something else,' she snapped before walking out of the room, stopping to pick up her letter.

In that intense moment, the significance of that letter placed strategically so fell into place. The letter had been a trap set for me, knowing I would read it. Over two weeks had passed since my father's internment, and she was frustrated. If I didn't give her money soon, she showed me she could humiliate me by applying for a job. Just three weeks ago, I would have dragged her to the church and begged her to marry me. But now, with my father gone, the desire and madness had suddenly and spectacularly left me.

I was free. I didn't love Eve anymore if I had ever loved her. What was this madness, this infatuation I had for her? Her beauty, her mystification, or was it the fact she, like the money, had belonged to my father? But now everything was mine while the desire to possess it had gone.

Sophia would be here tomorrow.

'I wish they would hurry and do something about the balcony,' began Eve. 'I miss not being able to go out there. It was so wonderful to eat and relax together out there.'

She had laid a table in the dining room. Through the windows, the sun filled the room, warming it like an oven. No cool air coming in even though the front windows were opened, as were the kitchens, but it was not enough. The dining room sweltered and drawing the curtains from the sun's rays only seemed to make it worse. I was glad we were only having a salad.

When should I tell Eve that Sophia will arrive tomorrow? Now, I had my secrets from Eve.

'I really appreciate you planning on giving me a lump sum of money. Of course, you agree that if Dominic had amended his will, I would now be a wealthy widow with nothing to worry about for the rest of my life.' Walking off, she knew I was watching her as she left for the kitchen.

Yes, I thought to myself; I had offered to give her half, but then I thought about it. They had only been married just over two months, and two months in monetary terms did not I felt merit a fortune. A couple of hundred thousand should serve her well; an excellent investment for the little time she spent with him. I am sure this brief affair wouldn't destroy the rest of her life.

'This is nice,' I said, turning over the salmon. 'It tastes different from what we had before. And the flowers, they are nice too.'

'Yes, I thought we should have some flowers. Dominic always brought me flowers.'

While I was pretending to eat with an appetite, I felt her watching me.

'I am going to write a letter to my bank and ask for money to be deposited into your account,' I smiled.

Eve heard, but she made no response except to stab at her food; there was definitely something on her mind, and I did not know if I wanted to hear about it.

'Sophia probably told you I was going to get married.'

'Yes, she said something about that.' I looked up. 'Who has proposed to you?'

'You. You asked me to marry you. Do you remember or had you forgotten?'

'Eve, you know that would have been a mistake. A son marrying his father's wife. One of the deadly mortal sins.'

'Yes,' she murmured to herself. 'We met at the wrong time.' Her silence was entombed with sadness, but not for long. This woman was a survivor. 'Do you know what I miss?' she asked, smiling.

I looked up with interest, glad the subject had changed to something not so heavy.

'And what is it you miss?'

'You.' she grinned. 'The way you used to be. You've changed. Now you've become more thoughtful, but wiser. You used to share all of your thoughts with me, but now you've become silent.'

'Have I?'

'Well, have you, haven't you Aiden? You used to be weak, but charming, and now you are so much like your father.'

'I don't think I've changed into my father.'

'I often think about what it's like to be rich, and then I think of Gerard, and then Dominic. They were both powerful. Money makes you powerful, and now you are the same. People who are rich like to keep their money.'

She regarded me with her dark grey eyes while running her fingers through skeins of thought. Cold, clear, calculating eyes. Time to change the subject.

'The flowers are lovely. Where did you get them from? The market.'

'The flowers, oh yes, the flowers. No, I didn't get them from the market; I went for a wander past some gardens. They were in someone's garden.'

I laughed, foreseeing a mischievous outcome.

'Don't tell me you stole them out of someone else's garden?' I burst into laughter.

'No, I won't tell you that because that didn't happen. I knocked on their door and pointed to the flowers and showed my purse. But I didn't pay for them, which was, I suppose, the same thing as what you were thinking. The lady gave them to me for free and then pointed to my face.'

'I can understand that. She was giving you the flowers

because you are beautiful. She was probably saying your beauty was lovelier than the flowers.'

'Thank you, Aiden, but what is beauty if it can't do anything for you? My looks given by nature are free to everyone else except me. I must take care of my features; so I must not stay in the sunshine for too long. I must eat all the right foods and go to bed early. Also, I must remember to moisturise my skin. I must remember my beauty, if not for myself, then for others. You have had my beauty, Aiden, every day since you have been here. Tell me, what is my beauty worth to you?'

'I never thought of it that way, but I suppose you could be right.'

She was still staring at me, but this time in anger.

'And that's what I mean; you have changed.'

'But not for the better?' I suggested.

'You're right. We should not be having this conversation.'

She went to move from the table to clear up the plates; there was going to be another course of fresh fruit.

'Aiden,' she paused, her voice soft, and her eyes willing me to remember. 'You once told me you loved me. Do you still love me?'

I stopped scrapping up all the bits of salad on my plate, knowing that what had been, was just a second in time. The fashion had passed, and it had been good, but not anymore. Not now, as the season of love had been overtaken by the madness of it all.

'Yes, I still love you, Eve; you were good to my father when he needed it. I hope one day it will happen to me.'

'Just when you need it,' murmured Eve, taking up the plates and moving to the kitchen.

18

When Sophia first told me she was coming here, my instant reaction was one of trepidation. As far as I could see, there were going to be more problems, and yet with Sophia, she always came with that breath of fresh air. I was pleased she was visiting. She would tell me what she saw, and always she made sense.

Going to bed now, I felt excited, and this was noticed by Eve. Finally, I had to tell her that Sophia was coming. Eve looked at me; her eyes dedicated to how I was taking this.

'You should have told me earlier. I would have got the room ready, and now I don't have any time.'

'But Eve,' I frowned with amusement. 'There is no need to worry.'

She understood my meaning in an instant and blushed quickly. I had never seen her redden up like that before.

'So, that's why you are in such high spirits. I should have guessed. Do you think it's wise?'

'How do you mean?' I asked, running my hand through my lengthening hair. I must get myself a haircut, but who do

I go to in this country? I don't want my hair to be cut too short.

'I mean, you and me. We are—'

'Oh Eve, you cannot hold me to that, especially when I was ill. I was out of my mind if you remember. I am sure I was not making any sense to you.'

'You do not know my mind.' Her face darkened with sheets of anger.

'You cannot accept the word of a madman; besides Eve, you don't love me. Kindness and concern you might have had for me, but love, no Eve. You are too sophisticated. While I am such an oaf, you would get bored with me in a moment. But it's very flattering that you should think of me as a potential partner. Besides, you were married to my father. How do you think that would look to others?'

'I have never cared what others think; it's my life to do with as I like. But it doesn't matter now. I thought you had no one in your life and being married to me would help you adjust—'

'What?' for now I was laughing from relief, feeling I had got myself out of a very tight corner. 'You would marry me until I found someone else or found my feet. That's very generous of you.'

And there I was, still laughing while she left the table, still laughing while I heard the water running in the kitchen, and still laughing, knowing I had caused an injury to her pride. When was I ever going to grow up? But then, I didn't care because in a few hours, Sophia would be here.

I HAD WANTED to meet Sophia at the airport, but she assured me she would be okay. Much of her life in modelling had meant she had to do lots of flying all over the world. While Eve went out to buy the food for the evening, I was in my bedroom sorting out my room. Sophia would need space, knowing that she would bring an entire wardrobe of clothes with her.

'If you need any help,' I looked into the kitchen when I was taking out some papers and other rubbish collected over my stay. 'Please let me know.'

Looking up from the oven, Eve nodded. I had not asked what she was going to cook for tonight, for it seemed like an insult. If we didn't like it; I was going to take Sophia out for a meal. I never realised how much I had missed Sophia. Gracious me, how I missed her. Eve, though, was keeping very much to herself. I was grateful for it. But it wouldn't be for too long. I had given Eve a letter to post to my bank if they needed any other instructions. Two hundred thousand should do Eve nicely, giving her time to move on to find herself another husband.

The taxi dragged itself up the hill and before it stopped, the door opened as a tall, leggy blonde climbed out. Waving her arms excitedly, she called to me. Her faithfulness and devotion inspired deeper feeling. My wait was over; I could not get to her fast enough.

'Sophia.' I wrenched open the door, smiling and waving as well.

This tall beauty with long legs and fabulous long hair was running towards me as pleased to see me as I was to see her.

We crashed together, still standing but laughing, and then I swept her off her feet and spun her around.

'I guess someone must have missed me,' she gasped and laughed, her bright blue eyes looking into mine.

'Might have, can't say for sure.' My eyes twinkled while

my heartbeat was agitated, like the wings of a hummingbird. 'You look great, Sophia.' I pushed her away from me for a better examination. 'What have you been doing to yourself?'

'I start the course in just a few weeks. I've been accepted by King's College London, and I am now a full-time student, well, in a few weeks' time. Are you proud of me?'

'I should say I am. Let me look at you. It's so good to see you. You look absolutely fabulous.'

'Yes, you said. There is someone watching us. I thought you said Eve had left.'

'She will. She's just waiting for the money.'

'So, you are going to get rid of her? I mean—'

'It's okay, I know what you mean. The situation between us has become complicated.'

'In what way, Aiden?'

I sighed. This was becoming very uncomfortable, but it was better I explain to Sophia and especially about my part. I told Sophia nearly everything as we collected her luggage from the taxi and walked to the house. All the while, Sophia listened, saying nothing until I finished.

'You are not in love with her anymore.'

'If I ever was, perhaps in the beginning.'

'What does she say about it? Or more to the point, was she in love with you?'

'No, I don't think she was ever in love with me, as I don't believe she was in love with my father. I believe she's one of those people who intimately understands what love is. There's a name for it?'

'Are you looking for the word schizoid? I don't always hold with giving people labels. Sometimes, I think some people are just born evil. We had better get into the house before Eve becomes too suspicious.'

The person who greeted Sophia differed from the one I

left only five minutes earlier. All smiles and charms, Eve took hold of Sophia's hand and pulled her into the dining room.

'I must apologise for the mess outside the villa. The police were supposed to have given the okay with the balcony so we could get on with our lives. It gets very hot in here, but I have managed to cook something for us to eat.'

'You shouldn't have put yourself to so much trouble. Aiden and I discussed about dining out.'

'But I've gone to all this trouble to cook you something,' said Eve. Her ready smile quickly vanished.

Sophia looked at me. I shrugged, meaning it was entirely up to her now.

'Then we'll stay and have something to eat. Next time you cook, I will help. We can't have you working away and feeling yourself to be a grudge.' Sophia was on her best behaviour.

'How long are you staying for?' Eve asked with interest as they walked, keeping Sophia by her side.

'For as long as Aiden needs me. I don't really have any plans; it depends on Aiden. Can't we put the table outside in the garden to eat? It will be much more refreshing.'

'I don't know,' said Eve, her mind was carrying her somewhere else.

Following me upstairs to the bedroom. I closed the door and looked at Sophia.

'She doesn't seem too bad,' whispered Sophia. 'At least she's not turned into a monster yet, but then, she never will, considering how beautiful she is. I think you might be making this ogre thing up?' she tapped me gently on the nose. 'To get more attention from me.'

Putting my arms around this leggy blonde, I pulled her to me.

'What do you see in me, Sophia? What did I do to attract you to me? You should have left me years ago, and yet you hung around after everything I did to you.'

'Yeah well,' now she looked embarrassed and goofy. 'You were worth it. This thing which I was supposed to be having with your father, it's okay Aiden, I spoke to Dominic about it. We both knew it was your personal conspiracy theory.' Then she laughed.

'I am so sorry,' I said, shaking my head. 'I don't know what came over me.'

'Jealousy. You have always wanted everything your father had. It's better known as the Oedipus condition.'

'That's so boring, Sophia. Especially when you know how I aspire to be different. I never thought I could be boring.'

'You were just being you. And now the infamous incident is over. We can get on with our lives.'

'Except someone is still here,' I said, looking at the bedroom door and wondered if Eve was listening.

'Just pay her off, like you said you would, and then forget about her. And we, Aiden, can get on with the next part of our lives. That's if you wish.'

Looking into Sophia's beautiful blue eyes, pushed all the terrible memories away.

'I won't let you go again. This time, I have well and truly grown up. I feel so different from what I was before. It's crazy how just a few weeks can make all the difference.'

It's not that we didn't want to eat dinner with Eve, we just forgot the time. The reminder came when Eve knocked and asked if we were coming to dinner that she had cooked.

'I have been trying a new recipe out,' she said when we sat down at the table. 'Aiden, will you do the honours and serve the wine? I thought we should drink red because it's said to be better for you, although to be honest, I prefer white, but anything for a healthy life, yes?'

She laid the table outside in the small patch of a garden to the side of the villa. Sophia and I sat side by side while Eve placed herself opposite us.

'I read that it's no good eating salads when the weather is hot,' said Eve. 'In hot weather, it's better to eat hot curries than cool salads, so that's what I have made. And curries are very good for you with all the herbs and spices in them. I have made it purposely hot; the idea is you will sweat, and it's the sweating which cools you; interesting, isn't it? The same as, if you have a headache, you should hit your foot, so you forget the pain in your head.' Then she laughed.

Sophia and I laughed too, politely, and also because Eve was revealing this side of her humour.

'Is it too hot, Aiden? You will get used to it; I promise.'

I don't like curries so I don't know why I should put up with it, but Sophia, who had travelled the world, had expanded her diet and now she was shovelling it in.

'Okay, Aiden,' said Eve, getting up from the table. 'I'll get you something else if you can't endure a bit of heat.'

Grinning at me, Sophia showed me how much heat she could put up with. I nodded sarcastically, thinking to myself, more fool her.

In came Eve with a plate of salad, for which I was grateful. I did not care if it was fish again. The only thing that mattered was if I could eat it.

After the strained feelings with Eve, I welcomed another step into a more normal relationship. We had forgotten about the past, and I was grateful for it, as I was grateful now for Sophia's company. With her being here, it was going to be easier than being alone with Eve.

Deep into the night, we sat and chatted like old friends,

pouring wine, and talking across the candlelight. I had never known Eve to be quite like this. Open and kind and interested in everything we talked about, especially Sophia.

'It sounds like you two are already married,' commented Eve.

I shrugged gently. 'Why not? We get along all right.'

It was at Eve's suggestion that we toasted the recent changes. Relaxed, Eve became that older sister to Sophia she had always wanted. I was regarding these two by candle-light. Looking at Eve with her raven black hair hanging down her back and I was reminded of those two and a half months ago when Eve walked spectacularly into my life. Sophia was lovely, but Eve was perfect.

'If everyone had money, lots of money, I believe everyone would be healthy,' began Eve.

I knew what she meant by that. Her money would be on the way once the banks accepted and verified my wishes.

'Everyone would be happy—Aiden, you are happy, aren't you?' Eve's eyes centred on me. 'Now you have come into possession of your father's fortune. You have everything you want. The money and now Sophia. Haven't you felt the difference now you are rich? We were only talking about money before you arrived here, Sophia, weren't we, Aiden? Life is so much more pleasant when you have money. In fact, I was prepared to marry anyone in order to have money. I do hate not having money. Not having money makes you sometimes go nutty and do things which you would not normally consider doing. It can be very embarrassing. I should know that.'

Her smiles at me caused Sophia to look deeper into this meaning.

'Oh well,' said Eve, pouring out the rest of the red wine into our glasses from the second bottle. 'I take it we are family. Oblige me, Aiden. We are a family of sorts. Aiden has been very good to me—you have to know this if you don't already. Being penniless can make you desperate. Personally, I believe secrets are better out in the open than left to fester. Dominic, too, had secrets. The truth is, I married Dominic for his money. Yes, I know, raise your eyebrows.'

'I don't see anything wrong with that,' interrupted Sophia. 'If you were prepared to make his life happy, then I see nothing wrong with it. And you made his life wonderful.'

'Absolutely. You can fall in love with someone if you are grateful, and I would not be surprised if that's how most marriages start if people believed in being honest with each other. I think the time has come when people should be honest with each other.'

'Yes, I am inclined to agree with you. Not everyone can find happiness, so why not make the most of your life?'

'To go back to what I was saying, I feel the need to tell you everything.' Eve gulped down her wine. 'I offered myself to Aiden in marriage. Aiden knew why I was proposing to him, didn't you, Aiden? Because I was desperate. But do you know what this wonderful man was prepared to offer me? Do you think I have drank too much? Who cares? You only live once. He has made a settlement to me of two hundred thousand pounds. I will be able to buy myself something small but nice, and with the rest, if I invest it well, I shall be able to live off the money for the rest of my life. What do you say to that, Sophia? Isn't this man wonderful?'

'I think he is.' Sophia took hold of my arm and curled herself around it and then stretched across to kiss me on my lips.

'She has changed,' said Sophia when at last we went to our room.

I had not drank as much as Sophia. On this occasion, it seemed to be a girls' night as to who could drink the most.

'I think I could actually like her. She has come out of herself, and I think you're wrong.' Sophia sat on the bed and now taking off her shoes. 'She is certainly not a schizoid or a psychopath or whatever else there is, like a sociopath.'

'You are right; money makes a difference, especially when you don't have any.'

'Well, look at you. You thought the world was much better when those that had kept their money to themselves. I don't know what I am talking about. You know that curry was very, very hot, but I found I could stand it. It's a pity you couldn't. You don't know what you're missing.'

'I am prepared to miss such things as that.'

'What surprised me was how honest she could be by telling us she was never in love with Dominic. I believe I judged her wrong about a lot of things. It must be hard for her when she is so beautiful.'

'But you are also beautiful, Sophia.'

'But no way as lovely as Eve. From what I understand, being beautiful did her no favours. It's a shame. A myth that being beautiful will open doors for you. She wants to take me shopping with her to the market tomorrow, just the two of us. Will you be all right here on your own?'

'Of course. Having you here is a tonic.'

'When will we be going back to England?'

'As soon as I get the money side all straightened out and into my bank.'

Still not feeling one hundred per cent, I was eager to get into bed. It was an enjoyable evening but too long. Sitting between two beautiful ladies, I wondered at life; one day, it reduces you to begging on your knees and the next, it makes you a king. But it would be good to get away from here. It would be good to get back home and start thinking about a future which without my father would be difficult and yet, now that I was rich, everything was possible.

Another golden day started my world off well. I figured that in two weeks, Sophia and I would be back in England and picking up on our lives. It would be good to put this awful ordeal behind us. Eve had intimated that we should keep in touch, but I don't think so. We had done a great deal of making up by going through misunderstandings about what we said, but then not what we really meant. But none of this, to my mind, was enough to satisfy a close relationship.

Eve, though, was getting on well with Sophia, which surprised me after these two women had shown hostility towards each other. They kept on touching each other, leaning across the table, and touching each other's hand; I put it down to the fact that both of them must be drunk, and probably wouldn't remember what they did or said. When we leave Italy and say our farewells, I am going to put my foot down about having anything further to do with Eve.

Back home, Sophia and I never have breakfast. But here in Italy, Sophia was awake in the early morning telling me she was to breakfast with Eve.

'Go ahead,' I said, waving her off. 'I don't mind how much you eat as long as you don't complain to me you are getting fat.'

But the biggest surprise was, Eve was going to cook and eat breakfast as well. Inconceivable to accept she had an enormous appetite because there was nothing to her.

The two ladies were out at ten to spend the rest of the morning and afternoon shopping. Sophia was filling me in on the details as she walked about the room, taking clothes from her partially unpacked suitcases. First, they were going to buy some food, and then stop for luncheon. Next, they were going to buy some vintage clothes or just look. Window shopping. This was right up Sophia's street. She had a fancy for some costume jewellery, a few more articles of clothes to add to her oversized wardrobe, and other knickknacks. Still resting on the bed, I heard the two ladies giggling excitedly and knew I might have some problem when it came to parting them. But let them enjoy themselves while they can because I was enjoying the peace and catching up on extra sleep. They would be home by five, and I would imagine still wondering where this friendship had come from.

It was nearly six when they arrived back at the villa in a taxi. My immediate thought was they had come back drunk.

'At last,' I muttered to myself, opening the door preparing to tick them off.

It was Eve who was out of the car first and paying the driver. Stopping where I was, I watched as the driver went to the back door of the car with Eve; they were getting something from the backseats. As I continued to watch, I saw to my concern it was Sophia.

'What happened to her?' I asked, hurrying across.

'She will be fine. I think she had a bit too much to drink last night. It's nothing to worry about, Aiden.'

'Let me.'

I took hold of Sophia's right arm and wrapped it around my shoulder. Between the cab driver and me, we walked her to the house and to the sofa.

'Aspettare.' It was one of the few Italian words I knew.

Coming back from the other room, I handed the taxi driver another couple of notes. He shook my hand and said a few fast Italian words, then looked at Sophia. It was obvious he was saying something about her health.

'You've made a friend for life,' remarked Eve when the taxi driver left.

'Tell me what happened to her.' I demanded.

'Oh, Sophia will be okay after she's had a good night's sleep. I think we overdid it last night.'

'But you both seemed perfectly okay last night.'

'Travelling. Travelling can take it out of you with dehydration. I think we ought to get her up to her bed and let her sleep.'

'What exactly is wrong with her?' I took up my darling in my arms.

'She complained of feeling nausea and headachy. We went to a pharmacist and asked if he could give her something. He thought she might have caught a bug. Luckily, the pharmacist could speak reasonably good English. Which reminds me, Aiden; what are you going to do about Pantelleria?'

'What about it?' as much as I love Sophia, she was still a weight. 'Can you get the door for me, please?'

'Perhaps we should open the windows for her and let in some fresh air. Do you always have the shutters closed, Aiden?'

A gush of warm air came rushing in. When Eve leaves the room, I will close the shutters.

'Shouldn't you consider what you are going to do with Pantelleria?' Eve continued like it was a complaint.

'Thank you, Eve. I can see to Sophia for now.' The villa in Pantelleria is now mine.

'If you need me,' Eve was by the door, 'just call. I think we overdid it last night. Oh well, I better leave you two alone.'

She closed the door quietly on us both and then disappeared rapidly down the stairs.

Sophia opened her eyes when Eve had gone. I had never seen her like this before, pale, and weak, for she was always so healthy. Feeling her head and then her wrist, not that did any good, I was trying to find out how she was.

'What happened?' I asked when I saw her eyes.

'Just me making a fool of myself.'

'You never make a fool of yourself. Something has made you ill. What can it be and when did it happen?'

'I will be okay,' she smiled, pleased I was worried about her.

She knew how much I hated illness; I never go to the doctors. One step towards the doctors means two steps closer to death. This was one of my sayings. Sophia knew every one of my sayings; I said them often.

Sitting on the bed beside her, I picked up her hand and began stroking it. Worrying didn't do any good. She was all I had now that my father had gone.

'So, you felt sick? Do you want any water? Are you hungry?'

'No food for me. I wouldn't mind if I never ate again.' And then she saw my face and smiled. 'Of course, I will be as fit as I ever in the morning and ready to eat that poor horse. Don't worry about me, Aiden. It's just one of those things. I shall be all right. It's probably as Eve said, travelling, drinking too much last night and the over excitement.'

'Yes, you're right,' I said, patting her hand. 'Can I get you anything, and I mean anything, a banana, a piece of fruit or even a drink of milk?'

'No, I shall leave food alone for the rest of the day. It won't do me any harm for a few hours. You have something to eat and be nice to Eve.'

'I am always nice to Eve.'

'That was not what she was telling me.'

'And what has she been telling you?'

'Go, have something to eat, Aiden, and then I will tell you later. I am so tired.'

I found Eve in the kitchen busy taking up pans and frying something. Awkwardly, I let my presence be known. She was pleased to see me and let it be understood that she also was worried about Sophia.

'We were having a great time,' began Eve, taking a spatula from the drawer. 'We had bought some food from the market and then we were going to have a coffee; it was going to be my treat. She was excited, and the only person she could talk about was you. She thought you had changed; I said to her you had, and that she should be proud of you. Oh, you know, the things women talk about when they're together. I won't go on anymore because I am sure it will make your head swell and for poor Sophia, impossible to live with.'

I was frowning all the time while she spoke, not noticing what she was doing or even what she was making. I didn't even think to ask if she wanted any help.

'Oh, by the way, I am making omelettes. Something light to eat. Perhaps that's where I went wrong. I cooked too much because I judged everyone was hungry. Heat can make someone ill. This is something I should know.' She raised her eyebrows, thick with irony.

Our evening meal came with a bottle of white, although neither of us expressed a desire to drink. But movement of hands across the soft gossip between friends took up that bottle and poured. I was on my second when I realised what I was doing. Eve laughed when she heard me muttering annoyances to myself.

'Aiden, you must admit that just lately, it's been a pretty tough time. Perhaps we needed a drink. Actually, I am going to be honest; I needed a glass or two. And if you are interested, Aiden, I am truly afraid of the future. Whenever I have been on my own, disaster has always followed. Anyhow, I am not your responsibility anymore; you've got Sophia, and I know you will take care of her. In a way, I envy her—'

She watched me, her indelible eyes still calculating.

'Yes, I'd better go and see Sophia.' I said, trying to be as natural and normal and not notice that her seductive eyes were appealing to me. If things had been different, if Dominic had not been Eve's husband, and if I did not have Sophia, then, perhaps. Yes, perhaps if our lives had run into one another.

'Right, I should not try to delay you. You are a very special person to me, Aiden. I can't think how lucky I am that I know you. You had better go and see her and give her my best wishes. Tell her—no, let us keep that a secret.'

I was at the door and opening it when Eve called to me again.

'Aiden, have you ever thought what it would have been like if I had accepted your offer of marriage?' She sighed. 'God knows why I didn't accept it. Oh, I know, I was still married to Dominic. But if you were to make the offer now—'

I went out of the door and closed it before Eve finished what she was saying. As I went down the stairs, I could hear Eve's laughter coming from the dining room.

Yes, I shall be glad when Sophia and I are on our way home.

19

Sophia slept well that night. I did too, but now and again I roused from strange dreams. Occasionally, I leaned on my hand to look at Sophia sleeping. Peaceful, her breathing was easy while her face was relaxed. Earth bound angel; she had just visited her cousins before returning to earth.

How quickly illness leaves, packing its case to be sent on its way. I awoke to an empty bed, patting frantically beside me and finding only cold sheets.

'I am absolutely starving,' said Sophia, coming from the other side of the room, dancing hotfooted on one leg, pulling on her sandal. 'I feel wonderful. Whatever it was has disappeared, and I am glad for that. You have no idea how miserable I felt.'

'I think I might have,' I interrupted. 'It was not so long ago when I was ill.'

Giggling, Sophia chatted with health while enjoying all the vagaries of wellbeing that came with that lift. While I—I was somewhere else. Remembering how good Eve had been to me when she was probably anxious about her own future and what she was going to do with herself and how she would manage. My father had once told me about Eve's fear of poverty and how it drove her obsession to get rich.

'I never realised how bad her life had been,' my father told me on one of those earlier days when we were on better terms. 'Eve has suffered. Her parents sacrificed her for their two sons. If she knew I was telling you this, she would be mortified. I am so angry. They sold her as a slave—no, that's not right. What I mean is they prostituted her.'

I promised my father I would never speak of this, not to anyone, and especially not to Eve. No wonder she had gone looking for a rich man who could save her. It made me understand her better.

'We are going shopping,' said Sophia, before going downstairs. She came over to me to rest a kiss on my brow. 'For the window shopping we were supposed to do yesterday. And then we are going for lunch—Eve's treat. The restaurant is supposed to be patronised by artists. Aiden, do you think we should have our portraits painted? I know it sounds vain, but it's something I would love and have always wanted. Sorry if I am gabbling on. Anyway, I've got to go now. I'll bring you something nice if I can find anything.'

When the door shut, the house fell silent. Getting out of bed, I was just in time to watch those two walking, arm-in-arm, heads together from my bedroom window. It painted a wonderful picture of conviviality. Eve on the right, with her silk hair tied once more in a plait, tapping away on her back as she walked next to the slender blonde but strong Sophia. Her blonde hair was also plaited but only half the length of Eve's. Even though they appeared so different, they could, I felt, be sisters. My feelings softened towards them with grateful smiles, although aware that Sophia in her flat shoes was still several inches taller than the raven-haired maiden.

Watching them go down the hill until they disappeared made me think about my day ahead, and what I was going to do. For something pleasing, my thoughts drew back to the unlikely sisters. Conversely, different to each other in height, hair colour and personality, yet, they had somehow found that elusive fellowship. Did I approve of this? My feelings said I did while my experience of Eve said she could be kind as she could be calculating. People who have been damaged are usually complicated.

Drowsy sleep came readily to me and strange with dreams. I climbed into bed, relieved that I had nothing to do. Was I lazy? So wonderful to be in bed. I was still half in that other world. A reverie of dream clouds was pulling out and prophesying.

'Beware of her,' said Eve to me, pointing at Sophia. 'She is dangerous.'

I awoke with a start and heard the two ladies were back. There was a bag by the side of my bed begging to be opened. Sophia had already come to see me and found I was asleep. This disappointed me. Taking up the parcel, was I supposed to open this now? This was exciting.

A pair of cowboy boots. I was astonished that Sophia bought them for me, but delighted. Getting myself fully dressed, I tried on these boots and walked them about the bedroom, seeing how they felt. And they felt good. I had always wanted a pair of cowboy boots but never had the courage or the inclination to buy them for myself, mainly because I thought my father would rebuke me for my vanity. But I am not a child anymore and nor am I in obedience to my father; I am a man, and one with substantial wealth. I can now cater to my vanity.

The boots were two toned. Red on the top and tanned about the foot part. Calf length with a long red suede dragon running up the sides. Standing in front of the mirror, I was mightily impressed with how I looked. I was going to wear them this evening to show Sophia how pleased I was. She deserves one big smackeroo right on her lips.

'THANK YOU, SOPHIA,' I said, grabbing hold of her arms to kiss her. 'This is the best present ever. How did you know what I wanted? And how did you manage to find them here?'

'It wasn't me, Aiden. It was Eve who suggested I get them. She said she would not be surprised if you wanted cowboy boots.'

'It was your idea?' I asked, looking at Eve, who was standing to the side watching, her eyes silently observing me as if she had not expected this.

'Sophia,' cried Eve. 'I told you I didn't mind if you took the credit; I said it would be more special if you allowed the idea to come from you.'

'Did you pay for them?' the elation which I had only seconds ago dispersed, and the magic balloon with all its joy had popped into disappointment.

Sighing, Eve looked resigned at the rest of the gifts which became a mountain of displeasures.

'Yes, I paid for them. But what does it matter? Aiden, you don't seem to realise what you've done for me. I am so grateful to you that I begged Sophia to let me have that honour. Oh, Aiden, why can't you see this for what it is? Two people have desired so much to make you happy. So please be happy, then we can all be happy.'

Prodding me from behind Sophia reminded me not to be ungrateful; everyone needs friends. And it was that a great gust of air in its mantle of thoughts which changed my disposition and reminded me this was the here and now. The battle of yesteryear had finished and now we must draw up plans for an entirely different future if we wanted to succeed. Perhaps I would not entirely rid myself of Eve, but designing new plans would be better for everyone.

'This time,' grinned Sophia, 'I shall cook dinner. And it may be better than last night,' she winked at Eve.

'What are you making, a salad?' I teased.

'No, I thought we would have another curry. But not for you, of course. I thought I would make you a—' and then she grinned wildly.

'A salad,' I laughed.

Perhaps it was good that we should spend some time together to reassess our relationship. Eve had received a letter from the landlord telling her that tomorrow the builders would be here to fix the balcony, this time with steel posts and rails which would be secured to the wall. Eve said she would be pleased to use the space again, but what I can't understand is why she would want to go out to the place where her husband had died. Showing the letter to Sophia and me, we viewed the letter with distaste. Again, I was reminded of what had happened that evening, and how my push had thrown my father to his death. Eve looked at me, saying nothing. She was always watching me now. From my side, I viewed her observations with the fault that I also found in myself. Then I thought about the future which I stole from her. This knowledge was something I had not spoken to Sophia about. Shame, that word kept whipping me. I loved my father, but I did not want him back.

Are we still pretending that nothing had happened? Is

that what we do with our lives? Pretend that nothing has happened so we can move on.

'You should use the money wisely you received in compensation,' nodded Sophia after congratulating Eve. Eve had received another twenty thousand for the price of Dominic. 'We must get on with life; it's up to us the ones who are left to do this, and we must do it well.' Her arm around Eve's shoulder gave the comfort of a good friend.

What was this feeling I was having?

'Yes,' whispered Eve. 'I still can't believe that Dominic has gone.'

The two of them left me to walk about the small garden, discussing the terms of grief and loss. I left them to it because my thoughts were for myself.

I could not feel any worse than I already did, and I could see a future in front of me where I would always be punished for the accident. Eve's eyes when she saw me on the balcony were something I found hard to face because I knew what she was thinking: he killed Dominic, but I shall forgive him for a price. Easier for her than for me. Her dead eyes said a thousand things. And I knew what she was thinking because I had already been there only days before. The reverse had happened that day only a week before, when my father had to make that call on whether he would save me. I couldn't go through it again; I chose not to save him.

While sitting in the dining room with the curtains open, the temporary scaffolding was still holding on to my blame. I hated it as I hated the person who looked at Dominic waiting for him to fall.

To hell with abstinence. I was going to have a drink tonight because I needed it.

'Just checking,' said Sophia. 'You don't want any of the curry I'm making, is that right?'

'Correct.' I preferred a liquid dinner.

It was a quiet meal; the two ladies spoke to each other while I sipped my wine. Chatting for comfort, they occasionally glanced across at me as if they were taking my temperature. Salads are salads; there is nothing to be said about them, so I didn't. After we had eaten, it was an early night for us all.

'I was thinking,' said Sophia, sitting in front of the vanity bureau. 'Of asking Eve to come and stay with us when we return to England.'

'No, Sophia. Have I not made my thoughts clear on this issue? She is not coming to live with us. If you invite her; I am leaving. Do you understand that?'

'Yes, I know you don't want her. I understand that perfectly, although I don't understand why you've taken against her—'

'Let me remind you it was you who did not like her at first. Do you remember?'

'Yes, I remember. But there is something called forgiveness; we all need to be forgiven once in our lives. What's the matter with you? You've been in a funny mood ever since we returned, and Eve has been so kind to you. She thought about the boots, remember? And she was the one who paid for them. She begged me not to tell you. She wanted me to take the credit. But I can't Aiden—do you know how afraid she is to live on her own?'

We looked at each other, but I would not budge one inch from my position.

'Why have you become so hard?'

'I have learnt that when you open up and try to be nice,

this is when you are the most vulnerable, because people will move in and take over. Please, Sophia, let us drop this conversation. Eve is able enough to look after herself without intervention.'

'You don't want her to stay with us, not even for a few weeks?'

'No, not even a day.'

'Then you are hard.'

'Hard. I must be hard for the two of us.'

'No, Aiden, not for the two of us just for you, because I am determined to stay and be there for Eve. She needs me.'

'You are going to stay here?'

'As I said, yes.'

'What about me? What about us? You are choosing her over me?'

'I will be back eventually, but Eve needs me now. I asked her if she would like me to stay and she said yes.'

'You have asked her already?'

'Yes, I have. I guessed that you might have something to say about Eve, and so I offered.'

'What about your studies?'

'I will catch up with them. I will explain that a great friend needs my help.'

'Oh, Sophia, you fool. You would leave me for her?'

Hearing my voice, Sophia quickly put her arm around me.

'It won't be forever, Aiden. I just want to help her get on her feet until she can look after herself.'

Saying nothing, I got into bed and turned on to my side. How did it happen that Sophia had chosen sides? What had Eve said to her to pull at Sophia's heartstrings and make her choose so unwisely? I would have to have a word with Eve about this.

Moving closer to me from her side of the bed, Sophia touched my shoulder and then stretched out to put her arms around me, but I was unmoved; she had chosen her side, let her stick to it. A minute later, she drew her arms away. I lay there, still on my side, thinking about it. It wasn't her fault that she had a soft heart; this was one of the qualities I loved about her, but when I turned over to make up and apologise, I found her asleep.

Something awoke me in the night. A noise gave me the impression someone was trying to break into our room. When I reached out to know if Sophia was well, I found she wasn't there. I switched on the side lamp and discovered Sophia was on the floor.

Leaping out of bed, I found her crunched up in agony, moaning. Her skin was deadly white while her lips were dry. I felt her; she was perspiring. My touch brought her from unconsciousness. She opened her eyes and looked at me.

'What is the matter with you? You can't lay here on the floor. I'm going to put you back in bed and then get the doctor.'

'I'm sorry, Aiden.'

'Sophia? Talk to me.' I was terrified to see Sophia fall into delirium.

A sharp knock on the door before it opened found Eve standing there in her nightdress. She looked at Sophia and then quickly hurried to her and touched her forehead.

'I found her like this,' I said babbling, impressed with Eve's calmness. I was afraid I was going to lose Sophia. 'I don't know what is happening to her. She was perfectly okay when we came to bed. Oh Sophia, please don't be like this.'

'It's probably the same bug that's going around town. I spoke to someone in the market who told me that his wife had been ill,' said Eve. Her face was very white. I could see she was as scared as me. 'Poor Sophia. She was like this yesterday, but not half as bad. You say you found her on the floor?'

'Yes, I don't know what she was doing—fell out of bed, I guess?'

'She was probably dehydrated and wanting some water. She's also very confused.'

'What do we do for her? She's not going to die, is she?'

'Nonsense don't even think that and please don't say it again for Sophia's sake. She probably can hear you. Sophia? You are all right; there is nothing to be afraid of. You have picked up a bug, that's all it is. The fever will pass and then you will start feeling better.'

'How can you be so certain?'

'Because this is what happened before,' Eve smiled. 'She will be fine, Aiden, I promise you. I heard you two arguing earlier. What was that all about?'

'We were just discussing our differences, that's all,' I said angrily, wondering why she wanted to know, and now I was also feeling defensive.

'Was it about me?'

'It was. How did you know?'

'Just a guess.' And then she smiled. 'I told Sophia not to worry about me. I would be all right, but she said she would not like to be in my position as she would also find it difficult. Wasn't that sweet of her to worry about me? You are very lucky to have such a sweet girl as her. It's a wonder you haven't lost her to someone else?'

'What are you talking about?'

'People like Sophia can be hurt easily by inconsiderate men, Aiden. That is all. Oh look, Sophia seems to have gained consciously. Sophia, how are you feeling now? Give me a hand, Aiden. Do you feel sick, Sophia? Help me, Aiden,' demanded Eve.

Still weak, but at least Sophia was conscious now; she complained of stomach-ache when she sat up.

'I'll get her a glass of hot milk. Rest is the best thing,' said Eve, going to the door.

'Wait, Eve, I want to talk to you.' there was something which baffled me about this situation. 'What do you think is wrong with Sophia?' I whispered to Eve just outside the bedroom door.

'My guess is that she has a bug; I don't think there is anything sinister going on. And another thing, she has been worrying about you. You've put her through hell these last couple of months; Sophia was telling me this while we were out shopping. She said she did not know what was going on with you and that you frightened her.'

Spiteful whispers: I felt Eve was spitting them out at me.

'She is a lovely young woman, Aiden; you should treat her right, otherwise, you will lose her. I'll just fetch the milk.'

Returning to Sophia's side of the bed and sitting down to be near her, I picked up her hand and held it as I looked at her. She looked beautiful with her hair loose around her face, like a mermaid. I always judged her to be healthy.

'I am sorry, Aiden; I don't know what came over me. In the morning, I felt great, and then—'

'So, when did this start? Eve told me you had a bug.'

'Yes, that's what she told me. What I know is that I felt dreadful. I awoke with sudden pains. I don't understand what's happening to me. It feels like an alien has climbed inside, and it's frightening. This is the second time it has happened; I feel like I am losing control.'

'You should see a doctor,' I said thoughtfully, then was reminded that Eve did not think it was essential.

I walked Sophia to the bathroom because she felt sick again and met Eve coming up the stairs. She nodded and smiled. I could not help thinking she was pleased, but that was probably my acid sentiment towards her. If I lost Sophia, my God, if I lost her—

'I'll put the milk on the bedside table,' Eve said, looking gently at Sophia. 'She's looking better, though. Strive for health, Sophia. This is what we should be doing.'

More exhausted now after clearing her stomach, I walked Sophia back to the bedroom and helped her back into bed. How weak she was.

'Thank you, Aiden. I appreciate everything you are doing for me. I don't know why I feel so ill. Eve thinks that once I get through the worst of it, then I shall be back to my usual self.'

'Yes, I know what Eve says.'

Sophia drank the milk gratefully, but remarking that it tasted of bananas. For some reason, I was not quite sure why; I took the glass away from her to smell it. It definitely smelled of bananas.

'Do you mind?' I asked, sipping the drink for myself. There was nothing bitter about it.

'What are you doing?' Sophia laughed when she watched me. 'Detective work? You suspect Eve of something. What is it, Aiden?'

'I don't know, but I don't want to lose you, Sophia.'

'You won't, I am not going anywhere yet. Besides, I am going to be thirty this year. Thirty,' she said. 'What have I done with my life except look pretty and wear clothes to get other women to buy them? I haven't done much with my life when there is so much to do.'

The thought that I could lose Sophia from something no better than negligence had an overwhelming effect on me. Sophia was mine, and I was going to do everything to protect her. Helping her back into bed, I crept to the other side and snuggled up against her, holding her in my arms for the long night to be over. I would let no one damage or hurt her. No one.

It was getting late when I awoke and went downstairs.

'How is Sophia?' Eve enquired when I arrived downstairs.

'Still tired,' I went to the window. Was this going to be the last time I would see the temporary support around the veranda?

'It is good for her to sleep,' she smiled, clearing away the last of the dinner from last night.

Had Eve waited for me to arise to do this?

'Sit down, Aiden. I will get you something to drink. What would you like? Some coffee. I am having coffee. Dominic always preferred tea in the mornings. I've got coffee bubbling. I bought a few things yesterday. It's wonderful to have money.'

'I hope the bank transfer will be done by the next week.'

She smiled and dipped her head to one side. 'That's very kind of you, Aiden. You are good to me. And that's what we must remember, the good in people.'

I waited for Eve to return. She brought two cups of coffee and putting them on the table she sat opposite to me. We sat in silence for a minute; I was trying to gain some confidence and the right words to say while Eve watched me silently, smiling as if something amused her.

'Sophia told me last night that she wants to stay here with you.'

'Yes, that's what she told me. Do you have something to say about it?' She picked up her coffee and sipped it.

'Yes, I do. I want her to come back with me.'

'That's what I told Sophia she should do. Return to England with you.'

'She thinks you need a friend.'

My hands, which had been clenched, were now resting on the table. I was making my moves, but they were not as successful as Eve's.

'Don't we all need friends, Aiden? I believe I have been a good friend to you—'

'What have you done for me?'

'Kept quiet. Wouldn't you say I have kept quiet in order to protect you?'

'Kept quiet about what? What's there is to be quiet about? I have done nothing wrong.'

Bending her head down, an annoying smile hovered on her lips. She had a secret that she was desperate to tell, only I had to say the wrong words for her to deliver.

'Oh, Aiden,' she breathed, looking back at me and giving me the full animation of thought in her beautiful grey eyes. 'The things we tell ourselves to make everything right. Your father told me what happened that night.'

I frowned. What was she talking about? I had nothing to fear except her deception.

'What happened on what night? I do not know what you are talking about.'

'Your mother.'

'What about my mother?'

'Do I have to tell you, or can't you remember? Think, Aiden, think about that night when your mother committed suicide.'

'No, I don't know what you are talking about and neither

do you. You are trying to put lies in my head. What do you know—that I don't?'

'But you do know, Aiden; it's a pity you choose not to remember or perhaps safer not to care?'

My eyes were on hers, mesmerised by what she was saying. I wasn't sure if she was threatening me?

'My father wasn't there, so how could he know?'

'Yes, you are right. And I should get us something to eat,' she said, getting up from her chair.

'No, Eve, it is my right to know what my father told you.'

'But as you said, he could have it wrong. He was not there. You were. Do you remember?'

It was on my tongue to tell her she was wrong, but I was prohibited. I saw my mother staring back at me, and then I saw her going to a desk and taking out a collection of pills she had been saving. It was supposed to have been a game to punish my father, and she was not supposed to die.

'There is nothing you can do or say to me,' I looked at Eve. 'Dreadful memories. That's what they are. I cannot be held responsible for others peoples' choices in life. I was only nine years old. What was I supposed to do? You cannot blackmail me, Eve.'

'I'm sorry if it comes across as that. I just wanted you to know I know everything about you, and that I forgive you for what you did to your father. Because I saw you, Aiden. I saw you push him; I heard him calling for you to help him. I heard you apologising to him, but that you had no choice. And when he fell, I saw you climbing down on the broken veranda and pretending to fall.'

'Your word against mine,' I bluffed. 'There is nothing you can do.'

'Except to keep that which you love. Oh Aiden, when you promised to marry me, I was still in shock. I couldn't tell you how I felt for you at the time, but I have feelings for you. And I love you more than I loved your father. Marry me, Aiden, you promised to marry me.'

'But I love Sophia.' I frowned.

'Oh yes, I know what you are saying. We all love some-one, but it is me who will make you happy. I know how to make men happy. Aiden, please, I am begging you. I have begged no one before. Do not turn me away.'

20

Sophia was sitting up in bed and looking considerably better when I returned; she was desperate to be well and get on with her life. When she saw me, her pleasure came with the clap of her hands. This was her way of letting me know how well she felt. But I could see this was not the complete truth because she was struggling. Her skin was still grey as her eyes were still sad.

'I've got to take you away from here,' I told her, walking angrily into the room.

'Aiden,' called out Sophia. 'It's not Eve's fault I am ill.'

'Oh yes, it is,' I said, returning and bringing the suitcases.

'I am not leaving yet, Aiden, and neither are you. Don't you remember you promised to stay to make sure the transfer goes through?'

'I remember what I said, but I can do it back in England. What I can't do is look after you while she's around.'

'Oh Aiden, really. What's the matter? Why are you so angry?'

Sophia was following me with her eyes as I walked backwards and forwards, collecting our clothes and putting them in our suitcases.

'She is going to take you away from me.'

'She can't do that,' Sophia giggled. 'She can only do that if I agree to it. What are you so afraid of, Aiden? Because you appear to be afraid, but I can't see why?'

'Eve wants more money.'

'Then why don't you give her some more money? You've got enough to give her without ever missing it.'

'She was with my father for less than four months. What I have given her is handsome enough. Enough to set her up in some sort of business or until she gets herself another husband.'

'I think you are overreacting.' Sitting up in bed, Sophia looked like a little girl with her blonde hair around her shoulders.

'Perhaps I am, but I would sooner overact than lose you.'

'You won't lose me.'

'Are you coming back to England with me?'

I stood with my arms crossed, giving Sophia an ultimatum.

'Not if you are going now, no. I've made a promise to Eve that I would stay with her. Help her pick a villa; she says she wants to stay here to be closer to Dominic. Don't you understand she is still grieving for him?'

'What I see and hear is that you don't love me.'

'Don't be silly, Aiden. You know I love you. Haven't I been telling you forever how much I love you?'

'But you're still not coming back with me?'

'No, I'm not.'

For a few seconds, my temper persisted. Was this a question of one will over another? Because if it was, then it was stupid. I always knew Sophia had a mind of her own, but this was a damn idiotic time to show it.

Lying on the bed beside Sophia was not profitable. We could not stay up in this room until Sophia decided it was time to go home. The serpent downstairs had to be faced, and it was to be faced sooner than thought because an hour later there was a tap on the door with Eve asking if she could come in. She looked at me and then at Sophia, then shrugging her beautiful shoulders, she went across to sit down on the bed beside Sophia.

'Aiden, I thought I would give you a break; I will sit with Sophia while you take a walk around.'

'You think I would leave Sophia alone with you?'

'Yes, why not?' and then she laughed and looked playfully at Sophia. 'Aiden thinks I am dangerous. He thinks I will try to murder you. But look at me compared to you. What can I do to you? Oh, I know I should not be like that because Aiden's fears are very real to him. Aiden, honestly, I know we haven't seen eye to eye just recently, but do you think I would hurt my best friend? How badly you must think of me.'

'Aiden,' Sophia called from the bed, now happy she was with this new best friend. 'There is nothing for you to worry about. I promise you. I just caught an awful bug.'

I didn't know what to say to Sophia, and from where I was looking by the door, the two of them were already chatting, nodding, and smiling. Could I have it wrong? Was I imagining these things? Had my fears taken substance?

'I will look after her,' said Eve, rushing downstairs to catch me before I left. 'No way am I going to hurt her.'

'I will give you whatever you want?' my hand was on the door ready to leave.

'What I want?' Eve grinned. 'I told you already what I want. But you have refused me.'

'Not me; I mean money.'

'Yes, money. I know that's what you mean. Hurry home, I am cooking everyone something nice for dinner.'

'What, for Sophia as well?'

'Yes, of course, why not? Would you rather she starved to death?'

She was laughing when I left the house, laughing at me and my silly fears.

I should have saved my mother, but I didn't. I watched her take every pill and then less than ten minutes later; she was slumped on the floor. It was a grand game my mother was playing to frighten my father; he certainly needed to be afraid. My father was supposed to have come home an hour later, but he didn't. Two hours passed and then three, and young as I was, I knew I had to do something.

'Bad timing,' I overheard my father say to one of his friends when the funeral was over. 'She should not have committed suicide in front of our son, and she should not have made him responsible for her death. She was weak. There was never enough that I could do to show her how much I loved her.'

Walking quickly to the town centre, I tried to put every memory out of the way, just like I had done over the years. I was trying to decipher why Eve wanted to remind me of it. We began bartering about love, but then about money with one another after my father's death. The price of her silence threatens to take so much from my future.

I went and had a coffee at a bar and sat at a table by myself and stared into nothing. We cannot make others live if they set themselves on their course for death. I loved my father as I also hated him, but in the end, it was not his fault that my mother killed herself.

Oh, what do we do with ourselves and our minds? We try to live the best way we can to make something out of what was just sadness.

Hurrying back up the hill to the house, whatever time I had left with Sophia, I was going to make the best use out of it.

Eve was in the kitchen when I returned home; I had been out longer than I thought.

'Sophia is asleep,' she came into the hall when she heard me. 'Don't wake her. Let Sleeping Beauty sleep. It will do her good.'

'Eve. How much do you want? I will give you whatever you ask for.'

'Oh, Aiden, you just don't understand, do you?' and then she laughed while I ran upstairs.

21

S leep had restored Sophia so much she wanted to come down and eat with us. It didn't matter how much I refused; she was going to do what she wanted.

Still unsure of herself on her feet, I helped Sophia to change and then guided her down the stairs. We were met by an overwhelming smell of pleasure, the tang of Indian spice. The kitchen was filled with cloves and vanilla that anyone who didn't have an appetite would conjure one up just to enjoy the food.

'What have you cooked, Eve?' asked Sophia as she took her seat at the table. I was there with every movement she made.

'Rice pudding. I got the recipe from one of my new friends. It's full of goodness and sits gently on the stomach.' And then she looked at me. 'I was uncertain about what you would like, Aiden. A dish full of fruit, maybe? You like your fruit, I've noticed. So, for you some figs. I hope you will enjoy them.'

'I shall enjoy mine,' said Sophia, picking up her spoon.

The look Eve threw to me was something to be suspicious about, and then she smiled as if she knew I was already heavy with paranoia.

'Now Aiden, I hope you will behave yourself. I'll bring in the dishes. There is a bottle of wine for you Aiden to undo. You don't have to have any.'

'I would like some,' said Sophia, now sufficiently animated.

'And I would like some, too. Will you do the honours, Aiden?'

On a tray, Eve produced the three dishes and served each dish to our places. With each dish she placed, her eyes stole to me, knowing I was watching her. There was a strange game going on.

'Let me try,' I said to Sophia, just as she went to put her spoon into the dish.

'Let Aiden try your rice,' said Eve. 'Aiden doesn't trust me.'

It was the sweetest rice pudding I have ever tasted; too sweet for me, making me wonder why so much sugar.

'Aiden, don't eat it all,' rebuked Sophia, looking at Eve and laughing. 'What are you looking for?'

'Aiden is looking for poison; he thinks I am trying to poison you.'

A spiral of giggles from Sophia, and then she stopped.

'You aren't trying to poison me, are you, Eve?'

'No, I am not, Sophia.'

'Why would you think Eve would poison us, Aiden?' asked Sophia, frowning.

'He believes,' began Eve, still looking at me. 'That if he does not have you, then he will have to turn to me and ask me to marry him.'

Looking down at her rice, Sophia began eating, not knowing what to say.

'Do you really believe that Eve is trying to poison me?' asked Sophia when we were back in our room.

'Yes, I do.'

'Oh, Aiden. This sort of thing will make you go mad. Just give her the money she wants and move on.'

'I offered more money, but she says she does not want it anymore. I don't know what game she is playing, Sophia. Please Sophia, why don't you come back with me now? We can start our new life together and be happy.'

'Because I made a promise which I intend to keep. Besides, it won't be for much longer. A day or two and we will head back to England.'

She took hold of my hand and held it between her own. I wanted to believe Sophia because, in her world, reality was much kinder.

What Eve had said about Sophia having a bug and that she would get over it appeared to happen. Sophia was so much better the following day, and even more so the day after. I had received information that the money to Eve had gone into her bank account.

Now Eve knew that the money was actually in her account, she looked more relieved and even happy. Perhaps I had imagined the poisoning and Eve's determination to destroy me. Especially now that Eve told Sophia that she did not need her anymore. Those bizarre passions I had vanished—well, almost. But it didn't matter now because our bags were packed, tickets booked, and in our minds, Sophia and I were already travelling back to England. The ordeal was almost over. But we could not run away without something of a celebration. Tonight, Eve was determined to cook us something special to eat.

Again, distrust grew. She was going to make an Italian casserole. Once more, she was given the recipe from a friend.

I could smell the wonderful aromas of a casserole rolling up the stairs as Sophia and I collected everything of ourselves from the room. Sophia was sitting cross-legged on the bed. She had a scrapbook of her time in Italy, photographs taken when she had accompanied Eve, and notes also detailing her time in this wonderful country. Her mind was somewhere else thinking about her Italian holiday, forgotten was her little scraps with illness. The future had arrived, and it was wonderful.

'Dinner,' called Eve from the bottom of the stairs.

'We should go down.' Sophia took hold of me by the hand. 'We should, because Eve has set me free from my promise.'

'There's nothing to stop you going whenever you want,' I said. My face was dour.

'Oh, Aiden, nothing is going to happen to me. Eve promised me, knowing how paranoid you had become.'

'Nothing is going to happen to you because I will not allow it. You are mine now and I am going to make sure I take care of you.'

Sophia leaned to kiss me on the lips, then ruffled my hair as we left the room.

'I'll bring the casserole in once you have served the wine,' Eve said to me.

It smelt better than it looked, but I had no appetite. Carefully, Eve put the dishes down in front of us.

'What do you think?' Eve asks, looking down at the two of us.

'It looks absolutely delicious.' Sophia smiled. 'I wish you would allow me to help with the cleaning up. I feel so guilty you've done all this for us.'

Eve returns her smile, but her interest was more for me as her eyes locked on me to see how I was taking it.

'Are we all eating the same tonight?' I ask.

'Yes, we are all eating the same, Aiden. Is that a problem for you? Do you want me to get you something else?'

'No, except I wouldn't mind a glass of water with this. Would you excuse me for a minute?'

'No, stay where you are, Aiden. I'll fetch you a glass.'

We watch her as she leaves for the kitchen. In a few seconds and she would be back.

'What are you doing, Aiden?' whispers Sophia.

Without a word, I switched plates, giving Eve's plate to Sophia and Sophia's to Eve.

'Why are you doing that?' Sophia looks perplexed.

'Here you are,' says Eve, passing me the glass as she sat down.

'To the three of us,' I said, taking up my glass. 'May we live forever and live life well—'

Again, Eve looks at me with wisdom in her eyes before she picks up her fork to eat. I watch as Eve eats her first mouthful; then I watch as she swallows it. And then she took another mouthful. Satisfied, I eat slowly, all the while I watch Eve and then Sophia. I stared at Eve with bated breath. Looking for any reaction, then she finished her meal. I watched as Sophia enjoyed her meal. I too ate my food and waited.

'Aiden, I thought you would like to see the photographs

that you and Dominic took on Mount Pellegrino.' She passed the pictures across one by one.

I saw my father handsome in his poses and felt the kick of pain that I would never see him again.

'Did you know Dominic took a picture of you hanging on to the mountain?' asked Eve, passing me the one. 'I had the film developed. I thought you would be curious to see the pictures taken that day. Imagine taking one of your son who was about to die. But what does it matter now when it's all memories, Aiden? We are made of memories. Now eat up, Aiden, you don't want—' Eve's eyes suddenly widened as she retched, and then vomit shot from her mouth, splashing onto the table.

'Nooo—yells Eve, as her head crashed to the table.'

Sophia looked on in horror. Then she turned to look at me.

I feel a burning from deep inside. It was then I knew what she had done. Her witch's brew was meant for Sophia and me. My head hit the table with a thud. Paralyses ran throughout my body; I am dying, and so is Eve. Poor Sophia, poor hysterical Sophia, but at least she will live.

'Aiden, Aiden, Aiden—'

I can hear my name echoing in my mind. Echoing through time and into the bleak black darkness of the abyss. Is a man's fortune worth his life?

REVIEW

I would appreciate it if you reviewed my book as this would make my day.

Thank You...

Printed in Great Britain
by Amazon